Naeem Murr

THE GENIUS OF THE SEA

WITHDRAWN

V
VINTAGE

Published by Vintage 2004

2 4 6 8 10 9 7 5 3 1

First published in 2003 by The Free Press

First published in Great Britain in 2003 by
William Heinemann

Vintage
Random House, 20 Vauxhall Bridge Road,
London SW1V 2SA

Random House Australia (Pty) Limited
20 Alfred Street, Milsons Point, Sydney,
New South Wales 2061, Australia

Random House New Zealand Limited
18 Poland Road, Glenfield, Auckland 10, New Zealand

Random House (Pty) Limited
Endulini, 5A Jubilee Road, Parktown 2193, South Africa

The Random House Group Limited Reg. No. 954009
www.randomhouse.co.uk/vintage

A CIP catalogue record for this book
is available from the British Library

ISBN 0 099 44999 4

Papers used by Random House are natural, recyclable
products made from wood grown in sustainable forests.
The manufacturing processes conform to the environ-
mental regulations of the country of origin

Printed and bound in Great Britain by
Bookmarque Ltd, Croydon, Surrey

For my Uncle Bishara

O God, I could be bounded in a nutshell, and count myself a king of infinite space, were it not that I have bad dreams.

—HAMLET, II, ii

THE FLAT was on the sixteenth floor of Hicks House, one of the five tower blocks of the Windsor Estate. The day's last light clung to the rococo mirror above the gas fire – a mirror more suited to a country estate than to a council estate in Wapping. The same was true of the sideboard, which looked like a mahogany jukebox. Either side of the chrome and smoked glass coffee table, which was the only new piece of furniture in the flat, were a green, shell-back armchair and a fat sofa, upholstered in burgundy velvet. On the sofa, their heads at opposite ends, their legs intertwined, lay two eleven-year-old boys, Daniel Mulvaugh and Galvin McCulloch.

Flicking a balled-up sweet wrapper at Daniel, Galvin said, 'What shall we name it, then?'

Daniel, who was staring at the entrance to the kitchen, answered vaguely: 'Name what?'

'The monster.'

Daniel didn't respond. His mother had been in the kitchen, crying, for almost two hours. As he tried to get up, Galvin pressed a bare foot against his chest, pinning him.

'What shall we name it?'

'Why are you asking me?' Daniel said. 'You always name them.'

'The Magdala.'

'If you knew what it was called, why d'you bloody ask?'

Daniel was trying to remember what the man at the school gates looked like. *I knew your mum before you were born*. Daniel thought he might be a bender, but the man didn't ask him to go anywhere and just seemed embarrassed.

'The Magdala –' Galvin's voice, which had started to break, slipped a couple of octaves and he cleared his throat. 'The Magdala, right, can destroy the whole world.'

Pushing Galvin's foot off, Daniel got up, went to the kitchen entrance, and looked in. His mum was still on the stool, hunched over. He checked her bare feet for the plaster that she put on the backs of her ankles where her shoes rubbed. They were there, the right one flapping loose. He wished he could cry himself, but what he was feeling wasn't a feeling exactly. It was *this*: Mum, broken in front of the kitchen window; tattooed arm helping him up from the pavement; the man's sweet, heavy scent of tobacco. What he wanted to remember was what the man looked like.

He'd never seen his mum cry. He wished he could go to her, but she'd told him to sit with Galv while she was making their tea. She wouldn't look at him, had spared him that. She would have looked through him, as she did sometimes, into the past, into the world of the old photo he'd found in a handbag she was throwing away: beneath the portrait of a stern old man posed his mother, a beautiful girl playfully pouting her lips into a kiss, lifting the abundant curls of her hair away from her neck. Daniel kept the photo under his wardrobe – evidence of a time about which she'd never spoken.

The floor quivered, sending a shock through his nerves, and he put his hands out in case he fell. He knew his mind was being bad now, a spinning sensation in his chest. Dr Simmons had told him to do *the stop*, to think of football or girls. He could take the medicine, but it made him sleepy, and he wanted to remember the man's face.

He returned to the sofa. As Daniel lay down, Galvin set the soles of his feet against Daniel's, and the two of them sawed their legs back and forth.

'The Magdala is the Beast of Avunta,' Galvin continued.

'No.' Daniel wanted a simple story, not this.

'Yes,' Galvin insisted. 'Listen: but now all the other seers are dead, right – 'cept me – so my mind is the only way between this world and the dreamworld.' Galvin narrowed his eyes, trying to pierce the eye of logic's needle with the thread of his imagination. 'So the beast can only come into this world *through* me, right. So I have to dream you so you can get into the dreamworld to fight it 'fore it has a chance to get out.'

'That can't work.'

'Why?'

It irritated Daniel that Galvin was always so forgetful about these things. 'You said I become *her* in the dreamworld.'

'Well, I'll make you yourself.'

'You can't change it; not once you've said it.'

'She can fight it, then.'

'Don't be stupid.'

'Her beast can fight it.'

'Her beast's in *this* world; our beasts are in our dreamworlds. You can't just change it like that.'

'Then *your* beast can –'

'It won't obey me. You know that.'

'I *can* hold you in my mind as yourself. I can dream you as yourself.'

'No, you can't.'

'Why? Why can't I?'

'Once you've said it, you can't change it.'

Daniel was tired of this. He wanted something simple, a distraction. He looked towards the kitchen again, a tightness in his throat. 'You can't change it.'

She was gone. He was sure of it. This realisation was like his dreams of falling. As he went to get up, Galvin locked their legs together. Daniel freed himself. He knew she was in there, but a silence that was the absence of her silence filled the flat. It assumed Galvin, subsumed his noise, because there had never been a world without him. But his mum had been in a world without Daniel, was there now, a sexy girl diverting the deluge of her lovely hair, showing whoever was taking that photograph that she wasn't afraid of the old man above her, or of anything.

He hurried to the kitchen. She was standing by the counter, peeling potatoes. He checked her feet – the plasters on the backs of her ankles. Her hair, then, shorn and spiky as ever. He helped her cut it every second Monday, using the half-inch attachment on the electric clippers. It was the same woman, his mum.

When she'd got off the bus and had seen him talking to that man beside the school gates today, she'd made the strangest sound: as if a lined hook deep in her throat had been tugged; torn out, the little gout of her voice. Taking hold of Daniel, she'd tried to carry him as if he were a baby. He was ashamed: all the mums and kids watching, the man following, calling her by a posh name he seemed to think was hers, Galvin running alongside. Daniel struggled, slipped in her arms, and she tripped over him, the two of them collapsing to the pavement. Galvin came to them. The man reached down, and Daniel took his hand. But his mum kicked out, screaming at the man to go away, revealing her hidden voice, which Galvin said was Scottish, like Galvin's dad's, though Galvin had to have been too young to remember.

Galvin, too, hit the man, while the man kept repeating that strange name, as if he were delirious. But Daniel was in another space: his hand in that hand. The man held on loosely, so Daniel could move his fingers against the callouses and hard skin. It was like one of the hollows in the horse chestnut.

Then those East End mums, with their brutal bosoms, waded in. They were unable to resist a good fight, though there was no love lost for his mum, who they said took on airs and who, with her close-shorn head, depending on their mood, either was a bloody lesbo or had the cancer.

His mum got to her feet and snatched Daniel's hand out of the man's. Galvin clung to them both. It was then, as his mum dragged Daniel away by the collar of his school blazer, that the man called his name – *Daniel* – as if he were going to say more, explain something.

Daniel now cupped his own right hand and brought it up to his face, the hand that had been in that man's, and on which Daniel had been husbanding the odour of sweet smoke. But the smell was sharp and rank. It was the smell of Galvin's foot.

'Mum,' he called from the kitchen doorway.

'I'm getting the tea ready.'

'Who was that bloke?'

'I don't know what a bloke is.'

'Who was that man?'

'Tell Galv to go home after we have our tea. His mum's going to be worried.'

'She knows he's up here.'

'You're too old to be in the same bed.'

'Why?'

She didn't answer.

'But it's *Fawlty Towers* tonight.'

'He should go down. She's not well.'

'She's always not well.'

'She's not happy.'

'She's always not happy.'

'It's hard.'

'He kicked it eight years ago.'

'Speak properly, Daniel.'

'Eight years.'

'It doesn't matter. It's hard.'

He wanted to ask her what she knew about things being hard in that way; what she knew about his own dad. But she wouldn't answer and he was afraid she might start crying again.

'He doesn't like going down there.'

'Tell him that after tea he has to go home.'

'That man knew you,' Daniel said. 'What did he call you?'

She got a can of baked beans out of the cupboard. A pigeon landed on the sill and flared its wings. Daniel took hold of the doorjamb, hoping his mum wouldn't notice. He didn't want to get the fears again; they had kept him awake because he'd become convinced that in his sleep, thinking it was a dream, he'd jump out of the window. And, after all those nights without sleep, it became a waking dream, a nightmare: abrupt images of himself falling through windows, doors, dark shadows – any kind of opening – into the sky. Dr Simmons had prescribed sedatives and told his mum he should join the scouts to get some male influence in his life, and Daniel had gone with his mum to see a man at the social services. She'd begged the man to move them to a ground-floor flat. Awful, how that man had looked at her. Daniel knew it was the one thing she couldn't bear, to be thought a liar. *The ground floor is for old ladies in wheelchairs, not for people who can't be fagged to climb a few flights of steps.*

Daniel wanted to go to his mum now but felt too afraid to do so, as if there were no way across to her. He was aware of his own image in the mirror over the mantel, and didn't want to look at it directly because he wasn't feeling all right and sensed that, if he looked, he'd somehow echo himself – an echo that gets louder. So he returned to Galvin, lying on the sofa.

His friend was staring at him anxiously. Daniel could still smell Galvin's feet on his hands, a new smell, like Galvin's new voice, the bump in his throat, the acne, the grease in his hair.

'I'll weaken the Magdala,' Galvin said. 'I'll use my dream powers 'gainst it and I'll weaken it, right, much as I can 'fore it gets out. But I can't stop it getting out, not in the end. And if you don't kill it, it'll destroy the whole world.' He hesitated, thinking. It came to him. 'And the only thing that'll kill it, right, is the Sword of Gorag. So we have to go on a quest for the sword. And if I fall 'sleep you have to wake me, else the Magdala might get out. It can get into the world while I'm sleeping. And the thing is, the thing is –' Galvin was caught up in his imagining now. 'The thing is that *her* beast guards the sword. Your dream self. *Her* beast. The only woman you can ever truly love. That's what guards it.' Galvin was clearly delighted at this inspired realisation. 'So when you kill it to get the sword, right, you kill her.'

'I can't kill her,' Daniel said.

'You can,' Galvin said. 'You have to, even though it means you'll be alone forever. *She* is what you have to sacrifice to save the world.'

The boys stared at each other for a while, Galvin's face greedy, almost cruel, until Daniel said, 'Or I can kill you.'

His friend frowned.

'If it can only come out when you dream,' Daniel explained, 'I can kill you. Then it can't come out, can it.'

'But that would kill her too.'

'No, it wouldn't.'

'Yes, it would.'

'No. You said –'

'I don't care what I said.'

'You said that you're just a way between the worlds. That's what you said. She wouldn't die.'

'But I'm the only way you could ever get to her. I'm the seer. I'm the meeting place. I'm the only way you two could ever meet.'

'But she wouldn't die.'

'You *couldn't* kill me.' Galvin looked desperate.

'You have to go home tonight,' Daniel said.

'Why? *Fawlty Towers* tonight.'

'Mum says you should go home.'

Daniel looked towards the kitchen. He got up again, determined to take hold of his mum. But he wanted first to know with some other sense, sure and deep, that she was *here,* in the kitchen, would sit with him tonight on the sofa as they watched *Fawlty Towers*. The throttled throbbing of his heart got worse. He couldn't feel that she was in the flat at all. He went to the kitchen.

Empty. It was empty. She was gone. Not on the stool or by the counter. She was gone. He felt dizzy. The room seemed to list. Taking hold of the doorjamb, he slumped down, then lay himself prone on the lino. He couldn't catch his breath.

The floor shuddered. His mum's bare feet, the plaster. She'd been standing on the counter getting a bowl off the top of the cabinet. The water tank had hidden her. She shouted for Galvin to call an ambulance. Daniel then felt her arms slide around his chest, the weight of her body anchoring him, her damp cheek pressed to his. Softly she began to sing, and her voice, regressed by her fears, became the voice of the girl in the photo, of the woman whose name that man had called – burred, beautiful, and strange.

1

THE RECEPTIONIST at Palm Court gave Daniel a smile well beyond the call of her duty. He was thirty-eight, apologetically tall and attractive, with a thick head of unruly black hair. He regarded her with an expression habitual to him – as if she reminded him of someone and he were trying to work out whom.

Signing in, he said he knew where to go.

On entering the main corridor, Daniel drew together the lapels of his coat. He became aware of this gesture and it troubled him. It was, he realised, his mother's: loving, superstitious, and proprietary.

He wanted a cigarette, but was trying to quit and had cut down to six a day. He'd already smoked four and had a sense he might need the other two later on.

The desolation of the sanitarium – locked steel cabinets, whitewashed walls, the smell of ammonia – was of the same species as his own and increased his nervousness. It had always seemed inconceivable to him that this Victorian mansion had once been someone's home.

A second after he'd entered a section of the corridor thrown into darkness by a faulty fluorescent tube, a massive man loomed out just beside him. Shocked, Daniel flung himself against the wall.

A catatonic with a stricken, pox-scarred face was jammed between two empty display cases.

Daniel moved on, increasing his pace and, just as he looked back, fearing the man might have followed him, he walked right into a tiny nurse who'd emerged from one of the rooms. It wasn't a hard collision, but she seemed hurt, throwing her hand up to her forehead.

He took hold of her elbow. 'Are you all right?'

'My fault,' she replied.

Removing her hand from her brow, she checked it. There was blood on one of her fingers, and Daniel saw a tiny cut above her left eye.

'What happened?' he said.

She gave a little nod towards his chest, and he looked down to see the Parker pen in his breast pocket.

'I am *so* –'

'It wasn't your fault,' she insisted, 'really. It's just a scratch.' She glanced now at his hand, which was still cupping her elbow, and he released her. An awkward few seconds ensued.

Pointing back down the corridor, he said, 'There's a patient –'

'Ah.'

'In between the –'

'Yes, yes, I was . . . Thank you.' She hurried off.

Daniel didn't move for a moment. He felt terrible, but re-felt also, with something quite different from regret, the soft percussion of her body. Lovely voice, he thought, accent of some kind. Pretty girl too. Her odour lingered – a clean, soapy smell. Suddenly a cry pulsed through the corridors.

Gone then, that cry, with its eerie suggestion of his name, and the nurse gone, and the house so still.

He walked on. He'd come without hesitation when Sally had called. A year. She'd written, letters that were essays into pure observation. He knew what she wanted: to begin with an exchange of their sensibilities, divested as much as they could be of bias, history, and personal reference. To begin. But though he'd been trying to strip himself of exactly these things, he'd never responded. A full year. The loss of her had resurrected the other losses: his mother, the dreams of the empty flat, where she was, *wasn't*; of Galvin, his dear friend, who had been, in the end, the one to fall.

All the sadness of this year, and the anger – incandescent. And yet, when Sally had phoned, the sound of her voice had caused him to sit on the floor as if he were being informed of a death. Come on Tuesday, she'd said, three o'clock, her tone that of a secretary setting up an appointment.

He now entered the spacious common room at the back. It shook with the explosions, rattling gunfire, and Stuka screams of a war film being watched by a cluster of patients – most of whom were standing up, for some reason, like a crowd around an accident. The sunlight lancing in through the French doors revealed the room's mealy air.

This was where they usually met. She loved the light

from the stained glass and used almost always to be sitting on the stone sill of one of the large windows. She wasn't there, though, and he looked around for her. Cross-legged on the tiles of the fireplace, scribbling into a notebook, sat a patient Daniel had seen almost every time he'd come. A wasted man with haunted eyes and huge, powerfully useless hands, he always put Daniel in mind of the tortured protagonist of some Russian novel. A couple of times he'd entered this room to find his wife engaged in anxious conversation with this man, and had felt a stab of jealousy. Just beside Daniel, at the Ping-Pong table, sat an Asian woman he'd not seen before. She was poring over a scattered pile of pictures she'd torn from old calendars – a junk on a jade ocean, a chain of mountains like fractured vertebrae, a stag emerging from the misty waters of a loch – each picture, within this shattering sound of war, a vista into being beautifully alone. Just as he was struck by the consummate sanity of this escape, she lifted her hands and addressed the pictures in some delicately elaborate sign language.

A shout drew his attention to the little chapel area at the side of the room, and he saw Amir, a male nurse he knew well, on one of the pews. He was trying to soothe a frantic old lady who was clutching a balsa-wood aeroplane. Amir noticed Daniel at almost the same moment, smiled, and managed to call out, 'She's in the conservatory,' before the woman struck his mouth with the fuselage.

Daniel waved his thanks and felt a churn of guilt as he

went out into the cold and sunny garden. He'd forgotten again to bring a gift for Amir, who'd been so reassuring when his wife had first been admitted three years ago, even writing to Daniel in his own time to let him know how Sally was doing. Amir often surfaced in Daniel's thoughts, had appeared a few times in his dreams. Of course, there were obvious reasons for this, not least of which was the proximity of this kind, compelling, and attractive man to Daniel's wife, whose breakdown had left her so vulnerable. But it was also because he'd been struck by the rare quality of Amir's humanity. Daniel had once heard that, at any given time on the Earth, there lived only thirty-six truly just men. If so, then Amir was one of them – the one condemned, for obscure reasons, to live out his life here, selflessly, among those suffering the hermetic egoism of madness.

Daniel glanced up into the clear blue sky, so unusual for London in early March and, as he looked back down, his vision smeared with the sun, he noticed, at the west end of the garden, a man sitting in a deck chair. Despite the cold, his feet were bare. He wore only pyjamas and a cap, the brim of the latter casting a shadow that completely hid his face. The sight of this man stirred something in Daniel – a memory, a dream, something – but the imminence of his meeting with Sally made him too nervous to attend to this feeling for long.

By the time he got to the conservatory, Daniel felt as if he could hardly draw air into his lungs. Their last encounter had been a disaster. After one of her perfunctory phone calls, she'd come to him, entering their home as if it belonged to a dubious stranger. He'd planned to paint the sitting room in time for her visit. He'd bought the paint, cleared away the ornaments, and pulled the furniture in towards the centre of the room. Then something – the same part of him that had refused to write back to her – had resisted, and it was this devoid, contracted place she came into. She perched herself at the edge of the sofa in front of the elaborate tea he'd prepared, her legs fused, her hands woven in her lap, and her lovely, ash blonde hair plaited, wound up, and pinned back so tight it seemed the full tension of her being depended upon the purchase of a single hair slide.

'I'll have it all painted in a week or two,' he'd said, instantly annoyed at himself for making excuses.

She didn't respond, just fixed her remarkable eyes, one brown, one green, on Daniel and waited for him to be quiet before making her fiercely timorous declaration: 'Dr Kenton has released me, Daniel, but I asked him if I could stay on at the home to help out and he said that I could.'

Silence. There it was: she was better; she was not coming back. He almost fell to his knees, almost took her hands, almost begged her, but managed to hold out until it came – anger, helpless, inflating him with the vacuous courage of despair.

Pouring tea calmly into her cup, he said, as if it were really of not much importance to him, 'Can I at least visit? You do seem a lot better.'

'Write to me, Daniel; let's write for a while.'

'Oh, you know me' – he smiled, a smile he'd felt breaking up at his lips like a fragment of ice from some frigid undercurrent – 'I'm not very good at writing.'

'I can't stay long.' She clearly wanted to leave but seemed physically unable to, as if, here, she were in thrall to him, as if, if he chose it, they would have to live out their lives performing in this peevish and stifling drama.

It was then that he noticed she hadn't touched any of the tea, realised that she wouldn't. When he used to visit her at the sanitarium before she'd asked him not to come anymore, he'd also never been able to bring himself to eat or drink anything in that place.

As he'd sat there, keeping her and himself in suspension, a word had come to him, beautifully new and suggestive: grief. How many lifetimes, he wondered now, would one have to live to learn every word as well at that?

Daniel shut the conservatory door quietly behind him. There she was, the sight of her another collision – all their collisions, loving and otherwise, remembered in one flinch of the nerves. She hadn't seen him yet. She was squatting in a bed of daffodils, a child ruining her party dress in the mud, a bunch of the yellow flowers cradled in her arms.

He called: 'Sally.'

She turned her head to him, then checked her watch, surprised. 'You're early.'

'Am I?'

She seemed relaxed, which relieved him. Standing, she shed the child, ascended years, arrived finally at the brittle grace of one who has lived a little too long. As on that last visit, her hair was tied back in a tightly wound plait, her lovely face breaking out of it, naked, dehiscent.

As he went to kiss her cheek, she shied, clearly afraid he might seek her lips, and said, tapping her fingers against his wrist, 'Didn't I buy you a watch?'

'It was automatic,' he said, following her out of the conservatory and across the lawn towards the gardener's cottage.

'Meaning?'

'Bit morbid.' He was being terse, to punish her – how childish.

She frowned, confused. 'Morbid? Because it was automatic, you mean?'

He didn't answer.

Softly, dryly, she said, 'You're the one who should be in here, you know.'

Just as they reached the cottage, Daniel indicated towards the man in the deck chair. 'Who's that?'

'Not seen him before,' she replied, barely glancing over as she shoved the cottage's ill-fitting door open and led Daniel into a single shadowy space cluttered with her life – ornaments, keepsakes, pictures, photographs, an antique stove, a table set for tea, a single bed. While he took a seat at the table, she carried the daffodils to the sink, laid them on the draining board, and began to prepare the tea.

Silence then, which he found painful, for at the heart of it was that flinch from his kiss, his own helplessness. He looked at her hair again. It had become paler, pearly, seemed unreal, wrapped in such tight convolutions, as if she could just have reached back and removed it, handed it to him, that relic of another life and self, that shell of what had been her sex.

He wanted to be strong, to ask her, as if it were an effort for him even to be curious, why he was here. And yet he wanted also, desperately, for her to know that in the three years she'd resided here – in this last year particularly – he'd been able to feel for nothing but what he'd lost. It had made social work a nightmare for him. He'd found himself increasingly incapable of responding to the lies and half lies of his clients, or even to those things that couldn't be true but were. He couldn't find a way to believe what he was being told, to believe, more frankly, in their lives. *I'm jolly bloody well going to set fire to her.* He'd laughed. Laughed at that Indian woman's anger and despair because it had to be true, and because it was so badly done. While here it was, his wife's slender back, like a paleontologist's dream, lovely bone of life. If only he could return to this at night, after the Grand Guignol, the Indian woman with her thick accent saying, I'm jolly bloody well going to set fire to her.

'*Gorgeous* day,' he said.

Sally glanced back with a smile but didn't otherwise respond. She was selecting a few of the daffodils for a small vase. Astonishing, after everything, how it had endured, that self-possession of hers, the way she engaged herself absolutely with whatever she was doing. Even her breakdown; even that she'd engaged with so completely it had almost destroyed her.

'So,' he said, 'apart from the fact that you're living in a garden shed on the grounds of an insane asylum, how are you?'

'It's not a garden shed,' she said, as she brought the vase of daffodils to the table.

'It's a nice little place, actually.'

She remained in front of him. 'It is a little dark, but you should have seen it when I moved in. Did you ever meet the old gardener?'

'No. I did meet his breath a few times, though.'

'Couldn't help that. He had stomach cancer.'

'I'm surprised *anything* survived in his stomach.'

She examined his face as though she were looking through curiosities in a box, picking them up, putting them down. 'Anyway, he lived in this place for almost fifty years, and when he died, apart from a few bits and bobs, they found nothing in here but a skeleton.'

'A skeleton?'

'A dog,' she said. 'It was under the mattress at the base of the bed. They buried the bones with him.'

'Good Lord. Well, that's going to be an interesting find in a few thousand years, isn't it: *Homo canis*. I want to be buried with the penis of my favourite horse.'

She smiled, but vaguely.

'You know,' she went on, 'he had an old mattress that he must have used for the full fifty years, and on it was this perfect little impression of him. Perfect. You could even see the outline of his toes – you're laughing at me.'

'I'm not laughing at you.' This was *so* Sally. 'I'm just –'

'Anyway,' she said, 'the point is that you'd think it'd be good that there wasn't anything in here – for me, I mean, moving in. But the oddest thing about someone who has nothing in his home is that it makes it so . . . well, so unbearably intimate somehow.'

'Too intimate for *you?*' he said.

Her smile was deeper this time. She seemed to have found it, the thing she would buy, would keep.

'Even for me.'

She went to the fridge and opened it.

'Oh, damn,' she said. 'I'm going to have to run up to the house.'

'Do you want me to go?'

She shook her head. 'I'm always afraid they'll realise it sooner or later.'

'Realise what?'

Pulling the door open, she threw back, just as she stepped out, 'That you're completely mad.'

A few moments after she'd left, Daniel stood up. As he did so, a movement in the room startled him. It was his own reflection in a mirror he hadn't seen for years: her old bathroom mirror from before they were married, the small oval one at the heart of an elaborate art deco frame.

The dimness of the cottage held the blaze of grass at its threshold, the door like an opening of sunlight in deep space. He thought of stepping outside to have a smoke but knew she'd be back soon. On her dresser, he noticed his own photograph huddled among others, a black-and-white in which his face was half obscured by the shadows of leaves. Her father was there, too, the man who'd thrown a pot of boiling tea over her bare back when she'd bumped into his chair as a child, whose scars – whose face – she still bore.

Intimacy. Daniel thought of the old gardener alone for fifty years, of his mattress; of Sally's mattress then, and a fleeting desire to be that – her impression, even to the toes. Unbearably intimate? Not for his wife. Intimacy functioned as a kind of dialysis for Sally.

He picked up the photograph of her father, who looked so happy, washing his Rover with his two swimsuited daughters. The little girls had been caught like large fish in his powerful arms, hysterical with joy. Lie? Was it a lie, this picture? It was the picture she'd chosen. Except for their hair, the girls might have been twins. It happened then, as Daniel was examining the picture, like the instantaneous resolution of an optical illusion: not laughing but screaming; their father's eyes sinister, his smile vicious; not joy but horror, unequivocally. Then, just as quickly, just as completely, joy again. Here was the reason she'd selected this photograph. Like his mother, she would not have a lie near her. He knew from Jill some of the awful things her father had done. But Sally never talked about her father and rarely brought up the past. She lived as much as she could in what engaged her at any moment. Not that she eradicated the past. Indeed, Daniel never got the sense that she wished anything different, not her father's most brutal acts, not her breakdown, not the day after day of Daniel's letter not arriving. She regarded such things simply as the yield of her life, and she kept them – her scars, that oval mirror, these photographs, even his longed-for letters, even letters that never came she kept. With the capacity few have to truly delegate their emotional history to *things,* she was a woman who surrounded herself with the tropes and totems of her life's intimacies.

Damn her. He was having a conversation with her as he always did while she was not here, as her body was with him when she was absent, as her voice would be panned now for weeks from the residue of his waking. She'd done this on purpose. She knew him. He wouldn't speak to her but would speak into the empty room that she was.

His own half-shadowed face stared back from the oval mirror. Damn him. Why couldn't he have written back? His regret now, encountering the flesh and blood of her, was so extreme it displaced him, placed him in the oval mirror. This was what he'd become, not a man with no reflection but a reflection with no man. A lie. He wasn't the one who couldn't respond. For a full year he'd spun hundreds of letters out of his head – observations, formulations, longings. He had so much to say about his love, but had not said it, not written it.

Suddenly it struck him: Sally couldn't live without this kind of response. With whom then? The Russian? Amir? Stop. He had to stop this.

Now, through the open door of the dim cottage, he saw her coming out of the house with the bottle of milk. Sitting down, he watched her traverse that blaze of grass. She halted and chatted for a while to the man in the deck chair before resuming her approach.

As she entered, he said, 'What were you talking about?'

'What?' She gave him a confused look.

'What were you talking about with that patient?'

Her face became overcast, almost angry, which frightened him. He remembered when it all started, how irrational she became, how things he'd never expect would make her hysterical.

'Please don't, Daniel,' she said. 'Please please *please* don't.'

The ensuing silence was painful.

He tried to think of something safe: 'Nice of them to let you stay here.'

She went over to the kitchen area and switched on the kettle. 'Yes,' she said.

'So, you're the gardener now – officially?'

'I am.'

'You're happy here?'

She wrapped the rest of the daffodils in a sheet of

newspaper. He didn't think she was going to respond, but she finally said, 'Well, I've gained a certain calm, I suppose. Nowhere for me to retreat to from here. It's sort of my last stand.'

'Your what?'

'Do you remember Mabel?'

He nodded.

The kettle boiled. She filled the teapot and brought it over to the table.

'She told me once that whenever she got really depressed she'd take a long walk and make a mental note of all the places it might be possible to kill herself.'

'Mabel?' He was surprised. 'She always seemed so unbearably chipper to me.'

'It's not that she *wanted* to do it. She just needed to know that she could if she had to.'

'And you –'

'No, I don't mean me, not like that,' she cut in. 'I just mean that that was *her* last stand. Mine's just a little more prosaic.'

'Well, are you absolutely sure it is your last stand? I mean, couldn't it be your almost last and if-I-have-to-come-over-there-you'll-get-the-back-of-my-hand stand? Couldn't it?'

She smiled but looked disappointed.

'So, what do you think my last stand is?' he threw out quickly.

'I don't know – to be heartless? What do you think?'

'To have a pair of knockers.'

'You can't take anything seriously, can you?'

'I *am* serious. A change of sex. I'd become a woman: I'd be totally unreasonable; I'd make sure my period would last three weeks of every month; and I'd ask my husband in the middle of the filthiest sex if he loved me.'

'That's not "a woman," that's me.'

'Yes, darling, becoming you is my last stand, that's why I love you.'

Despite the lightness of this declaration, she went visibly cold and busied herself filling the milk jug.

All the pain he'd managed to liquefy with his facetiousness recrystallised. He looked out of the door to see the form of that man – with whom she'd spoken – on the lawn. She *had* spoken to him. In the bright sunlight the man appeared two-dimensional, like a photograph from which the face had been carefully cut out, so exactly placed was the shadow cast by his cap's brim.

'The garden at our house has gone to rack and ruin, I'm afraid,' Daniel said, without the strength to attenuate the reproach in his voice.

She didn't respond, and remained at the sink, though there wasn't anything more for her to prepare.

'Sal –'

'It's not *our* house anymore, Danny, it's *your* house.'

She couldn't look at him. He sensed that things were very precarious now and sat still and quiet while she brought over the milk jug and placed it on the table.

Everything was ready. She sat, bent over a little, biting at the skin around one of her nails. Why was the silence so often hers? It bothered him, but he couldn't find a way to make it his own. Jill also chewed the skin around her nails. When the sisters were together, he could see those two shy little girls in that unhappy home: feral, clinging to one another, gnawing at their fingers. They still communicated with their eyes and little flickers of expressions, and were physically very close, as if their bodies belonged as much to each other as to themselves. They looked alike, but Daniel had become attuned to their differences. Sally had more of her father's features, the strong nose, the almost hawkish aspect of his eyes. But she had that Pre-Raphaelite hair, and had inherited a certain expression Daniel had seen in photographs of her very beautiful mother. It was an acute awareness of beauty. Looking out of photographs, Jill and Sally's mother seemed like a woman who was looking into a mirror, trying, always failing, to find a single flaw. It was the very paradox of this inherited expression asserting the beauty of Sally's odd, sharp, asymmetrical features that made her, even at a first encounter, so physically compelling. But that expression hadn't made it through to Jill, though Jill looked much more like her mother, had a face that was a kind of elegy to that original beauty, marred just slightly, like a lovely face with a cut or a bruise, by certain of her father's features. No, Jill had no awareness of or belief in her beauty. What she had was that stubborn flaw at her brow, that expression of brave intransigence.

'I'm worried about you,' Sally said at last.

He almost laughed. 'You're worried about me?'

'I know what you're like,' she said. 'Are you seeing people?'

'Seeing people?'

'I mean just people, friends?'

He was irritated at this condescension. 'I see Rich. Actually, it's Jillybeans's birthday today. What is she now – six?'

'Five. I made her a little dragonfly costume for her party.'

'Nice. Apparently, Laura has –'

'Why didn't you write to me?' she said.

He'd expected it, but not this directly.

'It wasn't –' His voice lost traction and he cleared his throat. 'It wasn't my idea for us not to see each other.'

'I couldn't see you,' she said. 'Not for a while. Every time I saw you, it made me feel poorly.'

Poorly – this was institutional code, the term used for the patients who'd had lapses. He hated to hear her say it. More than any food, it was the language of a world, the understanding of the nuances of that language, that made you a part of it.

'So, what do I make you feel now?' he said.

'That I'd like you to be happy.'

'I was happy when you called.'

She frowned and scraped at something on the table-cloth. It was an impatient gesture. On the table: sandwiches, scones, ginger cake, biscuits, cheeses, julienned vegetables. Ridiculously elaborate and – it struck him – none of it to be eaten: a culminating ritual. Daniel studied the table for a flaw, unable to believe that she'd done it, and so implacably, setting it into its final resonance with that impatient gesture. This beginning, the table just now perfectly set, was the end. These pristine arrangements of food were in their essence a disarray of things eaten, of crumbs, wine stains, coffee cups, and sputtering candles. And he was the last guest, had lingered, believing that this woman, beyond her duties as a hostess, had found him attractive and fascinating.

But she'd just made that impatient gesture.

'How often do you see Jill?' she asked.

'We work in the same office,' he replied, being deliberately obtuse.

'You know, I always wished we could all have lived together, you, Jill, and I. She's so much more sensible than the two of us. I realise it's awful, but I was often thrilled when she broke up with those dreadful boyfriends of hers.'

'She just didn't choose the right men.'

'You were glad when it was just the three of us, weren't you?'

'Well, it's every man's fantasy, isn't it – sisters.'

He was being flippant, but she responded seriously.

'I wouldn't have minded,' she said. 'Even –' She stopped herself.

'Minded what?' he pursued, amazed. The hostess, after backing him to the door, had offered an indiscretion.

'You were so different, Danny,' she said. 'Most of Jill's boyfriends reminded me of my dad.'

'You know, I sometimes think that the only reason you married me was because I was one hundred percent not your dad.'

'That's not true.'

'Anyway, Jill's boyfriends weren't abusive, none of them were.'

'Not in that way. But they were all so bloody *male*.'

'Morgan?'

'I don't think you understand Morgan very well.'

Her protective tone bothered Daniel; the tinder of his old jealousy began to smoke again.

'They didn't seem anything like your dad to me,' he said stubbornly. 'Abusive or not, your dad was a brilliant man and they were a bunch of bloody Neanderthals – Morgan excepted.'

'The only difference was that my dad was ambitious; but he was completely male. That's why he was the way he was.'

'Because men are brutal?'

'I'm not talking about men, I'm talking about him. My dad was the way he was because he wanted to have an imagination.'

'He was a scholar,' Daniel said. 'Famous. You're saying he didn't have an imagination?'

'He made himself one.'

'How can you *make* yourself an imagination?'

She tugged the hem of the tablecloth to remove a wrinkle. 'He was fiercely ambitious and smart. He was a pure male who surrounded himself with women. He was a good man who violated us. *Deliberately*. That's imagination by main force, Danny.'

Her face had become flushed. He couldn't tell if she was giving him this or taking it away. It was in her nature to develop such theories, though he'd never been sure if she actually believed them.

'Well, anyway,' he said softly, eliding it, 'that explains why Jill almost always chose men without imagination.'

Sally grimaced. 'Yes, but I just don't see how you could live with someone like that. Seems like hell to me.'

'And this doesn't?'

She looked at him, seemed merely curious. 'Is this hell for you, Danny? Am I hell for you?'

'No. No. But I can't say these last years have been exactly ecstatic for me either.'

She continued to stare at him for a while. It was a simple, discrete acknowledgment. He knew that she couldn't engage right now with the subject of his unhappiness.

'Oh,' she abruptly exclaimed, 'do you remember that awful fellow, the one who came to Richard and Laura's wedding with us?'

'Barry.'

'Yes, Baz. So horribly English. Still lived with his mother, didn't he? Don't you remember him and Jill having sex next door in that hotel? God, it just made me sick to hear them. He was like a bloody jackhammer. I couldn't stand him.' Sally was getting passionate. 'Those dreadful, racist jokes, that little gap in his teeth he seemed so bloody proud of. To think of him touching her. I hated it. I just –'

'Stop it,' he said gently. For a moment, he was dreadfully, precariously happy, to be able to say this to Sally. She seemed his wife again, leaning in close, gnawing at her finger. This was a lovely parenthesis from that finished table of tea things.

'You hated it, too,' she said.

'He must have gone on for an hour. As a general rule men don't like to be made aware of the astonishing sexual stamina of other men.'

'Sexual stamina, darling, results from a lack of empathy.' She smiled at him. 'You're just a very, *very* empathetic person.'

'I feel *so* reassured,' he said. 'Thank you, Sally.'

She got back to her point: 'But you hated it because it was her, too, because it was Jill, didn't you?'

She was being oddly insistent, which gave him pause.

'I suppose,' he reluctantly conceded.

She waited, wanting him, he could tell, to be more definite. He did have a proprietary feeling towards Jill. She'd provided ballast for his often painfully unbalanced relationship with Sally. She had earth in her. You could hear it in her voice, a loam. And Jill's clear and uncomplicated love for him, as much as it sometimes frustrated Daniel, also allowed some essential part of him to *be*, and to develop. He *had* hated those boyfriends, had hated listening to Barry having sex with her that night, but he also envied those men their superciliousness, their straightforward appetites, the way they would talk to him, with a flaccid belch and an appraising glance at his wife on the balcony, about what a goer Jill was. These men had simple lizard brains; they had to blink to swallow their food.

But he wasn't going to give Sally anything else.

Sally waited a few more seconds, then made her declaration: 'Jill *adores* you. She always has.'

The parenthesis had been closed. She'd said at last what she'd brought him here to say. Here they were, twelve years after she'd made that call and seduced him. Twelve years later she wished she'd given that old boyfriend just one more night so that Daniel's evening with Jill could have followed its otherwise inevitable course. Now Daniel knew why he was here. The hostess had become incontinent and impassioned in order to let him know that he was perfect for one of her other guests. Surely she had to be aware that every man who came here did so for her, for this hostess with the obscurely important and eternally absent husband, who worked her way into exquisite intimacies with her male guests in order to say, when they had started to pin her gaze and contrive reasons to take her hand, that *she,* that girl in the brown dress, *adores* you, would be perfect for you. Twelve years.

'When can I come to see you again?' he said.

She looked away but sat up straight. 'You should have written to me, Danny.'

'I could –'

'I want to start again.'

'Start again? With whom? Amir? With that bloke in the deck chair?'

'What?' She regarded him with amazement. 'No. Not – at least for now – with anyone. Don't get like this again, Danny. I was *never* unfaithful to you.'

He hated to feel it, that old, acid jealousy, intensified now by his regret. There was so much he wanted to say to her, all the things of this last year. She'd given him a chance, had asked him to write, to begin slowly, but he'd failed, hadn't told her the truth, had lived in sin with his love of her. Could there have been a worse deception and debauchery than the fevered celibacy of these last years?

'I know,' he said, standing.

She stood also, brushing down the front of her dress. She fetched the bouquet of daffodils from the counter and handed it to him. 'Put them in the sitting room, on the mantelpiece.'

Taking them, he walked to the door and hesitated again. There was nothing more that could possibly be said. The sun was in her face: she was squinting at him; her father's odd features. It was astonishing how unattractive she could look. He'd often tried to take hold of these moments as a way into ceasing to love her, but it was never any good. The silence between them was now so absolute that the pressure of it made him want to laugh. Even to say good-bye now would be a kind of lie. He walked out.

As Daniel passed the man in the deck chair, he was jarred again by that elusive familiarity. What had that man and his wife talked about? Still looking back at him, Daniel shunted right into an upheld hand. It was the old lady Amir had been trying to placate in the recreation room. Still clutching her aeroplane, she stared up at Daniel with dazzled love.

'Francis! She told me you wouldn't come. Peevish, she is.'

Daniel couldn't think how to respond.

Her gaze settled on the flowers, and her voice swooned, 'Oh, you brought him.' Putting her aeroplane down, she took the bouquet carefully out of Daniel's arms. 'Such a quiet child.' She laid the bouquet into the dry basin of an old birdbath. 'Never cried, 'cept in the morning. Then he was all glisteny.' Suddenly she looked back up at him, confused. 'Didn't you die in the war? I thought you all did. Bert did. And my Bertie.'

The pretty nurse who'd collided with Daniel in the corridor suddenly appeared. A small plaster covered the cut above her eye.

'There you are, Consuelo.' She spoke in a quick whisper, and he realised that her accent was Welsh. 'The doctor's not going to hurt you, now.'

'But my son's here,' the old woman protested.

'Oh yes, but he has to go.' The nurse threw Daniel an entreating look. 'He'll be back again in no time.'

'Do you have to go?' the old woman asked, deflated.

'Yes, but I'll return soon.'

'Are you off to fight again?'

'Yes.'

Yielding to the arm the nurse now placed around her shoulders, the old woman allowed herself to be shepherded towards the house. But, just a few yards away, she pulled free and looked back at Daniel, confused. 'They said you was dead.'

'They were wrong,' he called.

When she and the nurse were out of sight, Daniel lit a cigarette, flicking harder than he needed to at the flint of his antique steel lighter as if restarting his stalled self. He kept the lighter in his hand for a moment, drawing comfort from its solidity and weight, looking at his own face distorted on its surface. After taking a few deep drags, he moved on towards the house.

'Son.' A man's voice. Daniel turned around. It could only have been the man in the deck chair. Then Daniel saw them, the daffodils, which he'd been about to leave behind, lying on the birdbath; saw his wife still at the threshold to the dark cottage, twelve years away, a woman loved nostalgically by the sun, saturated, obscured.

'Thanks,' Daniel called to the man as he retrieved the flowers. The man didn't say anything more, just cleaned out the bowl of his pipe then, strangely, without filling or lighting it, lifted the stem towards the shadowed void of his face.

2

THE NEXT MORNING, Daniel woke with a shock and checked the clock beside his bed. Late. The third time in two weeks. Again he had no memory of the alarm ringing or of switching it off. He hadn't slept for most of the night, sweating, his heart racing. In these last few months, it seemed, he'd hardly slept at all.

Panicked, he threw on his clothes and ran downstairs. After lighting a cigarette, he snatched up his briefcase, which was just inside the door to the sitting room. As he was about to leave, though, the daffodils, which lay on the mantelpiece still wrapped in newspaper, snagged his conscience. He'd had terrible dreams last night, trying to get something back to someone, something they needed or they would die.

These yellow flowers; a reproach; something new. Nothing else in this room, this house, touched him any longer. He didn't even think anymore about those unwrapped paintbrushes, those paint cans sitting, covered in dust, unopened for a year now on that sheet of tarpaulin. A featureless room, a contracted room, with its furniture pulled in towards the centre. Not enough light for it to dilate, the room, him. Depression? He didn't feel depressed exactly, always completely there, intensely there. Here. He would try to cry sometimes but never could, would think, objectively, This is crazy, and yet it was as if he'd displaced the craziness into the house itself, insanity becoming a kind of familiar, this house alive, and lithe, and curling into his lap in the evenings. His little madness, soft beneath its chin, its eyes like nothing on this earth.

Put them in the sitting room, on the mantelpiece. She'd asked him to do it. Damn it. He threw down his briefcase, opened one of the sideboards, which was crammed with all the things that had once been on display in the room. He dug around roughly, and an old carriage clock fell to the floor, its glass face shattering. Then he found it, pulled it out, that crystal vase she'd picked up as a steal in some flea market. He took the vase to the mantelpiece and held it up for a moment, offering it to the daffodils. But they remained impassive, immobile, and it was too late now, too late for this. Putting the vase on the mantelpiece, he took up his briefcase and ran out.

3

HALF AN HOUR LATER, Daniel entered work with the feeling that there was not a single person in this vast, dreary, open-plan office not aware that he was late. And yet, his co-workers, interviewing clients, shuffling files from one place to another, gave him no more than their usual wink or smile, and those waiting to sign on or to be interviewed paid him as much attention as sad old or satiated young lions might pay a distant herd of wildebeest.

He searched for Richard and finally found him, hunched over, trying to hide his lanky body in one of the interview cubicles. He was reading a newspaper and furtively eating a jam doughnut.

'Looks like you're enjoying that.' Daniel sat to face his friend.

'I'd offer you a bit,' Richard said, 'but this here' – he held up what remained of the doughnut as if it were a jewel – 'is pure jam.'

'The point is to eat the jam *with* the doughnut.'

'I don't have a taste for pap, unlike you, matey.'

'How'd it go last night?'

Richard shrugged. 'Twenty screaming kids.'

'Did Laura – ?'

'Yes, she brought him.' Richard's mobile face, with

its slightly jutting ears and sad eyes, twisted into a grimace. 'He's an American. Episcopal minister. Looked like he'd been laminated. Where were you yesterday?'

'Went to see Sally.'

Richard became instantly serious, though he'd put the entirety of what remained of the doughnut into his mouth and was now trying to chew as unobtrusively as possible.

'You just went?' he finally got out.

'She called me on Sunday.'

'Should've given me a bell, matey.'

Daniel nodded.

'Was it all right?'

'She doesn't want to see me again.'

Richard cocked his head and squinted, as if he were hard of hearing.

'I mean ever again,' Daniel said. 'That's it.'

Leaning back in his chair, Richard raked his fingers through the wiry, salt-and-pepper curls of his hair. 'So how do you feel about that?'

'Tell you the truth, I can hardly believe I even went there. It's like it didn't happen.' Daniel thought of the daffodils, their spill of yellow in his bare home.

Richard, working dough from his teeth with his tongue, was clearly at a loss for what to say.

'How did you feel about this minister?' Daniel asked.

'Same I suppose. You'll never guess what his name is.'

Parodying a southern accent, Richard drawled, 'Nathaniel Vandemeer-LeGrand the third from Tuscaloosa, Alabama, at your service, sir.'

'That's never his name.'

'Bloody is, matey.'

'What does Jillybeans think of him?'

'Seems to like him. He's like someone off the TV. Big and handsome, looks really well fed, you know. Made me think of a black Angus.'

'Is he black?'

'No, but he would be if he were a bull, matey.'

'He could be a white bull.'

'I'm going for glossy.'

'You can have a glossy white.'

'Not on a bull, precious. I mean if a bull were white it would be a dirty white, wouldn't it – white with a touch of shite.'

They both laughed.

'That's what I'm going to paint my house,' Daniel said, 'white with a touch of shite.'

'Yeah, day you paint your house, matey, is the day I cease to be your example and superior.'

Daniel stood up and looked across the bustling main office to the entrance of his own. He felt overwhelmed by the thought of working today.

Glancing down at his friend again, he said, 'Rich, I did a terrible thing on Monday with this Indian woman who came to see me.'

'With a client?'

'Not *that*. Anyway, I'll tell you later. Do you want to go for a curry tonight?'

'Actually, a bunch of us are heading up to the King's Arms. You want to come?'

Daniel knew Richard well enough to sense the reticence in his invitation and didn't reply.

Clearly troubled by the false note struck between them, Richard said, 'Listen, forget the King's Arms. Let's go and eat.'

'Well, who's going?'

'Usual suspects.'

Daniel just stared at his friend, and Richard finally said, 'Look, what do you think about me and Jill?'

'You and Jill?'

'I don't want to tread on any toes, matey.'

'You're not treading on my toes.'

'Are you sure?'

'She's my wife's bloody sister.'

'We were a half pint of Stag away from a snog the other night. Truth to tell, me old matey, I've always had a bit of a thing for Jill, and I was hoping, after a few pints tonight, she might muster up a bit of a thing for me.'

'Why don't you just ask her out?'

'I'm British: we don't meet, marry, or reproduce without alcohol.'

'She's always liked you, Rich. You two would be good for each other.' Now Daniel had struck the false note.

Richard quickly filled the awkward silence: 'Do you know why I disliked him?'

'Who? The black bull?'

Richard nodded. 'He was brought up by his six older sisters.'

'So?'

'You could tell.'

'Why would that make you dislike him?'

'You could just tell that the only things he could really relate to were adoring women and a congregation. I just didn't feel I was in his ken, do you know what I mean?'

'Come on, Rich, you're the ex-husband of his fiancée. He's not going to dance the bloody lambada with you, is he.'

Meeting this with anxious recalcitrance, Richard said, 'I suppose I just didn't think he could feel for my daughter in the same way. In the right way. I don't want Jillybeans to be one of his bloody adoring women.'

'That's all right, Rich, he's not her dad.'

Richard now looked as if there were something he desperately wanted to say, but just at that moment someone pinched Daniel's bottom. He turned around. It was Betsy, an ample woman in her early forties with a voice that, as Jill had once put it, was like having a full body rub with warm coffee grains. She wore very low-cut dresses and touched expertly. Her sexuality was so overt it could have no ulterior motive and was given equally to women and men. Daniel would often seek her out just to sup at her vibrancy, which, as she held court at the information desk, was given perfect expression in the great well of her cleavage. That cleft itself separated a small yin and yang, tattoos that actually looked like little blue tears.

'Mutt 'n' Jeff were looking for you earlier, sweetheart,' she said.

'Christ, I'm going to hide in my office.'

'Ooh, I love a man who runs away.' She shivered her body in mock ecstasy.

He looked back at Richard. 'I'll talk to you later.'

Richard nodded.

'You coming tonight?' Daniel asked Betsy.

'I never lose hope,' she said, winking.

Daniel walked swiftly towards his office, but halfway there all the impulse in him congealed and he came to a halt. His wife wanted a new start. Without him. It had happened again: Galv, his mum, now Sally, gone. A distant roaring in his ears, the old vertigo. The room began to list; he was afraid he might fall. He closed his eyes for a few seconds and this disorientation eased. It occurred to him that he hadn't eaten since seeing Sally yesterday, and had barely slept. He continued on to his office but, just as he reached it, the door to the office beside his opened to reveal a strange conjoined creature made up of Daniel's large, phlegmatic boss, Morgan Bryce, and the diminutive Perry Linneker.

Morgan's gaze, which managed to be at once sympathetic and sardonic, fixed on Daniel. Aristocratically mannered, with a first in classics from Christchurch, Morgan had always seemed to Daniel more than a little out of place in this office.

'Dan-i-el,' Morgan sang out with camp affection, 'you're like our guest star, you know. I always expect to hear wild applause whenever you make an appearance.'

'I'm sorry, yes, my clock stopped.'

'I'd be happy,' Perry offered, 'to give you a call before I leave for work in the morning.'

Not even glancing his way, Daniel replied, through his teeth, 'Thank you, Perry, that's fine. It won't happen again.'

'Well, I'm glad to have caught you,' Morgan went on. 'Perry here was just bringing one of your cases to my attention.'

'How conscientious of him.'

'In-*deed*,' Morgan wryly agreed. 'The Lockley case. Do you remember the Lockley case?'

At Daniel's hesitation, Perry reminded him, with reticent, almost pitying, reproach, 'It *was* assigned to your office more than three weeks ago.'

'Right.' Daniel decided that being firmly vague might save him: 'With the father and the children and the . . . uh . . . the housing problem.'

'No, no, the *Lockley* case.' Morgan was getting impatient. 'Have all these people become indistinguishable to you?'

Perry, animated by his increasing delight at Daniel's discomfort, had become like Morgan's interpreter for the deaf, using not sign language but exaggerated facial expressions.

In a gesture of avuncular admonition, Morgan laid his

bearish hand on Daniel's shoulder. 'To misquote the bard from Hull,' he drawled, 'you, Daniel, say, "Be beautiful and I will embrace you." They – our clients – say, "Embrace us, and we will be beautiful." Embracing not been your strong suit lately, has it, Daniel?'

Just then Daniel glimpsed salvation emerging from one of the cubicles.

'Jill,' he called, throwing her a desperate look as she turned to him, 'the Lockleys?'

Jill hurried over to his defence. 'I've been dealing with that case,' she explained, adding casually to Daniel, 'You remember, the old woman who claims she's being abused by her son.'

'Oh, right.' It came to him now. He'd interviewed the mother a few weeks ago, a fierce ferret of a woman who'd littered dozens of delinquent children. He remembered how, like so many of those he interviewed, she would glance up at him only periodically before returning to the exhaustive labour of her claim. For her, he was like stubborn grime upon a mirror, grime she was determined to scour away with the angry frottage of her voice, to bring before her, at last, her own gleaming image.

'It's an obvious scam,' Daniel threw out, not intending his tone to be quite so derisive. 'They want to jump the waiting list, so she claims her son's beating her up and we have to get her into emergency housing. The Lamertons have made a career out of –'

Jill touched his arm. 'Lockleys, Danny,' she said softly. 'I mean the Lockleys.'

'*Do* you mean the Lockleys?' Morgan asked, the dubiety of this question instantly translated into the language of facial expression by Perry.

'The Lamertons is a very similar case,' Jill got in quickly.

With a glance at Jill, Morgan slipped back into his torpid, nasal irony, though it had something of an edge to it now as he addressed Daniel. 'You and Jill are like a married couple. Not only is she your memory, she's your apologist. Daniel, we have to keep a tight ship here. You're becoming rather forgetful. This isn't like forgetting to stack a shelf in a shop. If you forget *here*, people really suffer.'

With that, Morgan and Perry, as one, like a great fiddler crab, sidled away.

'Thanks, Jill,' Daniel said a moment later as the two of them found refuge in his office.

'Perry's angling for your job, you know.'

'He's bloody welcome to it.'

Daniel threw down his briefcase and slumped himself in his desk chair. She offered him a cigarette, which he took, and they lit up. 'The most frustrating thing is that they're right. I've lost it. I can't distinguish these people anymore. I feel as if I've seen every bloody one of them a hundred times before. I've become one of those social workers I used to hate when I came to this job. On Monday, this Indian woman –' He stopped himself.

'What?' Jill stepped a little closer. Around him, especially if he were upset, she would often move as if

her actions had been staged by some obsessively
controlling director. Daniel was aware of the effect his
presence had on her, and it frustrated him. She was
wearing a short tartan dress and a pair of white stockings,
an outfit Daniel had once offhandedly told her she
looked good in but which didn't suit her at all.

'What happened?' she said.

'I'll tell you later.'

'Where were you yesterday?'

He couldn't believe she didn't know and glanced at
her sharply. 'I needed a day off.'

'I found something that might cheer you up.' She left
his office and returned a moment later with her leather
satchel. From this she removed a framed photograph and
handed it to Daniel. It was an old picture of him, Sally,
and Jill standing on a beach.

'We went to Hastings, do you remember? Just after I
broke up with Simon.'

'Simon? Was he the bloke who'd memorised all of
Monty Python?'

'That's him. Funny to think now that every night some
other lucky woman is being treated to the unexpurgated,
one-man Dead Parrot sketch. Can you guess which part
of his anatomy plays the dead parrot?'

'Spare me, Jill, please.'

She laughed and squatted down in front of him to look
at the picture.

'Anyway,' she said, 'I was cleaning out my car on
Sunday and I found a roll of film under the seat. Do you

remember how devastated Sally was that we'd lost the photos?'

'She thought I'd lost them. She was bloody furious.'

'Isn't that a great picture? Hardly any of them came out. I've made a copy for Sal. She's going to wet her knickers.'

'When was this?'

'Seven years ago. I'd just bought my Mini, do you remember?'

He nodded. A subsidence in his chest: to see his wife leaning against him, calmly, as if he were solid.

'Is this for me?' he said.

'Yes. I thought it might encourage you.'

'Encourage me?'

'You can put it in your house somewhere, after you've finished painting it, which would mean, of course, that you'd have to take the wrapping off one of those brushes.'

'Jill, darling,' he said, rapid-fire, 'a paintbrush is a tool; a tool is designed to save labour; the ultimate tool, therefore, is what?' Before she could come out with anything, he leaned in towards her, placed his hand paternally against her cheek, and whispered, 'Something you never use.'

He could see that she wanted to riposte, but their proximity, his hand on her face, had robbed her of her voice. She was trembling.

He looked back at the photograph. What he remembered of that weekend was the three of them late at night in that bed and breakfast room. Sally had just come out of a bath, and they were all on the bed having a nightcap – he and Jill sitting up against the headboard, Sally lying across their laps. Her towel had fallen away to reveal that old burn scar on her back. Sally demanded a kiss from him, and a kiss from Jill, asked them then to kiss each other. They didn't, though. Didn't because they both knew that Sally, bridging their bodies, wanted to be that kiss.

'I went to see Sally,' he said.

'When?' She looked genuinely surprised. 'Yesterday?'

He nodded.

'Was it okay?'

'Yes. She seems better.'

'She *is*,' Jill said vehemently. '*So* much better; and she's happy there.'

This offended him, though he realised at the same time that he'd wanted to be offended, was glad to have this little bead of anger to roll in his fingers.

Instantly aware of the implications of what she'd said, Jill hastily recanted: 'I don't mean she's *happy*. I just mean she's much better now.'

'Don't pretend you don't know,' he said, irritated.

'Don't know what? What are you talking about?'

It was probably true that she didn't know what had happened: Sally wouldn't wish to put Jill in the position of having to keep anything from him.

'Did it not go well?'

'It went fine. She prepared a lovely tea and told me she didn't want to see me again.'

Jill flushed, bright red. She was chewing at the skin around one of her nails, and Daniel did what he hadn't been able to do to Sally. He took her hand out of her mouth and held it. He felt so grateful to Jill for this flush, this anger and struggle not to cry, which expressed the feeling trapped in him. Jill couldn't speak, caught between them as she had been since the night he and she would have got together if Sally hadn't lost her keys.

'It's been coming for a long time,' he said. 'It's the best thing.'

She still couldn't speak, though her face was composed now, almost surly. She retrieved her hand to wipe away the tears that had escaped and began to chew at her fingers again. Like Sally and so unlike her. While Sally – in part to save her sister – had engaged with her father's cruelties, Jill had, at nine years old, taken to punching him in the crotch so remorselessly he'd bought himself a batter's box. Twice she'd called the police on him, once the ambulance for her sister. It was Jill who'd cared for their sedated mother. All this had made her the consummate social worker. She could empathise but had also learned to protect herself (though she had her weaknesses, of which he was one). Earth. There was earth in her. Looking now at her lips, he wondered if you could taste it there, mineral, like blood, in her kiss. They'd come close to kissing on a number of occasions in these last twelve years. But there was only one really dangerous time: that evening five years ago when he'd driven to her flat to pick her up for the office party. She'd opened the door in her dressing gown, late, as always. While she was changing, he'd gone to the bathroom. There it began: with the wet imprint of one of her feet on the bath mat, the faint impression of three of her fingers in the steamed mirror of the cabinet above the sink, a pair of her knickers curled up on the floor, and a smell like suntan lotion. Simply: he stepped into her body, possessed it, felt it as his own. When he got out, she was standing with her back to him, wearing the little brown dress he loved on her, and was putting in her earrings. Walking past, he deliberately knocked into her, and she playfully pushed back. He then stood between her and the mirror, refusing to move. She went to shove him out of the way, but he defended himself, and they began to wrestle. He took hold of her wrists, but she tripped him back on to her bed, the two of them laughing and struggling. He trapped her then on top of him, holding her arms behind her. She clamped her teeth gently around his chin. It was too late for him: more than anything in the world he wanted *this* Jill, with one earring, in her brown dress, whose body he'd just been. As she made her ventriloquist threats, he released her wrists and gathered her damp hair in his hands. It was she who pulled away, that loyalty, stubbornness, pragmatism asserting itself. What would she say at this moment if he told her, 'Sally has just given me back to you; returned us to each other'?

He stared at Jill now, a look she met with sympathy, interpreting it, no doubt, as a look of despair. But what he was wondering was whether he could love someone other than Sally. Could he learn these new sounds, or had he spoken love in the language of his wife for too long? Was it possible to forget everything and learn to hear again, hear this woman's face, her body, her life?

'So, how do you feel?' she said.

'Jill, I haven't seen her for a year. We haven't been together for more than three years. In a way it's good. I really need to forget her.'

'No,' she protested, 'that's not –'

'You don't know me,' he cut her off sharply. 'I *need* to forget.'

After a moment, she said, 'When's your first appointment?'

'No appointments today. I'm doing that damn evaluation up at the Tower Hamlets office.'

'A bunch of us are going to the King's Arms tonight.'

'Rich told me.'

'You going to come?'

'I don't want to cramp your style.'

'What do you mean?'

He just smiled.

'Are you talking about Rich?'

'He's a great bloke.'

'He's also seriously on the rebound.'

'He named his daughter after you.'

'Oh, shut up, that's his mum's name.'

'Rich *adores* you, Jill. He always has.' He heard himself

repeating Sally's words exactly. What odd exorcism or revenge was this?

'I just want to support him, really,' Jill said.

'Support him?'

'They're off to America in a week.'

'Who?'

'Laura and Jillybeans.'

'With the bloody Texan?'

'He's not Texan, he's Alabaman or Alabameze or whatever it is.'

'How long are they going for?'

She was clearly surprised he didn't know. 'For good. They're *going*.'

'But Laura can't just take his daughter to another country. She's only known this bloke for two months.' Daniel felt terrible for Richard, but angry and perplexed also that Richard hadn't said anything to him.

'I'm going to talk to him.' Daniel got up, but Jill took hold of his arm.

'Listen, Danny, *listen*. Sit down for a minute.'

Daniel sat. He'd finished his cigarette and wanted to smoke what remained of Jill's. She never really smoked them, just held them in her hand.

'Danny, I think something happened, a long time ago. I don't think he even tried to get custody.'

'Happened? What happened?'

'I don't know.'

'What are you talking about?' It was infuriating him that she was being so coy.

'Look, Laura was going to tell me because everyone thinks she's being such a bitch, but I asked her not to.'

'You mean he did something? Like an affair?'

She shook her head. 'It happened before he knew Laura, when he was a teenager, and it was very bad. That's why she left him: she found out. I think the best thing is not to say anything. If he ever wants to tell us, he'll tell us.'

A sickening pang in Daniel's stomach made him feel dizzy again. Jill's face, right in front of him, suddenly appeared strangely rigid and ill-fitting, as if it might fall away. He recalled his own voice from weeks ago, telling her that she looked good in those white stockings and that tartan dress. Idle words to allay some little flicker of desire in him, or to propitiate some memory of his wife, or to bridge a momentary loneliness. Here they were before him now, those words, embodied, believed, wrong.

'Jill, have you got anything to eat?'

'I have a Kit Kat.' She fetched it from her satchel.

It tasted sickly sweet, but he felt a little better.

'Are you all right?' she said.

He nodded.

'Oh, I almost forgot.' Jill reached over and pulled a file from one of the trays on his desk. 'I wanted you to have a look at this. I got the oddest letter from some bloke up at the Windsor Council Estate.'

'Windsor? My old spawning grounds?'

'Oh God, yes. I always forget how common you are.'

'Which block's he in?'

She glanced at the front of the file. 'Hicks House.'

Windsor, Hicks House: his words, from his life. Again that strange feeling that this wasn't Jill. Her voice, he thought, I know her voice, and though he didn't want to hear any more, he needed to be sure of that voice, and said, 'Which floor?'

'Well, he's in a hundred and sixty-three, does that mean he's on –'

Daniel snatched the file out of her hand and stared at the address in disbelief – or rather, in confirmed belief.

'That's *my* flat,' he said, 'my mum's flat. That's where I grew up.'

'How funny,' she said, visibly taken aback by his behaviour.

'Yes, it's bloody hilarious, isn't it,' he almost shouted. It was just a stupid coincidence, but it was as if he'd known it the second she'd said Windsor, had known which block, which flat it would be, had known exactly what she was going to say, almost as if he'd willed it, or something had willed it. He didn't need this.

'You've gone pale,' Jill said.

The shame now, appalling, the memory, after his mum's burial, of flinging the keys out of the landing window, of turning away from the door in which had been everything and, perhaps, all he could love, leaving it. To strangers. A stranger *there*. He couldn't bear to think about it. Jill was standing in front of him. The tartan dress, the white stockings. He reached out and put his hand on the inside of Jill's thigh, almost at her crotch. Shocked, she stepped away. Neither of them said anything.

He returned the file to her and stood up, a frantic, thwarted energy inside him.

'Why am I still here, eh, Jill?' His voice issued as if from someone else, blithely comic, fake. 'Lived in Paris for a year. Almost got a French woman to smile at me once – it was an amazing moment. India, three years – three years on the crapper, that is, after a week in India. Australia – loved Australia. I loved that place. Why didn't I stay there? I always came back, Jill. *I always come back.*'

Jill's face was flushed. Silence threatened, and right now he couldn't stand that.

'So, what's this letter, then?'

'Are you okay?'

'Yes, I'm fine.'

'Right.' She spoke quickly, nervously. 'Well, this bloke, Amos Radcliff, lost one of his legs five years ago – severed by a beer barrel, of all things, that fell through a cellar hatch. I'll spare you the legless jokes. Anyway, since then he's been getting a disability allowance on top of a few hundred other benefits – including a pension. There's some confusion about his age. There are records of him being in the Star and Garter Veteran's Hospital just after the war, which would make him over seventy, but according to *these* documents' – she patted the file – 'he's in his early fifties.' Abruptly Jill raised both her hands palm out as if to stop the onrush of this information and sighed. '*Anyway*, seventy-year-old veteran Radcliff is someone else's problem. We're dealing with fifty-year-old, one-legged Radcliff, who hasn't worked a day since his accident.'

It *is* her voice, he thought. It is.

'So, since we have orders from our new *Führer* to integrate the disabled into the workforce, I sent Radcliff a letter telling him he had to come and be rehabilitated. And to this he sends a polite refusal – as if I'd sent him a wedding invitation. So, then I let him know that if he doesn't accept the place I'm saving for him, I'll have to withhold his benefits. And in response to that' – Jill opened the file, which Daniel was still holding, turned a few pages, and tapped her finger on a handwritten letter – 'he sent this.'

The letter's script was neat and rounded. He read.

My dear friends at the DHSS,

   I wish to express regret at my negligence towards you. Your generous and hitherto unconditional sponsorship has been invaluable to me. The real problem I have with rehabilitation is that I'm already habilitated – equipped, that is, with all I need for my vocation. I'm a writer. At this point in time, I wish to continue the experiments of Henri Gauche, who'd claimed, as a proud young man, that he could bring an entirely imagined human existence to life simply through description. A few young blades at his club challenged his honour over this – isn't

hubris the seed of all greatness – and he began work on a
fictitious woman called Elise Essouffle in 1896. After a
year of dedicated writing, his friends withdrew the bet,
and his family became worried. But it was too late. He
was obsessed. He was in love. A further seven abject
years of dedicated writing achieved nothing. But then,
one cold morning in March, sunk in the most profound
despair, he made a fractional alteration to the
manuscript and immediately felt the paper begin to
warm. Thus revived, he worked on for a further twelve
years, giving up his youth and irreparably corrupting his
health. In July of 1915, he wrote to a friend that the
paper had broken into a fine sweat. In the following
nineteen years, he lost that heat and sweat innumerable
times, and was driven even to attempt suicide (luckily, le
Ruisseau Bafouillant was more shallow than he'd
anticipated). One day, on the brink of despair and now
nearing complete blindness, he crossed out what he
thought was the word livid – in fact, the word he erased
was lurid. Suddenly, he felt the faint pulse of her heart.
Thirty years later, his tenacious life at last abandoned
him. On the morning of the 28th of July, 1965, Henri
Gauche's body was carried down la Rue Interminable to
the cemetery. Directly behind the coffin shuffled a
woman in black. She had a rather sour and suspicious
face, and stooped a little. Her dress was not ugly, but
well behind the times. 'Let's face it,' whispered one of
Henri's old friends to another as he nodded towards this
woman, 'his prose always lacked grace.'

> *My friends, your generous contribution to my*
> *sustenance will not be forgotten.*
>
> > *Your humble servant,*
> > *Amos Radcliff*

Far from amusing him, this letter now distilled Daniel's confused feelings, his shame, into a pure, caustic fury.

'You know,' he said softly, 'my mother worked every fucking day of her life.'

'Danny, that isn't his fault.' Jill was clearly shocked by his response. 'I only had you read it —'

'I'll deal with it.' Daniel slipped the file into his briefcase.

'What's wrong with you? Is this because he's living in your mum's flat?'

'That's got nothing to do with it.'

'Daniel, you're not in a good frame of mind right now. You don't need to take it out on this bloke. Just forget him. What does it matter?'

'I'll deal with it,' Daniel repeated, opening one of his desk drawers and filling his briefcase with files. 'I've got to spend the day at the Tower Hamlets office anyway. I'll drop by our man with one leg on the way home.'

He got up and went to the door. Just as he was about to exit, though, he hesitated. He wanted to say something to Jill, but couldn't even meet her eyes directly. 'I'll see you at the King's Arms tonight.'

Again he paused, needing Jill to respond, even if it

were just with 'good-bye.' She didn't. He hurried out of the building, and it wasn't until he got on to the bus to Tower Hamlets that he realised he'd left the photograph Jill had given him behind.

4

APART FROM JILL'S KIT KAT, all he'd had to eat today were a sausage roll and a bag of crisps. His morning at the Tower Hamlets office had passed through him like a fever. Fractured images: the way one man, as he spoke, kept using his right hand in a pincer motion to clean away the spittle that gathered in little foaming balls at the corners of his lips. The way a woman ate her lunch, a yoghurt, as if each mouthful were something shameful she had to hide inside her. All he'd been able to think about was that ridiculous letter, *already habilitated, your humble servant,* that voice, the voice of the man-with-one-leg, the writer, in his home.

The five high-rises of the Windsor Council Estate were now in sight. The grey clouds seemed to hold in suspension the lees of night. Despite what he'd said to Jill, though he'd always returned to London and still lived just a mile from this part of it, he'd not been back to the estate itself for twenty years. He thought of Eveline, that obsessive-compulsive woman Sally had befriended at the sanitarium, who spent many hours each day walking in a circle around a photograph of her dead brother, repeating over and over again that she just couldn't look at it.

Twenty years. Not since the day of his mum's funeral,

which was the very day his neighbour, Maggie, had told him of Galvin's death. Daniel thought – a thought that was never far from the surface – about the pain they both must have been in, physical and otherwise. Four stories up on that roof, what had been going though Galvin's mind as he'd unhooked his safety harness? And Daniel would feel a sickening shear in his chest whenever he imagined his intensely private mother forcing herself to visit old Dr Simmons, who would have started writing a prescription as soon as she'd entered his office, and whose final response would have been to tear it out of the pad and hand it to her. She drank gallons of milk of magnesia. He remembered seeing those blue bottles in the dustbin but hadn't thought too much about it. She must have known that something was seriously wrong, even as she'd sung that strange ballad down the phone to him – into his silence.

There were only three people at her funeral: the nice young mortician, who tried to get Daniel to look at her body before they closed the coffin; the bibulous priest who gave a eulogy in which he mistook Daniel's mother for someone else; and that stranger at the back, who Daniel had thought at first was a homeless man but who came to the cemetery also, standing some distance away in the shadow of a hawthorn as she was lowered into the earth.

After the funeral, Daniel went back to the flat, intending to sort through his mum's belongings. But he couldn't bring himself to go through the door. Why? Was

it because he was afraid he might discover what had kept
her so silent though all the years of his childhood? Was
it because the news about Galvin had offered, all at
once, a terrible chance to sever everything and be new?
Or was it simply because the pain was so extreme that it
had been purified through the powerful alembic of his
youth into a kind of ecstasy? There he'd stood, for what
seemed like hours. The feeling: not as if he were drifting
through space, but as if space, all of it, were drifting
through him. He'd thrown the keys out of the landing
window, a gesture that had felt wrong even as he'd done
it. It was dramatic, obvious, not enough. Nothing would
have been enough but to be standing there still, sixteen
stories up, before a door beyond which she and Galvin
were. And were, emphatically, not. In lieu of this, the
impromptu play, the keys flung from the window, the
man, who was not yet a man, walking away.

He'd expected someone from the council to tell him to
come and clear his mother's belongings out, but no one
ever had. Gone. As simple as that. His act. His non-act.
And when, one night, years later, he told Sally what he'd
done, it was as if he'd struck her – *Her things, all your
poor mother's personal things!* – and he'd been touched by
a terrible suspicion that he'd told her in order to fashion,
from his wife, the image of what he should have been
feeling, what he longed to feel, had made use of her as
drunks make use of alcohol: this glass, this woman,
contains what I would feel if I were human.

He passed a cluster of mackintoshed old men waiting

for the Derby Arms, which had been Galvin's local, to open. Never having known his father, Daniel had looked to such men when he was a child to transform his secret shames into legitimate hungers.

The sight of these men made Daniel think of the man who'd come to do some plumbing for his mother. Daniel, eight years old, had stood watching him, fascinated by his hands – a man's hands. While his mum was making tea in the kitchen, the plumber told Daniel proudly that he'd fought in Italy during the war. Encouraged by Daniel's naïve attention, he'd beckoned him closer and had whispered that at one time he'd had an Italian woman – *A beauty like you ain't never seen in your life, chief, a bloody countess* – perform, in exchange for a pound of flour, an intimate service for him in the ruins of some palace. The plumber remembered the alabaster child, the shattered chandelier. In the centre of it the cleft forms of him and this woman, this countess, doing *that* to him. She couldn't have known, Daniel thought now, that that moment would be, for this man, *the* moment of his life, that he would remember it for as long as he lived and, still half in disbelief that his life had yielded such a thing, pass it on as sacred to a boy. This image had gone into Daniel, the two figures among the ruined grandeur. He saw them as a grotesque iris, her supplicatory form becoming the arched pistil of his unfurled body. And when Daniel's mum had brought the plumber some tea, he told her, winking at Daniel, that they'd been having a man-to-man. His mum had then appeared to Daniel entirely different, the feeling at once arousing and sickening.

Such was his fathering.

Worse still, perhaps some of those old men were like Galvin, whom he'd betrayed. More than betrayed: he'd been the breach of Galvin's last stand.

But it wasn't old Maggie, so hungry, and so happy to be the first to tell Daniel that his friend had *fallen,* so much as that encounter with Galvin on the steps to the Derby Arms that Daniel would never forget or cease to regret. Daniel was there still, looking up into the naked longing of his friend's face, giving him the same polite *No, thank you*; as Daniel held still to the phone into which his mum, a little drunk, sang that Scottish ballad; as, even now, he stood beneath the horse chestnut while his wife, kneeling at the water's edge, tried to get him to speak, to say anything. It was not one ghost he would become but dozens in the living-back of his life, each the hull of an irrevocable moment.

He turned on to Church Street, terraced houses, endless iterations of the same squalid circumstance. Then he came to it, Our Lady Queen of Peace. He stopped, put his briefcase down, and lit up a cigarette.

Lilac was sprouting from the broken tiles of the roof. Beneath the parapet jutted gargoyles made featureless by acid rain. The windows and the main doors were boarded shut.

Who could imagine that he'd once been married in this church? That he'd stood at its altar beside that exquisite woman (wearing red stilettos with her white wedding dress) whose love he'd never quite been able to believe in? When they'd turned around to face the congregation after the ceremony, his eyes had fallen on Jill, who was looking like a bride herself, more beautiful than he'd ever seen her, her face flushed, at once passionate and solemn. At the reception, when he went to get Sally a drink, he heard violently raised voices. He looked back to see Jill and Sally involved in some kind of altercation on the dance floor. All the guests were looking on stunned. Suddenly Jill, screaming abuse, ripped off one of the shoulders of Sally's wedding dress. A general cry went up, and Daniel pushed his way back towards the two struggling women. Just as he got to them, Jill took hold of Sally's dress by the cleavage and ripped it off completely, in one smooth action. Now both sisters, unable to keep up their roles, were clutching each other and laughing. Sally had made her wedding dress like a stripper's costume, held together with Velcro, and there she stood in a gorgeous sliplike dress of red silk that matched her red stilettos. Soon everyone was laughing. A few moments later, Sally took hold of Daniel, whose heart was still pounding, and, in a shower of applause, they began to dance.

Now, as a few raindrops were cast like a handful of seeds on to the pavement, Daniel almost smiled. He loved Sally.

Reaching out, he took hold of the church's cast-iron gate. His whole body felt clenched. He wanted to wrench the gate off its hinges, to tear the boards away from the doors and windows, to open it.

A woman hurried by on the other side of the street, studiously not looking at him. Daniel released the rails and wiped the rust from his hands. After finishing his cigarette, he walked on.

5

A FEW MINUTES LATER, he came to it – the little park at the centre of a square of Edwardian houses, with its pond, once a paddling pool, and its ancient horse chestnut, from the branches of which he and Galvin had garnered chestnuts to play conkers, and ruled this scrap of grass. He'd been happy here, lying along the limbs of this tree while Galvin had revealed the secret, fantastic lives of all the people who walked by. What would Galvin have said about the couple who would be here at two in the morning seventeen years later? What would he have whispered to Daniel about the woman squatting like a child beside the water, and the man standing under the tree? What story would Galvin have told and the young Daniel believed? He could almost hear it in Galvin's voice – an older Galvin: *That man, Danny, that man is mad, and the woman, to save him, is acting out his madness. She's going mad to keep him sane. She's going mad because she loves him. She's believing in his madness so that he doesn't have to.*

Daniel leaned against the tree, letting his head, which felt heavy, loll back. Above him he could hear the wind in the leaves, the eddies that augured rain. It sounded like the sea. He closed his eyes for just a second, and when he opened them again he got the strangest feeling that he was alone in the city. Everything went very still for a moment, as if the world had seized. He could hear nothing, no birds singing, no traffic, no wind in the trees, only his own breathing.

Quickly he left the park and entered Walnut Street, which led straight to the Windsor Estate. A few minutes later he was at the entrance to Hicks House. Home.

The lift, reeking of urine, shuddering, squeaking, just as he remembered it, conveyed Daniel to the sixteenth floor. As the lift opened, Daniel felt, with a jarring pulse in his head, the whole building shift. It was the old vertigo.

Trying not to look out of the landing windows, he made his way to the flat door, but couldn't bring himself to knock right away. *Her things, all your poor mother's personal things!* He tried to reason himself through it. It wasn't his home anymore. He'd been to a thousand of these flats and knew exactly what he'd find in this one: the vinyl sofa, the pink impatiens, the gas heater with fake coals, the large model of the HMS *Victory* bought with Green Shield stamps, the Silver Jubilee commemoration plates, the barometer stuck to a piece of Land's End.

This he knew, and yet, right now, he was struck, made almost breathless, by an image, so vivid, of this door opening into *nothing*, into the grey sky above London and a sheer drop of sixteen stories to the street.

Feeling sickened and unsteady, he put his hands against the wall of the landing and closed his eyes.

Finally, he gathered himself and knocked. No response. This, he wasn't prepared for. He knocked again, waited, slowly succumbing to a feeling that was itself vertiginous – a dizzying mix of relief and grief. But as he was about to return to the lift, he heard the sound of the bolt being drawn. The door was cracked open, and a canny face appeared.

'Mr Radcliff?' Daniel inquired. 'Amos Radcliff?'

The face brightened.

'My name's Daniel Mulvaugh. I'm from the DHSS.'

A frown; confusion. 'Did you say Radcliff? Let me just see if he's in.'

Daniel put out his hand to prevent the door from being shut in his face. 'What are you looking for, Mr Radcliff – a mirror?'

The man scrutinised Daniel for a moment before fully opening the door. Looking down at his own body, he then exclaimed, with what appeared to be genuine surprise, 'Well, fancy that, here I am.'

Amos offered his hand. Daniel took it and was instantly disturbed by its unnatural strength. Almost at the same moment, he realised that there was something familiar about this man.

Amos, who was wearing red nylon pyjamas that were too small for him, wasn't much shorter than Daniel, but he appeared short because he was so thickset. While Daniel would have guessed he was somewhere between fifty and sixty, Amos was one of those spry, robust men who might easily have been older. His grey, unkempt hair and beard suggested a mild electric shock. His eyes and mouth brimmed with an impish humour that ran into his leathery face by way of numerous wrinkles. His broad, bare feet looked decidedly unprosthetic.

Taking Daniel's coat, Amos led him down the narrow hallway. The instant Daniel entered the sitting room, his whole body went hollow: nothing in the flat had changed – the '70s-style chrome and smoked-glass coffee table between the burgundy sofa and shell-back armchair, the squat, mahogany sideboard. It was all exactly as it had been the last time he'd seen it, more than twenty years ago.

Numbness for a moment, then a slow throbbing that began at his temples and spread down.

Turning to the man, trying to appear nonchalant, Daniel said, 'I knew the woman who lived here before. I was her caseworker. These things are all hers, aren't they?'

'Some of 'em, yeah,' Amos said as he threw Daniel's coat over the back of the sofa. 'The council was going to throw 'em away 'cause no one come to pick 'em up, so I thought, well . . .'

'Even those.' Daniel tried to keep his voice steady as he indicated the framed photographs cluttering the mantelpiece and sideboard. 'Why did you keep those?'

'Didn't 'ave the heart to chuck 'em. She looks nice, she and her boys. Funny, there weren't no pictures of anyone else.'

'Boys?' he queried but realised instantaneously that

Amos had used the plural because of Galvin, who was in most of his childhood pictures.

'Yeah.' Amos was surprised. 'You must have known she had two boys?'

'Oh yes, yes of course.'

'Anyway, now it's as if I knew 'em, know what I mean? When you get older you seem to have seen everyone somewhere before. Like you. Seems like I know you from somewhere.'

'I don't think so, Mr Radcliff.'

'Are you –'

'Don't *you* have any family?'

'Oh yeah . . . yeah.' Now it was Amos's turn to be evasive. 'Got a picture of 'em somewhere,' he mumbled. 'Anyway, sit yourself down, mate. I'll make you a nice cup a tea.' With that, he disappeared into the kitchen.

Daniel looked down at the sofa. On its left arm were still visible those Arabic letters that he had, one bored afternoon, worn into the nap with his fingernail, copying them out of a book on the Crusades. He went to the sideboard and picked up the photograph of him and his mother, taken in a booth in Euston Station when he was six or seven. For just a second he saw her not as his mother but as a woman his age now. What if she'd been merely a colleague of his? Would he have wondered why she kept her hair so short, almost shorn, why she was so reticent? Certainly it wouldn't be lost on him that, despite her indifference to her own appearance, she was a beautiful woman.

Daniel recalled now how constantly pestered she was by men, who'd call him Chief and Champ, and would refer to her, with a wink, as his sister, men who must have been encouraged by how little regard she seemed to have for what she possessed. Frigidly, without looking at the men, she'd tell them that she was waiting for her husband. She always wore a wedding ring. Where was it? Daniel looked around now as if he might see it somewhere in the room. Had it been buried with her? Daniel wanted to stop thinking about her but now couldn't get the thought of what had happened to her wedding ring out of his head. *Her things, all your poor mother's personal things!* Did this man have it? Had he pawned it, together with anything else of value? Daniel's thoughts were interrupted as he noticed, on the mantelpiece, a large framed photograph of him as a young man, which she must have taken during one of his university holidays. Afraid this Radcliff might recognise him, he went over and shifted it behind a big photograph of him and Galvin imitating the gorillas in Chessington Zoo.

It occurred to him then that there was something different about the room. It seemed smaller, somehow, and not just because he was bigger. As he tried to think what it was, his gaze fell upon a large steel ball that had been placed right at the centre of the mantelpiece. Picking it up, he hefted it in his palm, his own distorted image peering out from its gleaming surface. He found it strangely captivating, and felt an urge to slip it into his pocket. Disturbed by this, he hastily returned it.

Then something occurred to him and, after a glance at the entrance to the kitchen, in which he could hear Amos clattering about, he went to the sideboard and tried to open it. Its doors were locked, as they'd always been. Once, while his mother had been ironing in her bedroom, the paper aeroplane Daniel had been playing with had slid beneath this sideboard. Reaching for it, his hand had touched something taped to the underside. It was the key. As quietly as he could he'd opened it. The shelves had been cluttered with things. He'd noticed a pile of letters tied up with blue ribbon. From the lowest shelf, he'd removed a shoe box. For a boy, it had been a casket of treasure. That's where he'd found the old steel lighter he still used – because he'd had the presence of mind to toss it under the sofa. He'd intended to take a number of the other things too – a switchblade razor with an ivory handle and a yellow tin of Erinmore pipe tobacco – but his mother had come in. Then and the day that man had been waiting for him outside his school were the only times he'd ever seen her lose control. Those Scottish inflections had reared so fiercely she'd become someone he'd never known.

He wanted now to check for that key but heard the man returning and quickly sat down.

6

Amos put the tray on the coffee table. He sat opposite Daniel, in the shell-back armchair in which Daniel's mother had always sat, and poured the tea. Daniel recognised most of the tea things except for the mug Amos had placed in front of him, which was white with a big red heart on the side. Before his eyes, as the hot tea filled the mug, the heart paled from red to pink and the words 'I love you' emerged.

Amos poured his own tea and sat back, regarding Daniel with, it seemed, warm expectation.

'Well, Mr Radcliff,' Daniel began, 'quite remarkable, isn't it, what they can do with a prosthesis nowadays?'

'A what?'

'What's it made of – whalebone? Screw it off for me, let's have a gander.'

'I seem to have missed you somewhere.'

'Mr Radcliff,' Daniel continued, pulling out the file from his briefcase and opening it. 'For the past five years – correct me if I'm wrong – you've been receiving a disability allowance. I have here receipts for twelve new prostheses – an inordinate number; somebody actually queried it here. But I've discovered your problem, Mr Radcliff: you have nowhere to put them.'

Amos was listening as if Daniel were someone with just the bare rudiments of English.

'So?' Daniel prompted.

With a suggestive arch of his eyebrows, Amos reached up to the breast pocket of his pyjamas and removed a small leather pouch. After lifting it to his nose, apparently to inhale its odour, he opened it. The first thing he took out was a tin of tobacco, which he put down onto the coffee table. Then he retrieved a wooden pipe and a little cluster of wire instruments. He unscrewed the pipe's stem, flicked it a few times, and began to clean it.

'I went to a healer,' Amos confided.

'A healer?' Daniel said, looking down at that yellow tobacco tin and wondering how common a brand Erinmore was.

'Of course, I don't believe in them – I'm not completely insensitive to Locke, Hume, Brecht, and their ilk – but I have to tell you he was the genuine article. He had cobalt eyes, a pitch-black beard, and bright red hair. That has healer written all over it, doesn't it. If you're interested, he has a little flat above an undertaker's in Aldershot.'

'I'll bear that in mind, Mr Radcliff. Now if we can –'

'Don't mention my name, though. First time I went, I did a little faux pas. I was unused to the whole business, see, so when he fell into his healing frenzy, I thought he was having a fit. Shoved a spoon into his mouth. Chipped one of his front teeth. He wasn't a happy healer.'

'Well, he couldn't have been that unhappy if he regenerated your limb.'

'What limb? Oh, that limb. Well, to tell you the truth, I didn't exactly lose that limb.'

'Did you just misplace it, perhaps?'

'It was very sore.'

'Oh, really.'

'*Very* sore. I was hit by a truck on the South Circular – a bloody Frog. It was early in the morning, no traffic. Bugger was driving on the wrong side of the road, wasn't he.'

'According to this, Mr Radcliff,' Daniel said, referring to the folder, 'you were hit by a beer barrel. Was this truck carrying beer?'

'Come to think of it, it was.'

'You were also apparently in a cellar. How about this: The truck hit you into an open cellar, then turned over, spilled its load of beer barrels, one of which rolled into the cellar and amputated your leg.'

'Excellent. You should write for the BBC.'

'Do you realise, Mr Radcliff, the seriousness of this?'

'Of what?'

'You've been claiming, among other things, unemployment benefit, rent benefit, a pension, and a disability allowance for five years. Not only will you have to pay this money back –'

'You're not going to stop my payments, are you?'

'Not only will you have to pay this money back –'

'How am I going to live?'

'Well, I know this is probably an outrageous suggestion, but you could get a job.'

'A *what*?' Amos looked appalled.

Daniel slid the folder back into his briefcase and stood up. Though the last thing in the world he wanted to do right now was leave, he had to do something. That frantic, unfocused energy had threatened to become absolute despair in the face of this banality he'd encountered at the heart of his home – his life.

Amos seemed alarmed. He dropped his pipe stem on the coffee table and stood also, putting his hands out to placate Daniel.

'Listen,' Amos said gently. 'Listen. I have a job. I wrote to you. I have a job. I'm an artist.'

'Mr Radcliff, this government isn't in the business of patronage. You seem to feel that this money is owed to you.'

'Well, I come from a long line of those who've accepted the king's shilling for one thing or another. But listen, Danny, I can see in you a sensitive soul. It's as plain as day. I see in you someone who can understand. I have to be able to do my work. It's up to you. If you'll just forget me, those cheques, which you have to admit hardly keep me in luxury, will continue coming through that door.'

'I haven't got time to listen to this. I've had to work all my life, Mr Radcliff. I've worked hard. I've never taken a single unnecessary day off. I've never shirked my responsibilities. I've never accepted the "king's shilling" as you put it, except for services rendered. I've paid my taxes, and I have *never* been in debt.'

'I'm proud of you, Daniel. We're all proud of you,' Amos said. 'You're a pillar in the temple, you're a Moslem in the brewery, you're a eunuch in the harem, but –'

'Frankly' – Daniel's heart was beating so hard he was out of breath – 'frankly, I find it contemptible –'

'Contemptible is a shirker, my pillar, my solid oak. Contemptible are those gaunt demons that live on our backs and whisper into our ears.'

'I beg your pardon?' The grandiloquence of this reminded Daniel of Radcliff's absurd letter.

'You want to know about suffering, you want to know about dedication, then let me tell you a story, my friend. Sit yourself down.'

'I will listen, Mr Radcliff, but I will stand.' He realised, the instant he said this, just how ridiculous it sounded.

'As you wish. At least finish your tea. It's a pity to waste it.'

Daniel felt an awful tremulousness in his stomach. It was so hard for him to take this in. A man here, in this silent, female place, a place that had had no man and somehow smelled still of his mother. A profound sadness descended into him. What was he doing here?

He sat down. Just as he did so, he glanced up at Amos

and was disturbed by what appeared to be a sly look on that man's face. But in a second it was gone and Amos, affable once more, also sat, leaned across the coffee table, and rubbed his hands together.

7

'IVAN IVANOVITCH,' Amos began, 'was heir to a great fortune. As a young Russian noble, he used his vast resources to experience everything he could. He travelled the world, lived years of orgiastic excess in which he went further than Sade in plumbing the depths of human abjectness. But he also lived years of privation as a monk, mortifying his flesh, embracing lepers, drinking the spittle of consumptives, and so forth. He fought in the Napoleonic Wars, killed many men and was almost killed many times. All this before he was thirty. On his thirtieth birthday he retired to his country estate just outside St. Petersburg, and began to write. You see, my friend, he was driven by a desire to write the definitive thing. He wrote and wrote and wrote all day, every day. It absorbed him entirely. Behind his back, of course, he was being robbed blind by his relatives. Paper was brought to him by the cartload and, over the course of the next ten years, he filled the whole cellar of his mansion with sheets covered in his cramped hand. Finally, he moved himself and his desk down to the cellar in order to be among his carefully stacked and numbered sheets, and over the next decade he wrought them into a great work of fifty hefty volumes. Not once in that period, Daniel, did he leave the cellar. Food and bedpans were brought to him by Osip, his valet, the one servant who still remained loyal. At the end of that ten years, Osip heard him stamping up the stairs and waited in solemn anticipation. Ivan Ivanovitch emerged like some aquatic beast, the now bald dome of his head breaking the surface for a moment. He snorted. He frowned. He looked at Osip without seeing him, then about-turned and sank back into his world. More years passed. He wrought these fifty volumes into ten, these ten into three, these three into one – one slim volume. Then one Sunday, as Osip was putting on the samovar and preparing his master's lunch in the kitchen, he heard him ascending the stairs, his step light and unsure. Once more that bald head broke the surface, and he held that single volume in his trembling hands. He was a ruined man, wheezing, etiolated, his body covered in sores. But, again, his brow furrowed and he submerged. More years went by. He worked on that volume until he'd distilled it to a handful of pages, then to a page, then to a paragraph, then to a single sentence, then to a word. One word. *The* word. They have it now in the museum in Moscow, written legibly, but with a shaking hand on to a moldering piece of parchment. And that same word is carved into the monument set over his grave . . . *That's* integrity. That's dedication. Daniel, all I'm asking is that you forget me.'

Amos leaned in towards Daniel, and his voice became urgent. 'I have great work ahead of me. Great work. You have to do so little to give me freedom. What is nothing for you is life for me.'

'So what was the word?' Daniel asked, despite himself.

'What word?'

'What was the word?'

'Oh . . . Well, it's been so long since I've been to Moscow.'

Daniel stood. 'I can't believe I even asked you.'

Amos stood also, snatched Daniel's coat up from the sofa, and held it out as if to help him on with it. This action appeared to mock him, and Daniel felt indignant.

'The truth is,' Amos lamented, 'it just loses too much in translation.'

'Mr Radcliff' – Daniel tried to seem merely weary as he slid his arm into the right sleeve of the proffered coat – 'let me tell you that what you've done is a criminal offence and will be dealt with as such.'

At this, Amos put his own left arm into the other sleeve, and there they stood, squeezed shoulder to shoulder, bound by the straining cloth of the coat.

'You can't leave like this,' Amos said. 'We might never see one another again . . . Look, I know I'm wrong. I know I'm being frivolous. Please let's sit down. Let me find out at least what my options are. I think I might have some chocolate digestives. Let's talk.'

Daniel made a show of reluctance before he pulled his arm out of the coat's sleeve. Amos also divested himself of the coat, flung it back over the sofa, and hurried into the kitchen.

8

A FEW MOMENTS LATER he returned, carrying a small plate piled with crumbled up chocolate biscuits.

'I get the broken ones for half price at the Co-op. I have a mate there who drops a couple of packs while shelving every week.'

'Couldn't he drop them from a lower shelf?'

'His name's Rupert Tomchit. I think further than that he shouldn't be taxed.'

'All right. Well, let's get to business.'

'Before that, tell me a little about yourself, my friend.'

'I'm not here to tell you about myself, Mr Radcliff.'

'Do you mean here in my flat or here on this Earth?'

'I'm sorry?'

'You're an interesting fellow, my solid oak. I can spot a government official from a mile off. But when I saw you at the door, you fooled me completely. I made the mistake of looking at your face instead of at your shoes – so comfortable, so . . . brown. You see, you seemed lost, bewildered. You seemed sad. You seemed as if you were at my door on anything but official business. It even struck me for a moment that you were the Second Coming, not slouching towards Bethlehem but ambling from Clapham Common, set upon this Earth as innocent as a babe with my address in your hand, one hundred and sixty-three Hicks House.'

'That occurred to you, did it.'

'For a moment. But let me give you a word of advice: you can never trust a face. Shall I tell you how I learned that?'

'Well, you obviously *didn't* learn it if you let me in, did you.'

'Has anyone ever told you you're astute, Daniel – don't answer, it's rhetorical.'

'Look, is it short?'

'Is life short?'

'For God's sake –'

'Good. If you're sitting comfortably, I'll begin.' Amos picked up his pipe stem, squinted through it, then started to clean it again. 'In my wayward youth, my friend, the government, solicitous as it was, gave me full room and board in Broadmoor for a year or so.'

'What did you do?'

'What do we all do, Daniel?

'Anyway, the most feared prisoner was a bloke called Charley Samson, who later became known as Squirrel. I'll tell you, he was a beast of a man. Most of his features were suitably grotesque, but unfortunately for him he had curly blond hair and baby-doll blue eyes. He'd been a soldier in Northern Ireland, and during an engagement with a sniper in the streets, his M-16 had backfired. This had left his face covered in hundreds of little black-and-white scars, and had damaged his tear ducts so badly that tears leaked constantly from his eyes. He'd been in and out of jail almost all his life for various crimes of violence. Now he was in for good: just a few weeks before I arrived for my sojourn, he'd beaten his cell mate to death. This meant —'

'Why?' Daniel said.

'Why what?'

'Why'd he beat him to death?'

'Oh . . . well, you see, it was a sort of tradition at the Moor to give your cell mate a joke gift on the anniversary of him being locked up. My cell mate gave me a pot of honey — but that's another story. Samson's cell mate gave him a tin of caulking. They'd been cell mates for four years. I suppose that's what made him feel he could get away with it. I imagine he'd hoped, given that hair and those eyes, even to coax a smile from Samson.

'Anyway, after that, Samson was, of course, put into solitary. But he was allowed into the yard for the one hour we all had for break at one o'clock.

'Now, in the centre of the yard stood a single horse chestnut.'

'A horse chestnut?'

'Is there an echo in here?'

'I'm sorry.'

Amos took a second to regather himself. 'For the prisoners that tree was our seasons; it allowed us to still feel ourselves a part of the world beyond the walls. Walking past the cells, I'd sometimes see a man examining a leaf, feeling the relief of its veins, smelling its scent on his fingers.

'I don't mean to give the impression that these were good men, Daniel. A lot of them were brutal. I remember one time watching helplessly as a prisoner called Malachy made a very bloody attempt to sew his cell-mate's mouth shut with a piece of wire.'

'Christ,' Daniel said. 'Why?'

'Oh, he'd found a journal the poor sod was keeping; read something in it he didn't like. Used the wire from its spiral binding.'

Amos's face became grave and Daniel somewhat regretted now his former flippancy and condescension.

Amos stood, went over to the sideboard and retrieved something from inside a blown glass bowl. As he sank back into the armchair, he deposited on the coffee table between them a horse chestnut.

'From the tree?'

Amos nodded. 'Don't know why I keep these things.

'Anyway, so one day, of all things, there was a squirrel in it. Who knows how it had scaled those walls. I think many of us believed it had been born from the tree itself. Whatever the case, there it was in the branches, chattering down at all of us.

'One day, Samson, who usually kept to his own place in the yard – a little niche in which he stood like a grotesque sculpture, watching the world with his sad eyes, tears, as always, streaming down his scarred face. Well, one day he began to walk towards the horse chestnut. As he walked he seemed to be frowning self-consciously, and I remember feeling surprised, even touched, by his discomfort at the general scrutiny. He walked towards the tree in the way that you approach someone you've decided to confront, someone popular who'd glibly insulted you. His right fist was clenched, and I honestly believed he was about to punch the tree. Instead, he hunkered down and released from that fist a pile of crushed walnuts.' Amos opened his hand over the table. Daniel noticed, as his sleeve rode up, a couple of tattoos on his forearm.

'A friend of mine, Zarkees, worked in the office, which had a view of the yard. He told me he'd seen the squirrel come down to take the walnuts a little while after we'd all gone back to our cells.

'Each day, Samson coaxed the squirrel. Everyone stood away from the tree now, though, as you could imagine, it was a favourite spot. We did this half out of fear for this brutal, remorseless man, and half out of an interest as to where this was leading. After a few weeks, he managed to get the squirrel to come down during the recreation period, though it would still scatter at the slightest sound.

'As time went on, Samson extended the nuts further and further from the tree towards his habitual position in the yard, and in this way, slowly, he drew the squirrel towards him. All the prisoners were engrossed. I remember, at break, some of them running to get a good position.

'Day by day the squirrel came closer to Samson, who effaced himself in his niche, staring at it with an expression of what seemed to be fearful anticipation. I'll tell you, it was an amazing sight – not just him, but all those men, those misanthropes and miscreants, holding their breaths, absorbed in the movements of this erratic little creature. It used to make me think of my older brother, Toby, who'd remained absolutely stoic when he received the news of our younger brother's death, but when Bog died – one of our sheepdogs – he'd wept inconsolably.

'Anyway, one day, Samson placed the nuts on his shoe, obviously too nervous to hold them in his hand. He seemed to be trying to blend himself with the wall as the squirrel approached. There was such a hush in the yard. The squirrel stopped for a moment at his boot, sniffed, and then, like a bather into cold water, inched on to the black leather. It took a nut and chewed it, standing to do this, balancing itself. There were nuts all the way up the laces and into the tongue. The squirrel seemed content. For a moment it nuzzled itself beneath its arm.'

Daniel flinched as Amos whipped his arm out towards him. 'It was over in a split second. With lightning speed, Charley snatched it up by its neck and stuffed it into a small burlap sack that his other hand had produced from his pocket.

'I'll tell you, my friend, it was as if there were a fishhook dug into each one of our hearts, and a fine, steel thread that led from all these hooks to the small life trapped in that bag. He was holding our hearts in his coarse hand. This was perhaps his aim, the almost admirable ambition of his brutality. Every man in that yard stood mute and suffering.

'He walked up to the tree. I thought for a moment he was going to strike the bag against it. Some of the men inched closer, but in his hand he had us. He was smiling; tears coursed down his cheeks. He began to run. The men scattered before him, and then, with a great heave, he flung the writhing bag over the wall . . . Are you married, Daniel?'

'Is that a true story?'

'True? Course it's true. Are you married?'

'I *was* married.'

'Divorced?'

'She's divorced.'

'You didn't want to divorce her?'

'I didn't want her to be divorced.' Daniel had raised his voice and was irritated, he realised, not so much because of Amos's intrusiveness but because he hadn't wanted the story to end.

Amos tugged at his lower lip and seemed to examine Daniel. For the first time, Daniel looked straight into his eyes. They were cold and inhospitable. Amos himself seemed lost in them. How hadn't he noticed them before? Was it just that the rest of his face, so full of humour and warmth, could never have intimated such eyes? Daniel looked away.

'Where is she now?' Amos persisted.

'She's not anywhere.'

'Is she dead?'

'I suppose so.'

'How did she die?'

'She's not dead. Not yet.' Now he felt ashamed of himself. In his head he was asking her for forgiveness. He became aware that he was reinscribing those Arabic letters in the sofa's arm, and snatched his hand into his lap. This made him feel exposed, shy and awkward, as if he were a child again. What was wrong with him? As he looked up at Amos, the sense that he knew this man returned, but it occurred to him that this might just be because everything else was so familiar to him here. Noticing that it was getting dark outside, he checked his watch and thought of Jill with both contrition and longing.

'You know,' Amos said softly and with real sympathy, 'I met the first woman I ever loved in a hospital. She and I were being sewn up.'

Daniel stood.

'Where are you going?'

'I have to be somewhere.'

'But you're coming back, yeah?'

Daniel looked around at his home. He wanted desperately to go into the other rooms, to see – to open – everything. 'Mr Radcliff, it seems pretty clear to me that you've defrauded the government. I'm not sure how necessary it is for me to come back.'

'No, look, I can explain. I can explain everything.'

'Well, you can be assured that I, or someone in my department, will be in touch with you very soon.'

9

HE ARRIVED LATE at the King's Arms, which was, as always, almost completely empty. Daniel bought a round and joined Richard, who was at a table watching Jill, Morgan, Betsy, and Perry playing darts.

'How are things going?' Daniel had been about to add 'with Jill' but stopped himself.

'Not too bad, matey.' Richard looked very drunk.

'Tell you what,' Daniel said. 'I've had the strangest day.'

Richard, intent on watching Morgan throw his darts, didn't respond. Finally, he leaned into Daniel and whispered, 'Funny to think they went out, isn't it.'

'Who? Jill and Morgan?'

Richard nodded. 'Was it serious?'

'Two years.'

'But he's not exactly Mel Gibson, is he.'

'Well, you're not exactly Mel Gibson, either.'

'I know, but I'm more . . . I mean, he's more not Mel Gibson than I'm not –' He'd confused himself and started again. 'I mean I'm not Mel Gibson, but he's even not Orson Welles or someone like that.'

'You mean he's fat?'

Richard looked offended.

'Look,' Daniel said, 'he's clever, educated, and

charming. Sally adored him. I think Jill was a bit jealous actually.'

'Why'd it end, then?'

'Got a bit too full-on for Jill, I think. Tell you what, though, he wasn't a happy camper when she broke it off. Made her life hell for a while.'

'Really?'

'Yeah, she started going out with another social worker and Morgan got him fired. She almost left herself, but Sally helped her smooth things over. Anyway, it's hard to stay angry at Jill.'

'You're right there, matey. Laura's like that. One time she sold my best golf clubs in a car boot sale for fifty quid. Thousand nicker they were worth.'

'Didn't help your golf much, did they.'

'That's not the point.' He hesitated, frowning. 'What was the point?'

'You could forgive her.'

'Right, right. You know, she'd never apologise. I don't think she ever apologised once in her bloody life. But I was losing my rag, so she just grabs hold of Jillybeans, right, and goes into this whole routine about how she'd given me this kid and how useful she is. And Jillybeans was being so good. She was only about three or four, but she was completely deadpan, you know, while her mum was showing me how she could be used as a scarf and as a vacuum cleaner and that; and we both ended up holding her upside down by her ankles and seeing what kind of golf club she'd make.

'You know, one time –'

'Rich,' Daniel cut in seriously, 'you didn't tell me they were going for good.'

'They can't be out there for good, can they. I mean, fucking Alabama. I mean that bloke, he's not a bloke. She's not going to stay with him. He's got no sense of humour, holy as shite. But I'll tell you what, I did have this horrible dream the other night that I went into our bedroom and Jill was breast-feeding Jillybeans –'

'Jill was?'

'Yeah. No. Did I say Jill? Laura, I mean. Laura was breast-feeding Jillybeans. I thought it was Jillybeans, and it was in a way, but it was a kind of rounder, fatter baby, and I realised that it was *him*.'

'The white bull?'

'Black bull, matey.'

'As a baby?'

'Well, no. Well, yes, but not, I mean, him as a baby, but *him* as a baby, if you know what I mean. Him *now*.'

'Look, how can they move there? You've got a right to see your daughter.' He wanted Richard to tell him what he'd done, or at least tell him that he'd done something.

Richard looked down into his pint for a second. Then his eyes met Daniel's, and quietly, with an instantaneous and devastating sobriety, he said, 'Danny, I've lost everything.'

An awful moment: it was as if Richard had surfaced, for the first and perhaps only time, from his general ease and humour, from the lie of his life, with a single, salvaged, useless truth.

'But why?' Daniel said. 'Why can't you see her?'

Richard had focused again on the dart players and after a moment said, 'I think I'm trying too hard with Jill, matey.'

'Jill? Your Jill?'

'This Jill.' He pointed at Jill, who was about to throw her darts. 'I don't think she's interested.'

The first of Jill's darts landed so high up on the wall that Perry had to fetch a pool cue to knock it down. The second lost its feathers in her hand. The third hit the scoreboard.

'Sound the all clear,' Richard shouted. Jill slit her eyes at him.

'Laura could never hit anything either,' Richard said. 'Talk about uncoordinated.'

Daniel had always been aware that Jill was, in some ways, very similar to Laura. Their voices and laughs were deep and earthy, though Laura was much louder. They were both uncomfortable with their bodies and clumsy, especially when they were drinking. Looking at Jill, he felt he could see something of what Richard saw: a woman with the same name as his mother and daughter, and with the same voice, manner, and body as his wife.

'I'm going to miss Jillybeans,' Daniel said. 'Sally is too.'

'I was thinking I might take her to see Sally before they leave. Do you think that'll be all right?'

'Probably best to ask Jill. You know, I wish Sally and I'd had a kid.'

'Better you didn't.'

'I suppose I just wish I had something left out of me and Sally. Twelve years. Feels wasted.'

'It's not a kid you want: you want a six-year-old Sally you can take to the zoo.'

'She hates the zoo.'

'Your Sally hates the zoo. Six-year-old Sally *loves* the zoo, and if you buy her an orange lolly she'll worship the ground you walk on, sunshine.'

Daniel smiled.

'Or is it a six-year-old Danny, you want?' Richard threw Daniel a canny look. 'He'd love the zoo too.'

Daniel lit a cigarette and they both watched the players. After a little while, Richard said, 'Ay, what happened with that Indian woman?'

'Didn't I tell you?'

'No, you said you'd tell me. Wasn't anything naughty, was it?'

'No. No, she came in to see me on Monday. She's living with her mother-in-law and wants me to get her into assisted housing.'

'Get the mother-in-law into assisted housing?'

'Right. Turns out, she married this mother-in-law's son when she was sixteen; the son dies after a year and the mother-in-law doesn't want her to get married again.'

'Why?'

'Don't know, religion or something, she didn't tell me. But she marries anyway – some bloke from Delhi – gets pregnant, but then gets really sick and has a miscarriage.

Gets pregnant again; the same thing happens. And the third time it happens the miscarriage almost kills her; not only that but her husband leaves her.'

'Leaves her?'

'Trots off back to Delhi. Anyway, she's gutted and penniless, living in a council flat with this mother-in-law, who treats her like a servant; and one night they have a row and she finds out that the mother-in-law *caused* the miscarriages, had put some kind of homegrown poison into her food.'

'Jesus.'

'So, anyway, this woman's going berserk in my office, crying and saying that every time she looks at her mother-in-law, who's completely unrepentant, of course, she gets the urge to soak her in paraffin and set her alight. She'd come to see me because she'd almost done it the night before when the mother-in-law had fallen asleep on the sofa, had stood right over her with the bottle of paraffin and the matches.'

'Je-*sus.*'

'And you know what I did, Rich? I started laughing. I laughed right in her face.'

Richard leaned back, as if needing a little distance to examine this new Daniel.

'It's hard to explain. She was hopping up and down in front of my desk. It was like someone doing a parody of a crazy Indian woman. She couldn't speak English very well, so she was using all these Indian gestures mixed up with English clichés. It was awful . . . *awful*. And the worst thing was that at the heart of it, *trapped* in this ridiculous performance, was a real person – I could see it. I could see it. She wasn't lying. Her whole life had been destroyed by this bloody mother-in-law. She was never going to have children; she was never going to get married; she was going to die in a foreign country on her own in a miserable council flat. And I fucking laughed.'

'So what did she do?'

'Well, in a way it was a good thing because she was so shocked she calmed down. I just apologised and did all the right things and got her into a B & B until we could sort things out. And she was fine, I think. I think she just thought I was mad.'

'You are mad, matey.'

Richard put his hand on the back of Daniel's neck and said, 'You know what you need, you need a holiday.'

'I don't need a holiday, I need a new life. Lived my whole bloody life in this city. I've always wanted to go to Thailand or South America.'

'South America? Tell you what, I'll go with you. I've heard that the women in Brazil are the most sexually promiscuous in the world; and Bangkok speaks for itself, doesn't it.'

'I'm not looking for sexually promiscuous women.'

'I know, Danny. You want to go on a spiritual journey. But it's just a perk, isn't it, of going on a spiritual journey in those countries, that you happen to be surrounded by droves of sexually promiscuous women. Or you could go to the Ivory Coast: child slavery, half the population dying of AIDS. It's a laugh a minute there. You'd love it.'

'Piss off.'

'Rwanda? Now there's comic genius – massacring people in a church with machetes. Laugh? – I almost peed my pants.'

'That's the last time I tell you anything.'

Richard squeezed the back of Daniel's neck affectionately, and they were silent for a while.

Finally, Daniel said, 'I want to start again, Rich. I just want to go somewhere, have a clean slate.'

'What would you tell the people you met?'

'I'd tell them the truth.'

'Wouldn't be a clean slate then, would it? Anyway, you need to muster up a little more dramatic potential than, *I was a social worker who didn't like the rain,* matey.'

It hung in the air then: Sally. It occurred to Daniel that he'd probably tell people she was dead; and thinking this, for just the fraction of a second, he wished that she were.

He turned to his friend. 'I could murder you. That would add a bit of intrigue, wouldn't it.'

'Oh, Danny,' Richard protested mawkishly. 'You couldn't kill me.'

Jill appeared. 'I'm not bloody playing with them anymore,' she declared, picking up her gin and tonic, which was on the other side of Richard from Daniel. 'They're making fun of me.'

She took a sip of her drink, then sat down next to Daniel. He wondered if Richard had noticed this manoeuvre. Jill was tipsy. He could sense that volatile energy. She almost knocked over a couple of glasses just sitting down.

'Did you go to see that bloke with one leg?' she asked, snatching Daniel's cigarette and taking a quick drag before handing it back to him.

'Who's this?' Richard said.

'Oh, just some client.' Daniel found that he had no desire to talk about Amos.

'Living in *his* flat.' Jill pointed at Daniel.

'Your flat?'

'The flat I grew up in,' Daniel explained. 'Anyway, there's nothing wrong with him. Got two perfectly functioning legs, and he's trying to convince me to let him have his benefit cheques because he needs time to write.'

'What's he writing?' Richard said.

'Who knows. Gift of the gab, though. Here, what does *etiolated* mean?'

Jill shrugged.

'Well, you know when you're really unhappy,' Richard said, 'and you buy yourself four king-size Bounty bars and a family pack of cheese and onion crisps because they were the two things you loved most in the world when you were a kid, and you eat them all in one afternoon, and it's revolting and doesn't make you feel any better?'

Jill and Daniel just stared at him.

'Well, they should definitely have a word for that.'

'There is a word,' Jill said. 'Bulimia.'

The others were shouting for Jill to take her turn. She ignored them.

'Was it strange to be back in that flat?' she asked, giving Daniel a solicitous look, which the alcohol by turns undermined and exaggerated.

Morgan, Perry, and Betsy now converged on the table.

'Come on, Jill,' Betsy said. 'We can't let ourselves be beaten by these castratos.'

'I haven't managed to hit the bloody board yet.'

'It's true,' Betsy said, looking at Daniel. 'I've known people with cerebral palsy who have better coordination than Jill.'

'Cerebral palsy.' Richard nudged Daniel. 'Now *that's* funny.'

'No, it's not. It's bad taste,' Perry said, taking a prim sip from his rum and Coke.

'Bad taste,' Betsy said. 'From a man who gets *all* his clothes at Burtons.'

'I don't get *all* my clothes at Burtons,' he protested.

Now Perry turned his earnest attentions to Jill. 'I'll help you, Jill. It's the technique. You're not keeping your wrist flexible.'

'Not all of us are blessed with such limp wrists,' Betsy said.

'No, listen to Perry,' Richard insisted. 'It's a tiny little thing with a quick release. He's had a lot of practice.'

All but Perry laughed. He just looked perplexed.

'Dan-i-el, why don't you join us for the *arras*?' Morgan

said, scandalised at himself for risking the demotic.

'Yes, come on,' Betsy encouraged, 'just one quick game of male sexual aggression.'

'I'll come,' Daniel said, 'if you can tell me what *etiolated* means.'

Morgan answered: 'Pale, pathetic, bleached of sun.'

'God,' Richard said, 'we should have known that one. Describes everyone in this bloody country.'

'Etiolated, etched in grime,' quoted Morgan, 'ghost we the cities of our time.'

'It really turns me on when a man can quote poetry,' Betsy said, hooking her arm through Morgan's.

Leaning into her, Morgan intoned, with humid passion,

> *'No philtres could compete*
> *With your potent idleness:*
> *You've mastered the caress*
> *That raises dead men to their feet.'*

Clasping her throat, Betsy crooned in her best Bet Lynch, 'Ooh, I've gone quite moist.'

'You're disgusting,' Perry shouted.

Daniel had noticed a lingering glance pass between Morgan and Jill. He got up.

'I'll play,' he said.

As they made their way to the board, Morgan queried Daniel: 'Etiolated?'

'Oh, a client I went to see today used it.'

'You went on a home visit?' Perry cut in, with a glance

at Morgan. This wasn't part of Daniel's job.

'It was on my way somewhere and he's . . . disabled.'

'In what context did he use *etiolated*?' Morgan asked.

'Oh, he was spinning some yarn. He's a writer, apparently, when he's not being unemployed.'

'I had literary ambitions once,' Morgan said. 'At Oxford I wrote a full-length play set in the public privies at Charing Cross.'

'The whole thing?' Betsy said.

'Yes, the whole thing. Inspired by Beckett. Four hours of brilliant if rather oblique conversation between a man in a cubicle and a man at a urinal, whom I call – *deliciously* – Number One and Number Two.'

'Shouldn't that be Number Two and Number One?' Perry said, quite seriously.

'Oh, shut up,' Morgan muttered, massaging his own forehead as if exhausted.

Morgan always appeared a little weary in his large body, as if he'd just woken up after a night of debauch. Taking his turn, he threw his darts with accuracy and elegance. He seemed like someone who could have been good at anything. Daniel felt, and it troubled him, that this man could contain him, effortlessly. He understood what Jill – what Sally – had seen in him. Once, when he'd gone to Jill's flat to water her plants while she was on holiday, he'd pulled a volume of Rilke's poems off her bookshelf and had found a love letter from Morgan taped to the page opposite 'Tombs of the Hetaerae.' It was a beautiful letter, which made reference to the poem but was filled with gorgeous if rather gothic imagery of his own. Daniel had been to Morgan's flat a number of times, and the letter reflected the aesthetic of many of the objects in that place: a carved Madonna with arthritic hands; the cicatrix of a dead bird on a shard of slate; a contorted piece of driftwood, like some archetype of pain.

Jill, on a few drunken evenings, had talked to him and Sally about her love life with Morgan. On one night, Morgan had placed her shoes in various arrangements around his flat, and they had then taken turns making up the erotic scenarios these configurations suggested. Hers, Jill admitted, were crude and urgent. She was the woman, Morgan the satisfying agent. He, though, always imagined this woman, who was Jill, and not quite Jill, to be on her own, in an erotic reverie. He told Jill not what was happening to this woman but what she imagined was happening to her, what she longed to have happen. Another time, Morgan had explained to Jill that he'd carefully considered not just the lighting and colours of his home but the textures also. How many men, Jill had said, get you drunk, take you home, then blindfold you and lead you through a textural odyssey that ends just when and where you want it to?

There was something of artistic genius in this man. But, unlike most artists, Morgan had no desire to impress himself upon the whole world. He wished to engage his genius with just one person, one woman. It was this, in fact, that had caused Jill to end their relationship. She was simply not made to be the object of this kind of attention, to suffer, as she would have had to, in a thousand mediations, for his art. He was a genius whose archetype and audience was the woman he loved. But Sally, Daniel knew, would gladly have been so intimately engaged and consumed. He'd never seen her so rawly attracted to a man, so oblivious to the jealous glances of her husband and sister.

Now Perry took his turn at the board. Despite his lecture on technique, he held his darts in a clenched fist and flung them with a stabbing action. It was the ugly, functional manner of a person without any real self-awareness or aesthetic sense. His body was that of a young boy: thin limbs and a large head.

'That's an unusual release you have there,' Daniel said.

'Well, I have small fingers all of the same length.' Perry showed off his creaturely hand. 'Fingers, apparently, develop in the womb concurrently with the medulla oblongata, so this deformity suggests the possibility of mild brain damage.' Perry explained this without affect.

'You must be very proud,' Betsy muttered, as he flung his last dart. Betsy was a human taxonomist and referred to Perry as a prime example of the phylum GWH – gay without humour. He was obviously gay, though even in the liberal environment of the social services he'd never come out. He was also clearly in love with Morgan, and Morgan seemed to have accepted him as a sort of companion – one of those rigid, loyal, pragmatic companions who are beneficial for, if not essential to, the ecosystems of certain creative people.

Years ago, Perry had been on the verge of marrying the district nurse. Daniel remembered her – a haggard, angry woman – coming to the office every day to have lunch with Perry: boiled eggs and Ribena, a mean little Eucharist, which they would share in silence, eating with extraordinary punctiliousness, as if to express their mutual disdain of appetite. But then Perry, this man with, frankly, so little to him, had found a man with far too much; this man so soft lit and cleanly focussed that nothing of complexity could be imagined into him, had found a shadowed, multifold man. He'd placed himself then not in front of Morgan, like one of Morgan's women, but beside him, until Morgan had begun to feel him even when he wasn't there, like a missing limb. No doubt Perry thought nothing of the art, lighting, or textures in Morgan's home, but he'd make Morgan his evening espresso, would listen, without understanding, to his *pensées,* and would, perhaps, sometimes risk not switching on the light as night fell, so that the darkness, in its way, could merge them. Daniel read something almost gallant now into that meagre body and large head, into that man who understood his limitations and had found a way, despite them, to love and be loved.

'When you next talk to Sally' – Morgan addressed Daniel – 'will you tell her thank you for the gift. I'll get a note off to her this week.'

'Gift?' Daniel said.

Morgan looked surprised that Daniel didn't know. 'Oh, she sent me the most remarkable book. I'd talked to her once, *years* ago, about my interest in old texts by naturalists – in the drawings.'

'Drawings?' Betsy broke into their conversation to get away from Perry, who was pointing out that her ears were slightly deformed in a way that suggested a propensity to epilepsy.

'Of flora and fauna. Have I never shown you my collection, Betsy?'

'No, darling, and you know how much I'd *love* to come up and see your etchings.'

'They're not etchings,' Perry interjected.

'No, they're not,' Morgan agreed patiently. 'Wonderful, though – wonderful illustrations; the same plant or animal drawn by Maderer or Southward or McCasley looks completely different.' Morgan leaned forward and added as if in confidence, 'Actually, the ones that fascinate me most are the ones where you can tell that the naturalist has no real precedent for the particular plant or animal he's discovered, so the drawing then depicts not so much the object as his struggle to *see* it.'

Betsy sighed. 'Suddenly my collection of beer bottle caps doesn't seem so impressive. But I did get one of them while I was so drunk I fell out of a moving car.'

'You must be very proud.' It was Perry, with a rare, sly smile. Betsy and Morgan laughed, as when a child has understood something in the coded conversation of adults.

Daniel couldn't laugh, though, that old jealousy leaking its acid into his stomach.

'When did she send you this?' he asked.

'Oh, I just got it a few days ago.'

'Just a few days ago.' Daniel repeated Morgan's words as if to echo them away, and with them the realisation that his wife's talk with him yesterday had been just one of the decisions she'd made.

'I can't imagine where she got it from,' Morgan went on, becoming voluble in his enthusiasm. 'It's been out of print forever. It's by a man called Dewy Smythe – what a wonderful name, eh? He was a turn-of-the-century adventurer and herpetologist. It's full of reptiles drawn in his slightly ghoulish aesthetic; and the most wonderful thing is that at the back of the book he's put in a kind of bestiary of imagined reptiles. Most of them look like dragons or demons – *his* demons, I suspect.'

'He had demons?' Betsy said.

'Plagued by them, one would think. You see, he was married and had a kid, but never had any money because he used everything to finance his expeditions. So what he'd do is leave his wife and daughter with various friends of his. Of course his wife found this terribly humiliating. So one fine morning she smothers their daughter with a pillow, then wanders off and drowns herself in the nearest river.'

'He sounds like a *total* bastard,' Betsy declared. 'I hope he was eaten by a bloody crocodile.'

'Most likely was.' Morgan pensively pinched together

the wings of his nose. 'Disappeared up the Zambezi somewhere. There was a report, though, some years later of two native twin boys with blue eyes whose names resembled the Latin for *iguana* and *monitor*. Probably apocryphal. But then again, I have a sneaking suspicion that Dewy Smythe himself is apocryphal.'

'What do you mean?' Daniel was interested despite what he was feeling.

'Well, what remains of his life – a few letters, fragments of a diary, his drawings – is oddly . . . strategic. It tells you not too much and just enough, if you get my drift. I mean, it seems likely that the person who did the drawings was a naturalist of some kind, but my sense is that Dewy Smythe might have been this person's sort of alter ego. He's too well-imagined to be real. But the odd thing is that although, on some level I *know* he's not real, I still believe in him. He's real because someone *wanted* him to exist, which wasn't true of me.' He threw off this last comment so casually that Daniel didn't feel its significance until Morgan had gone on.

'Dewy Smythe *has* a reality. And that reality is another human being about whom I know nothing but that he or she wished, in some way, to be Dewy Smythe.'

It was so hard for Daniel to hear this, to find himself, in the face of his jealousy, so impressed by and attracted to Morgan's mind and sensibility.

'Tell Sally I'll take her up on her offer also,' Morgan said.

'What offer?'

'Tea. I've never been there. It's south of the river somewhere, isn't it? Perhaps we can go together?'

Daniel felt numb. Morgan was being delicate, kind, trying to keep everything aboveboard.

'Jill's going in the next couple of days,' Daniel said. 'Perhaps you can go with her.'

'I have to say,' Betsy declared, 'Sally is just *the* loveliest girl in the world. I always wondered what on earth she saw in you, darling.'

Perry, who was, for some reason, looking down at all of them along the shaft of one of his darts, as if it were the barrel of a gun, said, 'Well, she obviously didn't find it, did she, or she wouldn't have ended up in the loony bin.'

This astonished them all into silence. With everything else Daniel was going through, this pierced him. The very simplicity of Perry's features, which had, a moment before, perfectly expressed Daniel's pitying admiration, now filled him with a hatred so violent he feared, for a second, that he was going to take hold of Perry.

'I don't know why we come here.' Betsy, obviously feeling responsible, tried to clear the air. 'This place is such a dump.'

Morgan assisted her: 'I think that old bugger puts the dregs back into the barrels.'

Daniel looked over at Richard and Jill. They were thumb wrestling. Richard kept pulling her into him. A profound loneliness seized Daniel. He thought of Amos, his old home, wanted desperately to be back there again, and felt strangely close to that man, whose voice he could hear now: *She and I were being sewn up.*

He walked back to the table.

'It's your turn,' Perry called after him.

He didn't answer and sat next to Jill.

'I've beaten him five times,' Jill said.

'You're bloody double-jointed or something,' Richard protested.

The others joined them at the table. Betsy sat opposite Daniel, caught one of his legs between hers, and squeezed apologetically. He winked at her.

'You know what I've always wanted to do?' Betsy addressed the table. 'I've always wanted to buy an old double-decker, get a bunch of people together, and go round the world. Why don't we do that?' She stabbed her index finger into the table. 'Why don't we all decide to do that *here, today, now*? Get out of London, get out of the bloody rain.'

Richard began to sing, 'We're all going on a summer holiday . . .' A few of them tried to join in, but none of them knew the words, so their voices trailed off and things went quiet. The landlord watched them from the bar like an old dog. The rain began to lash the windows. Jill's hand, which was down on the bench beside Daniel's, touched his, or his touched hers.

10

JILL WAS ASLEEP NOW beside him. It had happened as simply as that: his wife's suggestion, then the act. Nothing had been said. After dropping Richard home, they took the taxi back to Jill's flat. In the taxi they debated Chelsea's chances of winning the league. She talked then, ransacking her satchel for the keys to her building, about one of the tenants who was refusing to pay maintenance charges. While they climbed the stairs, she told him about the old lady on the second floor who let her dachshund pee on the banisters. But as they entered her flat the silence flooded in on them. Their hurried kiss and the frantic, clutching sex that ensued seemed, more than anything, a struggle against this silence.

He got out of the bed. On the floor lay the small massacre of her clothes, the tartan dress and white stockings. There her bare back and bottom, pale, curved, cochlear in the dim room. He tried to invoke desire but couldn't; tried then to recall the times he'd desired her, so many in all these years, and to accept this as a fulfillment or culmination. It didn't work. Her body said nothing. He tried then simple recognition: this was Jill, whom he'd known for thirteen years, through her five serious relationships, the death of her parents, the nervous breakdown of her sister. But it seemed as if he could just as well not believe it as believe it. He was feeling the way he'd said to Richard he wanted to feel, shed to pure being, ready to accrue a new life: no Galvin, no Mother, no Richard, no Sally, no Jill. A stranger in a foreign city with a woman he'd met tonight, her home as meaningless as her language.

Certainly this feeling had been expressed perfectly a couple of hours ago, when Daniel had woken to find himself alone in Jill's bed. He assumed she was in the bathroom. Prompted by the dry ache of an incipient hangover, he went into the kitchen to drink some water. The instant he switched on the light, there was a crash. Jill, standing by the sink, had flung her arms around her naked body, and in doing so had knocked a few things from her dish rack on to the floor. Quickly she recovered herself, apologising and explaining that she'd been half asleep. But that image of Jill, with her face stricken, her hands clutched over her crotch and breasts, seemed to Daniel the truest image of the night – the one at the heart of all their blind and tangential energies. He saw blood on her breast. It was from her hand, which she'd cut on a knife that had been placed blade up in the dish rack. He bandaged it – a focussed and tender act that provided at least partial relief from that estranging moment.

Daniel now went around the bed to *see* her. Her face winced as she slept, as Sally's did, though there, at Jill's brow, even in her sleep was that little fist of recalcitrance.

Here she was. But for a set of lost keys, she might have been his wife. He might have spoken love in the language of this face, this body, this life. When she'd first started at the office, both he and Richard had been attracted to her, but she'd liked Daniel. Richard had started seeing Laura just weeks later, drawn perhaps to how similar she was to Jill. Laura the surrogate love; now Jill the surrogate loss. For months, Daniel and Jill flirted at work and, one night after the pub, he drove her home. Then, thirteen years ago, as they ascended the stairs, the silence had been not empty, evacuating them, but too full – pressured, as it was, by their desire for each other.

But at Jill's door sat a man in a heavy parka, his hooded head sunk between his knees. A derelict, Daniel assumed, or an old boyfriend. The man then, responding to their approach, did something unimaginable. It began with his ankles, emerging from those worn espadrilles, spread to his hands upon the floor as he pushed himself up, and culminated with a spill of hair as he drew back his hood.

There could not have been a better or worse way to meet her. She'd been a man who'd become a woman right in front of him. On top of this, the intense emotional and physical anticipation focussed at that moment on Jill was drawn by and diverted effortlessly into this more strangely, finely wrought Jill. Sally was there because the man with whom she was trying to break things off, desperate for her to come home with him, had thrown the keys to her flat out of the bus window.

Daniel remembered the first thing Sally said to him: 'Really, they're both brown with bits of yellow in them, but the left one has a lot more yellow, so it looks green.'

'They go very nicely with your face,' he replied. In truth, he'd not even noticed that her eyes were different colours. Ankles, hands, Pre-Raphaelite hair: he was at the coast still, had landed via Jill, who'd become, at that moment, no more than the way in, the crude metaphor for her sister, before more particular metaphors could begin to discover and name her.

Jill dug up her sister's spare keys. Sally lived just a half mile from Daniel so, at Jill's insistence, and despite Sally's protests, Daniel took her home.

After that, he cooled things down with Jill, telling himself, even half-believing, that it was unwise to get involved with a colleague. He felt cruel. Jill would contrive reasons to get angry at him. But it wasn't in Jill's nature to hold a grudge, and things soon settled.

He met Sally again at Jill's birthday party. They talked for most of the night. She gave him her number, but Daniel didn't want to cause trouble between the sisters, so he didn't call. It was she who called. She told him that she was pulling up the carpet in her flat and that, if he'd help her move some heavy things, she'd reward him with gazpacho and smoked salmon.

When she met him at the door, she was wearing what appeared to be a tie-dyed maternity dress, and she'd wrapped her hair in an old dishcloth. It was as if she were saying, *This* is how ugly I can be. Later, though, when the work was done, after a change of clothes, lunch, a few glasses of wine, he was brave enough to tell her how lovely her hair was. She said it was too long and asked him if he had a steady hand. She placed a chair on the linoleum floor of her bathroom, wet her hair, and allowed him to cut a few inches off the bottom. He remembered, as he then dried and brushed her hair, how still and silent she kept, her face iconic in that tiny but elaborately framed oval mirror above the sink. When he kissed her, she remained, for just a moment, unresponsive, with her eyes open, as if he were kissing not her but her image.

Daniel dressed as quietly as he could. But as he went to leave, Jill called. He returned to the bed and hunkered down.

'Where are you off to?' she said.

'Can't sleep.'

'Were you just going to leave?'

'I didn't want to wake you.'

Jill placed her hand on the back of his neck. She wanted him to kiss her.

Gently, he removed her hand and held it. Her cut had bled through the bandage.

'Please don't tell Sally,' he said. 'Please, please don't tell her.'

Jill stared at him for a moment, then withdrew her hand, and said, 'I won't.'

11

FROM HIS OWN OFFICE, where he'd been since six, Daniel listened to the main office come to life. He felt exhausted. After getting home from Jill's at four, he'd sat smoking cigarette after cigarette in the darkness, all his regrets resurrected: what he should have said to his mother when she'd telephoned and sang to him that night, to Galvin on the pub steps, to Sally in that little park and in those unsent letters. Three beautiful letters she'd sent him. And she must have waited, as his mother and Galvin had waited, for something, anything, a word. Gone. He'd lose Jill too now. She should have married Richard. They should have had a daughter named Sally, whom he could have loved purely. A fantasy: the young Sally, daughter of his closest friends, who would never become the empty vase, a throat longing for the bright flowers.

A tentative knock. It was his first appointment, almost half an hour late.

'Come in,' he called.

She entered, carrying a little boy who didn't want to be carried. As soon as she let him go, he ran full tilt into the side of a filing cabinet. Delighted by the loud bang, the boy took a few steps run up and did it again.

''Ere,' the woman shouted, 'pack it in.'

Melinda Dockford. He'd interviewed her a couple of times. She was somewhere in her twenties, though she looked forty, deep shadows under her eyes, her hair halfheartedly bleached.

'Bloody traffic,' she said. 'This is miles from the tube and I got 'im.' She pointed at the boy, who was now lying spread-eagled on the floor singing to himself.

'Yes, it's pretty bad out there.' Daniel opened her file and glanced at Jill's memo.

'So, why do you want to move?'

'I need a bigger flat,' she said. 'I 'eard there was some flats going down Roehampton.'

'The flats aren't any bigger there.'

She nodded towards the child. "E's got asthma. It's damp.' Then she leaned forward confidentially. 'They threatened to kill my 'usband.'

He checked the file again. 'You got married?'

'Well, 'e's not my 'usband,' she said.

'But he's the father of the child?'

She looked down at the boy and hesitated. 'Yeah,' she said, ''e's the father of the child.'

She'd repeated his words, he knew, because she was lying. By echoing, she implicated him, and the lie was shared.

'Look, if he's being threatened, that's a matter for the police.'

"E's got asthma. And I'm living with my cousin and she can't get up the stairs. She got a nerve problem and the planes set 'er off.'

'Melinda, I moved you from Tower Hamlets to Heathrow because you needed to look after your mum, right?'

'Yeah, she can't stand it neither; the planes mess up 'er 'earing aid.'

He glanced through the file again. 'Says here that your mum passed away in October.'

'Oh, yeah. I thought you meant my stepmum.'

Daniel pointed at the boy. 'How old is he?'

She examined the child for a moment, then said, 'Three.'

The boy protested: 'I'm four.' He then crawled under Daniel's desk and began to gather up the paper clips.

'You didn't have a child two years ago when I moved you, and now you have a three-year-old?'

'I'm *four,*' the boy insisted.

She was stuck for a moment and flushed.

He felt bad for her. 'Was he living with your mum?'

'Yeah, right. 'E was living with my mum.'

'Listen, there is, as you probably know, a long, long waiting list for flats, and most of the people have urgent needs. I had an Indian woman come in here the other day who was about to set fire to her mother-in-law.'

'That's part of the culture, though, i'n' it. Always setting fire to each other that lot. Lot's of 'em in the block. Bangladeshis. Stinks of curry.'

Something seemed to occur to her: 'So, you going to move 'er, then?' It was clear she now regretted not suggesting that she was on the verge of incinerating a close relative.

He examined her, the pale, bruised putty of her skin, her thirsty mouth, her vacant, shiftless gaze. No way in. No way into this life. Lies. Perhaps she just wanted to be by the park. He could understand that. She closed up her body a little, and he realised that he'd been staring and hadn't spoken for a long while.

'Let me ask you a question,' he said.

She looked at him.

'What's the happiest memory you have?'

'Why?'

'I'm just interested.'

She thought for a moment. 'Went to 'olland once with my boyfriend on this boat.'

'Did you like Holland?'

'Oh, you didn't get off the boat. The booze was really cheap, you know, and they 'ad a disco and that.'

'Is this the boyfriend – ?'

'Nah, this was years ago.'

'So where's he now?'

'Don't know. Lives in North London somewhere I think.'

'Do you miss him?'

She shrugged. 'Yeah, suppose.'

'What do you miss about him?'

'Good laugh.'

'Have you ever done anything you've really regretted?' he said.

'I once threw up on a bus conductor.'

'Were you pregnant?'

'Nah, it was a dodgy kebab.'

He thought for a moment that he was going to cry. He wanted her to say something, anything that was true. Or *seemed* true. A detail, he didn't know what, a way in: *She and I were being sewn up.*

'Look,' he said, 'I'll see what I can do, Melissa –'

'Melinda,' she corrected.

'Melinda. But I can't promise anything.'

She fluffed out her hair. 'You married then?'

'Yes.'

Clearly disappointed by how unequivocally he'd responded, she nodded, got up, and opened the door.

Realising that she was about to shut it behind her, Daniel called, 'Your boy.'

'Oh, yeah,' she said, and shouted, 'Come on, you.'

The boy was all the way under Daniel's desk, looking at him. He held his little hand up, his fingers splayed, his thumb jammed against his palm.

'I'm four,' he whispered. And Daniel wanted desperately to press his own hand against the boy's, to pull the child close and tell him he believed him.

12

Daniel cut through the little park and down Walnut Street. He'd escaped the office after Melinda had left, though he still had dozens of appointments waiting.

As he got close to the Windsor Estate, he became aware of the sound of excited voices. In the centre of a vacant lot at the end of Walnut, a crowd of children surrounded something. He went to enter the estate but then heard an eerie, high-pitched cry. It sounded like someone in pain. Quickly, he made his way over the rubble to the children, most of whom ran off.

It was a fox, whining and snarling, tied to a post. He wondered how they'd captured it. It was barely able to stand, one of its eyes swollen shut. A fat child with a crew cut stared fearlessly at Daniel. He was holding an iron bar, with which he suddenly struck the animal across its back. The fox squealed, staggered, and looked around as if actually surprised. Daniel lunged at the little skinhead, but the boy flung the iron bar at him, hitting his shin.

Daniel cursed, clutching his leg with one hand and snatching up the bar with the other. The little skinhead and the remaining children scattered.

The fox buckled on to its haunches. He reached for it,

but it snapped at him. What could he do? Release it? It was dying. He'd find a telephone. As he walked away, the children closed back in, the little skinhead picking up a slab of concrete. Daniel felt furious and hopeless. With the iron bar still in his hand, he limped back to the fox. It looked up at him, its one good eye blinking. Daniel struck it – a firm blow between its dark ears – and it collapsed.

Casting down the iron bar, he walked away, his shin throbbing. He saw now how young some of the children were.

13

THIS TIME THE DOOR was opened without hesitation, the sickening image of falling out into the sky instantly extinguished by the prosaic Amos Radcliff – barefoot, pyjamaed, beaming, declaring, 'Mr Mulvaugh, you came back.'

Daniel nodded, still shaken by what had just happened with the fox. Following Amos in, he returned to the sofa. Nothing had been moved from the coffee table – the tea things from yesterday, the chestnut, the tin of Erinmore, the pieces of the pipe.

Amos sat in the armchair, smiling and rubbing his hands together, as if expecting good news.

It then occurred to Daniel that this man *was* expecting good news. He hadn't even given a thought to Amos's case. Confused and embarrassed, Daniel now wondered what he was going to say. *I wanted to be back in my home; I wanted to hear your story.* He couldn't say that.

At last, Amos broke the silence: 'Can I ask you a question, mate?'

Daniel nodded.

'What's wrong with your trouble?'

'My what?'

'Your missus.'

'What do you mean?'

'Well, you said she was poorly.'

'Poorly? Did I say that?'

Amos leaned forward and whispered, 'Is it the cancer?'

This was how the women used to say it when Daniel was a child, whispering and always affording it the dignity of the definite article.

'Yes,' he answered; it seemed the easiest thing to say.

'Is it the vulva,' Amos said, 'or the breast?' He laughed. 'Oh, listen to me. I sound like someone at the Kentucky Fried, don't I: "Vulva or breast, me darlin'; white meat's fifty pence extra."'

'What?'

Now Amos seemed abashed, like someone from another culture who suspects he's committed a faux pas.

'It was ovarian cancer,' Daniel said. This was the primary cancer that had killed his mother. Answering with this made him feel he was at least saying something true.

'Funny,' Amos said, running his thumb along the edge of the coffee table, 'that's where they're vulnerable i'n'it.'

The *vulnerable* seemed wrong – right rather. The rest of it seemed wrong. Why was this man, whom he knew to be educated and articulate, talking like an East End huckster?

Amos sighed. 'It's the things that bring life that kill 'em: womb, breasts, ovaries, vulva.'

'Why do you keep saying *vulva*?' Daniel asked. 'Do you mean the cervix?'

Amos arched his eyebrows. 'What's a vulva then?'

'I'm not exactly sure.'

'They do 'ave a vulva, don't they?'

'Yes, yes, I'm just not a hundred percent sure what it is.'

Amos got up and went into Daniel's bedroom. He soon returned with a hefty book, which he dumped into Daniel's lap. It was Daniel's old *Shorter Oxford English Dictionary*. But it couldn't be. It looked ancient, the cover torn off, the pages foxed and falling out.

'Let's look it up,' Amos said. As he sat back down, he pulled a pair of steel-rimmed spectacles from the breast pocket of his pyjamas and settled them upon his nose.

Assuming they were reading glasses, Daniel handed him the dictionary, but Amos said, 'No, no, you read it.'

After taking another moment to align his spectacles, Amos assumed a look of scholarly concentration. Daniel got the impression that the glasses were helping him not so much to see as to hear.

He couldn't believe that this man was waiting for him to look up *vulva*. But waiting he was.

He thumbed through the pages. It *was* his dictionary. His writing crowded the margins: words he was trying to learn used in three or four sentences. He felt no vestige in him of the young man who'd done this.

He got to it. 'Vulva: The external genital organs of the female.'

'That's it?'

'Essentially.'

'Read it all,' Amos insisted. 'Read everything.'

Daniel sighed, but Amos seemed oblivious, his closed eyes tympanic behind those glasses.

'One. The external genital organs of the female, including the labia majora, labia minora, clitoris, and the entrance to the vagina. Two. In entomology, the orifice of the oviduct. Three. In conchology, the long and considerable depression often occurring behind the summit of bivalve shells at the dorsal part of the external surface.'

'Fancy that.' Amos took off his glasses and put them on the coffee table. 'A bivalve used to describe a woman's bits and pieces – a depressed one at that. Bivalve with the blues. God, that has to be bleak.' He laughed, then sighed like an old woman and added, 'Nothing about the cancer, then?'

'No.'

'Well, there you have it.' All at once, Amos seemed overcome with sadness, his antic energy draining. He tipped forward and rubbed his eyes hard with the palms of his hands as if he had a headache.

Daniel took his opportunity: 'What did you mean that last time about that woman being sewn up?'

Amos looked up at him, confused.

'Your first . . .' Daniel faltered. He couldn't say it, a simple word – *love*. 'You met her in a hospital.'

'Chloe?' Amos inquired. 'Are you talking about Chloe?'

'Yes. Well, I don't know.'

'In a hospital in Bangkok?'

Daniel shrugged. 'You said you were both being sewn up.'

'That's right.'

'Why?'

'Oh . . . oh, that's a bit embarrassing actually – what landed me in the hospital, I mean. You easily offended?'

Daniel shook his head.

'Well, you see, when I first left the ship –' Amos broke off, shut his eyes, and rapped his knuckles against his forehead, trying to remember. A second later it came to him. 'The *Dog Star*,' he declared. 'I was on the *Dog Star* out of Clydeside. Anyway, second I step on the dock this old Thai bloke comes up and tells me his girls are choice. I was with my cabin mate, Hamid.'

Already, Amos's manner and voice were changing.

'I told this geezer I was up for it and tried to get my mate to come.' Amos smiled. 'I remember Hamid asked me if I'd ever been to a prostitute.

'"Course I have," I said.

'Then he points out that I'm blushing like a virgin, which I was.'

'Blushing or a virgin?' Daniel said.

'Both. A twenty-six-year-old virgin – can you believe it?' Amos looked as if he were still ashamed. 'I'd been in jail, I'd fought in the war, but I was a little sensitive in regard to the fairer sex. I thought it would be easier with a foreign girl – especially 'cos it would mean we couldn't speak to each other.

'So, I told Hamid it was just a bit of fun. He replied that, oddly enough, having a red-hot wire shoved up his urethra as a result of a few seconds of sweaty degradation wasn't his idea of fun, and wandered off.'

'Sounds like a wise man,' Daniel said.

'One of the very few, God love him,' Amos agreed.

'But you did it?'

'Well, I followed this old bloke through the streets to a shantytown at the outskirts of the city, and finally into this lean-to made of corrugated iron. Inside it was an old woman and six naked kids. Course, being an idiot, I looked at the old bird and thought, Blimey, she's a bit ripe. But she shouted at the children and they all lay down in front of me. High up on their backs were written prices in what looked like lipstick; obscene phrases had been crudely tattooed below these prices in very badly translated English.

'Horrified, I turned to go, but the old man pulled me back round. As he did this, he reached down, took hold of one of the little girls by her hair, and lifted her off her feet.' Amos imitated this action, thrusting his fisted hand out over the table.

'Though her eyes were wide with the pain of it, this girl didn't make a sound. Just hanging there, she was, in front of me, having her mouth squeezed open by that bastard.'

'Christ,' Daniel said. He could almost see the child suspended beneath Amos's hand.

'Well, I've always had a wicked temper, Daniel. Just about ripped the bloke's arm out getting him to put the kid down. Then I chucked him across the room. He recovered quickly, though, and punched me just down here in my lower back before I could get out.

'I was lost in the streets for a while. I reached round to touch my back, which felt strangely wet, and when I looked at my hand, it was covered in blood.'

Daniel frowned.

Leaning forward, Amos explained: 'The old bastard had stabbed me.

'Anyway, cut a long story short, I eventually got to a hospital down by the docks. It was a Saturday night. You couldn't breathe in there for people. I was lying face-down on a table having the wound in my back stitched, and right in front of me sat this gorgeous woman. She looked Asian, though she was tall and had blue eyes. There was something else about her eyes, which I couldn't put my finger on at first. After a while I realised that the left was slightly less Asian – more Caucasian – than the right. A subtle difference – you'd hardly notice. Probably sounds weird, but this made her even more captivating.'

'Doesn't sound weird,' Daniel said.

'Anyway, this woman was having the back of her head sewn up, and in her lap lay this thick plait of black hair. One end was matted with blood. We didn't speak. They weren't using anaesthetic for either of us, and we just stared at each other as if we were competing for who could take more pain – an apt courtship as it turned out.

'She was done before I was. As the nurse went to put the needle away, this woman lifted the hem of her skirt, which had got torn somehow, and said something in Thai that made the nurse laugh. God, I was so young.'

'Twenty-six isn't so young.'

'I was a young twenty-six. I thought I'd die if this woman left, so as she got up to go, I called out, "You're not Thai, are you?"

'She stared at me.

'"You live here in Bangkok?" I said.

'And she says, with an Aussie accent, "You a sailor?"

'"I'm from England," I said – proudly, for some reason.

'"I know where you're from," she says, "Where are you going?"

'Her manner was so cold, Daniel, and her beauty so striking that it seemed . . . it seemed to have separated from her somehow, to have its own presence in the room – while she, Chloe, was the homely sister, into whose eyes no one ever really bothered to look.' Amos went quiet, absently pinching his own lips.

Daniel found the silence troubling, and said, 'So, she asked you where you were going.'

'Ah, yes . . . yes, and I said, "Anywhere but England."

'Then she asked me what I was running away from, and I replied – suavely, I thought – that I wasn't sure yet.

'She wasn't impressed.

'I asked her who'd cut her plait off.

'"My dad," she said. "Did it with his machete – which I wish he'd bloody sharpen once in a while."

'"Why?" I said.

'And she said, "Because it would have hurt less."

'Then I said, "No, I mean, why did he cut it off?"

'And she said, "I know what you mean, sailor."'

Amos went quiet again. Daniel could sense Amos's regret, still, at giving Chloe so perfect an opportunity to expose the gulf between her world and his.

'Anyway,' Amos continued, 'she then explained that he'd caught her in a bar with some Filipino sailors.

'She was about to leave, and not knowing what else to do to keep her there, I asked her for the plait.

'Well, this surprised her, and she now looked at me with a sort of grudging affection as she told me she needed it to cover up the wound until her hair grew back – wait.'

Amos got up and disappeared into Daniel's bedroom. Minutes passed. Daniel listened for the opening of a door or drawer, the shifting of furniture, but nothing. The silence became like a slow drip in his chest. He couldn't sense Amos in the flat at all. The old fears surfaced and Daniel took hold of the sofa with both hands. Sixteen stories up: he mustn't think about it. He concentrated his attention on the objects in front of him. The horse chestnut, its casing split to reveal the precious conker at its heart, looked as if it had been plucked from the tree yesterday. After running his fingers briefly over the chestnut's spiny casing, he took up the dictionary and flipped through its pages, wondering again what could possibly have happened to have so aged it. Then he examined the spectacles, discovering something he'd vaguely suspected: they had no lenses. He put them back down. For some reason, he couldn't bring himself to touch the pieces of the pipe, though he felt an impulse to smell them.

Finally – to Daniel's profound relief – Amos returned. He was holding a fraying plait of black hair. He seemed to half-offer it up to Daniel as he sat, but Daniel leaned away, repulsed. Amos put it down on the coffee table and sat silent for a moment. He looked as if he were attempting to discern something through the cold obscurity of his own eyes.

Daniel was deeply shocked by the plait, which seemed not like a relic but like something fresh, alive.

'Her name was Chloe Beausant, and we met, as we'd agreed, a few days later, in the Chin-Say Park on the north side of Bangkok. As we walked, she told me that her mother, who was racially pure Japanese but had grown up in Sydney, had flown the jade trade between Thailand and China, and had died a number of years ago when her Gypsy Moth crashed. Chloe had been thirteen. Her father was a Frenchman from Provence. She believed he'd deserted from the army during the war because he always ran a mile if he ever heard anyone speaking French.

'"No good in him," she told me. I remember so clearly the way she said it – as if she wanted the words to come out differently this time. "Strange," she said, "to have a father with no good in him."

'Fathers' – Amos broke off, addressing Daniel directly – 'how many of them are any good, eh?'

'Wouldn't know,' Daniel replied. 'Didn't have one.'

Amos reached down to the table and shuffled the sections of the pipe around as if they were the pieces of a small puzzle. Then he cleared his throat and said, 'You *have* a father.'

'I mean I didn't know him.'

Amos, still toying with the pipe, remained silent for so long that Daniel became uncomfortable.

'Are you a father?' Daniel was instantly aware of how oddly he'd put this.

Finally Amos looked up. 'Yes.'

'Do your children –'

'Well, that's a story for another time.'

Daniel nodded.

Amos continued: 'Chloe told me that, like a lot of people who aren't good, her father coveted goodness, wanted to have a kind of goodness near him that he could lay claim to.

'"For him, that goodness is me," she said. "And because he's such a lousy man, he can't stand to see me with other men. He's threatened to burn my face. He's threatened to kill me. And he's going to do it one day. That's why I've got to get out of here."

'"Why don't you come with me?" I said. I told her I was going to sail to Tahiti, which hadn't actually occurred to me until that very second – though I had met this crazy Kraut who had an old ketch he was selling for next to nothing.

'Amused more than anything by my excitement, she forgot herself for a second and so came into perfect alignment with her own beauty. I couldn't help myself. I kissed her. She didn't turn away, but she didn't respond either and, after I'd drawn back, she gently patted my cheek and said, "Listen, sailor, don't fall for me."

'"I've already fallen," I said. "It didn't hurt that much."'

'And she said, "You haven't hit the ground yet, sailor."

'I went to kiss her again, but she jerked away and said, "I have to pee." Then – I swear to God, Daniel – she hiked up her dress, squatted down, and emptied her bladder. It was just magnificent. I didn't know where to look.

'A few moments later, she was back at my side, and we walked on.

'"A lot of sailors," she says, "tell me they're going to take me to paradise, and the next morning they've disappeared. Either they're ridiculously deluded about their own sexual performances or they're barefaced liars."

'"Don't say that," I said.

'"Don't say what?" she said. "Don't say they're liars?"

'I didn't answer, and she said, "Don't say I've fucked other men?"

'Her eyes met mine with a fierce and provocative joy, Daniel, as if she wanted me to hate her. But as quickly as it had come, that cruelty was gone, and her face went pale, almost winced with remorse, though her voice was still cold. "Look, sailor," she says, "once you get the boat sorted, come and find me." Then she walked away.

'Can you hear it, Daniel, the way she said *sailor*?'

'Yes,' Daniel said. 'I can hear it.' *Don't say I've fucked other men*. He could hear that too, seemed indeed – which confused him – to remember it in a woman's voice, Chloe's voice.

'Good,' Amos said, 'I can't think of a better way to bring her to life than the way she said that word.'

'So you don't think she felt anything for you?'

'No, I think she did feel for me,' Amos replied, hesitantly at first but then with conviction. 'She *did*. And feared that, feared most that affliction of mine, my innocence. But I'm not sure she was able to feel that ecstatic fear most of us call love. She had more concrete fears to deal with.

'Anyway, that evening I went to the German, who lived on a ramshackle little houseboat in the harbour, and I bought his leaking old ketch for almost all the money I had.'

Amos paused, smiling. 'Half crazed, that Kraut, I'll tell you. You should have seen the paintings he showed me.'

'He painted?'

Amos laughed. 'Oh, they weren't *his* paintings, not by a long shot. I remember him saying to me, "If I could just sell these, I would be a wealthy man" . . . You know anything about art, Daniel?'

'Not really.'

Amos pointed up to the wall beside the window. Daniel now noticed a painting, half-obscured by shadow, one that hadn't been there when he was a child.

At Amos's smiling encouragement, he pulled himself up and – despite the painting's proximity to the window, which Daniel avoided looking out of – he went over to examine it. Its colours were vivid, blue-greens and pinks. It was of a window opening out on to a view of a few sailing boats. But the boats, Daniel could see, were not important. The subject was the window itself. It was a beautiful painting, though the colours were inimical to those of Daniel's world, and made Daniel feel almost disoriented. This feeling was further enhanced by the overelaborate, silver frame that encumbered the painting. In the lower-right-hand corner, it was signed, Henri Matisse.

Daniel returned to the sofa.

'Was he a forger?'

Amos smiled. 'Something like that,' he said quietly, 'but how I got that's another story.

'Anyway, I was desperate to get Chloe away from Bangkok, alone with me, and the weeks I spent fixing up the ketch with Hamid were agony. I kept finding her in the bars with other sailors. Hamid saved me from so many fights, pulling me back or distracting everyone with one of his great comic performances. You should have seen him, Daniel.' Amos smiled. 'Six five, with a shaved head and the most magnificent Semitic nose. I can still picture him vividly, those wild movements of his

rangy body. In the blink of an eye he became Hitler, W
C Fields, a woman in labour, a crazy evangelist – you
name it.

'But he was also a truly educated man – self-educated;
and a lover of animals. The cabin we'd shared on the *Dog
Star* was as crowded with beasts as it was with books. He
always insisted on having a creature from pretty much
every species. Drove me crazy, and as close as we were I
swore I'd never share a cabin with him again.'

'Sounds like a remarkable man,' Daniel said.

'He was,' Amos replied, a deep and tender respect in
his voice. 'He was. And the funniest man you ever met,
a comedian – but the *right kind* of comedian.'

'You mean he wasn't cruel?'

'No, I don't mean that, exactly, though he wasn't. No,
what I mean is that in my experience, Daniel, constant
humour usually derives from a retarded sensibility. In
most "funny" men, humour is just the flip side of a gross
sentimentality – one that has its source in the pathetic
image these men have of themselves as unhappy
children.' There was something now about the intensity
of Amos's gaze, the way he was saying this, that made
Daniel feel it as a reproach. 'Or humour is simply a
machine, as some develop a machine of bitterness or
kindness from the few resources available to them, a
machine that turns out – no matter what you put into it
– exactly the same things over and over and over again.
But this wasn't Hamid. He used humour either to return
others to a sense of peaceful perspective – he'd clearly

had to deal with a lot of violence in his life – or as a kind of lubricant, allowing that odd and oversensitive man to slip as little chafed as possible through life.

'I loved him, Daniel, loved him as deeply, I realise now, as I ever loved anyone. But, you know, I couldn't even tell you which country he was from.'

'Didn't you ever ask?'

'Well, he had the habit of sidestepping questions about his own life, and I never really insisted.'

Amos became lost in thought again. Daniel found the silence hard to bear. His mother's silence seemed to be pressuring in, and he realised that Amos's voice, in this place, had already become a kind of refuge. It cohered him, and he had the sense that it cohered the silence also.

Daniel looked down at the plait. It seemed to reflect a hard and brittle light from its weavings, as if the hair had turned to jasper, and that's how he felt her, hard and brittle. Chloe. The name echoed in his head.

'Chloe,' he said. 'Did Chloe – ?'

'Yes, yes,' Amos took up with renewed energy. 'So the ketch was finally ready and I went to look for her. I couldn't find her in any of the bars, but one of the barmen told me where she lived.

'The building was squalid. The door of the fourth-floor flat was answered by a white man, mid-fifties perhaps, wearing only a loose sarong. His muscular torso was covered in tattoos, his eyes were bloodshot, and I noticed what looked like a cluster of tears running down his left cheek. When I told him I was looking for Chloe, his manner became unexpectedly kindly. In his strongly accented English, he told me she lived one floor down. The second I turned around, I felt a tremendous shove in my back, and the next thing I knew I was lying crumpled on the next landing. Incredibly, I hadn't broken anything. I launched myself back up those stairs and kicked the door in. I had every intention of chucking him headfirst out of the window, but I was quelled by the strangest sight. On the floor, behind a low table on which lay a couple of opium pipes, sat a grieving, half-naked Thai woman. The white man was lying across her legs suckling at her breast. It wasn't at all sexual. She was cradling his head as one might cradle a child and crying. The tears I'd seen on his face were not *his* but hers, which were dripping down on to his cheek. *Hers,* Daniel.' Amos clearly seemed to think this of real significance. 'Neither of them took any notice of me.

'I found Chloe in one of the bedrooms, naked, her wrists and ankles tied together, a couple of nasty burns on her back.'

'Burns?'

Amos nodded. 'Looked as if they'd been made by an iron.

'Anyway, within an hour, we'd set sail.

'We had six days of sun and strong breeze as we headed up through the Balintang Channel. Every night Chloe had nightmares, in which she'd cry out in Japanese. She'd never tell me what they were about. My incessant amorousness was a burden to her. She treated me like a child, would try to calm me down, would sing to me even. But she was always looking out at the sea, always asking when we'd arrive.

'I remember the sight of her sitting at the prow, her question always the same: "How long before we get there? How long?" A few times I tried to kiss her, but she'd just turn her face away and, if I forced my mouth on hers, would remain impassive, her eyes wide open, as if I were kissing an image.

'One night, I went to her as she was lying asleep in her bunk. It was love – love, not lust, such love as only the young can know. She woke with a start as I touched her.

'I said, "Chloe, why won't you even try?"

'"Try what?" she said.

'I just stared at her. Finally she got up out of her bunk, took off what she was wearing, and lay herself down in front of me.

'I said, "I love you."

'She said, "I'm sure you do, sailor."

'I ran my hand just once gently over her face and along the length of her body.' Amos held his hand palm down over the table. Daniel could see it – *feel* it rather – her body beneath that hand, that relic.

'It was as if I'd made her, Daniel, and she were now finished, no longer a part of me. Then I went to my bunk.

'On the morning of the seventh day, we awoke to a strange light, an eerie silence and complete calm. When I climbed out of the hatch, I saw a yellowish sickness in the sky. I told Chloe to stay below. I tied on a lifeline and stupidly rigged the sails. For about half an hour, they remained completely slack, then, as I stood there staring up at the livid sky, the sails flapped once, twice, and began to tremble.' Amos snapped his fingers. 'It was on us like that. The whole mast suddenly collapsed – thank God it was as rotten as the rest of the boat or we would have capsized. I forced her into the waves. She almost upended. I was thrown into the ocean. I could hardly keep myself above the surface. Then, through a trough, I caught a glimpse of the ketch and of Chloe tugging at my lifeline. She kept slipping as the waves broke over the deck. At that moment, as if two huge hands had taken hold of my back, I felt myself lifted and thrown towards her.'

Amos reached down and pulled the right turn-up of his pyjamas over his knee. Running down the full length of his shin was a grotesque scar.

'My leg struck a cleat.

'Chloe tried to take hold of me, but do you know what I did? I hit her in the face, hard. I couldn't bear it that she was helping me. I don't know why. So there we were, on a small, sinking boat, in the middle of a typhoon, and she was lying on the deck, her nose bleeding, and looking at me with such hatred – *such* hatred.

'The boat was flooding. Another wave almost swept us off the deck. She got up and made her way to the open hatch, but the boat lurched, and she was thrown against the rusty metal edge of the hatch cover.

'I got her below. The water was ankle high. Her side was bleeding badly. The radio was ruined. Our only bottle of iodine had broken. The water was black with it, and that smell – I'll never forget that smell. After I'd dressed her wound as best I could, I got out on deck again and tried the flares. They were so old they burst into powder.

'The storm lasted two more days. The water rose to my knees. Why the boat didn't sink, I don't know. Chloe slept through those days, and when she finally awoke, she looked terrible, the skin beneath her eyes bruised, her face utterly white.

'When it was calm, I bailed out the boat, a bucket at a time. I set a course northwest and started the engine, hoping to hit China. Within a few hours the diesel was gone. I remember I was standing on the deck as the engine cut out. Then the silence . . .

'There were gulls sitting in the calm water. Chloe called out to me, but I didn't answer. I had no hope to give her. I knew I should go down to her, but I didn't. I couldn't. I moved softly about the deck so she wouldn't hear me – as if, if she thought I were gone, I could be gone. Do you understand? Would you blame me for that?'

Daniel didn't answer.

'Would you?'

'No,' Daniel said, almost a whisper.

'Then she began to curse me. God, she cursed me for so long, called me things I'd never heard even from the mouths of dockers. Her voice rose into a scream and all of a sudden choked. It was out of my hands. Do you understand?'

Daniel stared at Amos's hands, which were now clasped together at his belly. Powerful, worn hands, the nails too split, blackened, and broken ever to be new again.

'Could you forgive me?'

'I'm not her,' Daniel said.

Amos clearly required something more definite: 'Could you forgive me?'

Anger flared in Daniel. He hadn't meant to say *no* before, he'd meant to say yes – *Yes, I would blame you for that*. Now Amos wanted to be forgiven.

'No, I couldn't,' Daniel said.

Amos just stared down at the table, his hands capsized in his lap, his shoulders hunched. He seemed humbled and wizened – not the fifty- but the seventy-year-old Amos. And Daniel succumbed to an impulse of pity – a feeling he instantly resented.

Amos sat up, sighed, recovering his poise and shedding, with effort, the years he'd gained.

'At last, I went down to her. She'd obviously tried to get up. There was fresh blood all over the bed. Nothing was dry. Nothing was clean. I hung a sheet out in the sun, and with it I dressed her wound, which had begun to smell unbearably. She was so white. I tried to say I was sorry, but she wouldn't speak to me. She hated me. Within two days, she was dead.

'I carried her out on to the deck, dragged her really – my leg was such a mess – and released her very gently into the sea.

'A week later, suffering, besides malnutrition and exposure, from an infection in my leg that had made me delirious, I was found by an Auckland tramp. They took me to a mission hospital in Pekan.'

Amos leaned forward, stroking one of his eyebrows. 'Chloe still comes back to me, Daniel, in dreams. It's always the same dream. She's been washed up on a beach, her bones scattered, her skull in a rock pool, the sky reflected in the sockets of her eyes. And I kneel down to kiss her, and as my lips are about to touch her bared teeth, a crab emerges from her mouth. That's what she has to say to me, Daniel, and I can do nothing but watch it scuttle across the sand into the sea.'

Amos went quiet, a somehow involuted quietness, as if he were closing in on himself. Again Daniel felt a touch of panic at his silence and said, 'The hospital – how long were you in the hospital?'

14

AMOS SAID NOTHING for a moment, then answered, 'Long enough.' He seemed as reluctant to come out of his silence as someone exhausted would be to come out of sleep. But then he took a breath, unfurling his hands to examine his own palms. A sad, bemused look overcame his face.

'How strange – fate,' he said. 'Where you end up and with whom. How it changes your life. It was at that hospital in Pekan that I was first introduced to literature – introduced in a very particular way. By a nurse, Sylvia Brandreth – a little Welsh girl, she was, from Swansea. Anyway . . .' Amos sighed.

'She taught you?' Daniel prompted.

Again, Amos took some time to respond. 'Well, not taught exactly,' he said. 'You see, this woman thought it was bad for me to brood, so on the first day I was well enough, she brought me a pile of books. Of course I told her to leave me alone. Then she realised . . .'

'Realised what?'

'That I couldn't read.'

'Couldn't read? Why?'

'Lots of reasons,' Amos snapped, as if this still hurt his pride. 'Anyway, she hovered around me awkwardly for a while, then asked if I wanted her to write a letter to my family. I said no.

'"What about your sweetheart?" she says, and I wasn't blind to her searching look.

'"No," I said. I wanted her to go away. At that moment, Daniel, I felt as if the only reason I was alive was to give some form to Chloe's absence.

'But she didn't go, and after a moment said, "You must have thought you weren't going to make it."

'I said, "What makes you think I made it?"

'Right then, a dreadnought of a head nurse steamed in and informed Sylvia that there *were* other patients.

'But the next evening – her evening off – Sylvia came back. She was holding a book. Her makeup was over-done, and she was wearing a very revealing dress. She was obviously extremely uncomfortable in it, tugging constantly at its hem.

'She was so physically different from Chloe, her body compact and voluptuous. She had a little shield-shaped face, small eyes, and lovely, thick lips, her upper lip very slightly cleft; and I remember her hair clung to her head in dry, pale curls.

'She sat down next to my bed and asked if I wouldn't mind it if she read to me.

'I just stared at her face, and then – brazenly – at her bare legs and half-exposed breasts, causing her to squirm. It was an agonising and delicious feeling: heartless desire.

'Finally, something relented in me, and I asked her what she was doing in Pekan.

'She told me she never thought she'd leave Swansea, where she'd grown up, but had enlisted as a nurse during the war and had been sent to all kinds of places. Each time she'd returned home for leave, she'd felt more and more like the ghost of the little girl she'd once been, so she'd stopped going back.

'She asked me why I was so far from home myself, but I didn't answer. Just dying there in my cruel silence and in that tiny dress, she asked again if she could read to me.

'My shrug must have seemed vaguely affirmative because she did read. She read –' He broke off. 'Oh, what was it called?' Amos slapped the palm of his hand hard against his forehead. 'What was it called? Damn it. It was one of Thomas Mann's stories. *Damn it.*' Now he hammered his fist down on to his thigh, but it clearly just wouldn't come.

He gave up. 'Well, anyway . . . anyway, this began my literary education. She read to me every chance she could: most of Shakespeare, *Pride and Prejudice, Anna Karenina, Jude the Obscure, The House of Mirth, Precious Bane* – Are you a reader, Daniel?'

Daniel almost said yes. He'd once loved language, and there had been a time in the years after his mother's death when he'd lost himself in literature – fiction particularly. But as he read more, the authors seemed able to reveal and suggest less, became too human, their books a preserved rather than a living mystery; or was it just that what mystery they contained had resonated too inexplicably, painfully with his own?

'No,' Daniel said. 'Haven't picked up a book in years.'

'But you can read?'

'Of course I can.'

'You just don't?' Amos was clearly perplexed.

'Lost the taste for it.'

'Then you should have someone read to you,' he said. 'Sylvia read beautifully. She'd also define all the difficult words for me without ever suggesting I didn't know them. She'd pretend it was *she* who didn't know them. Then she'd look them up and read out their definitions, giving elaborate examples of the words' uses that I'm sure weren't in the little dictionary she owned.'

'To help you remember,' Daniel said.

'Yes,' Amos repeated softly, 'to help me remember.'

'After a few weeks, on finishing a wonderful little book called *Adolphe,* she asked me if I wouldn't mind listening to a poem she'd written – for me.'

Amos took a deep breath, then released his words in a sigh: 'Imagine her, Daniel, this woman, trying to inspire a dead man.'

Amos became abstracted, but a second later something seemed to occur to him: 'Do you want to hear it?'

'Hear what?'

'The poem.'

'You remember the whole thing?'

'Yes.'

'Well, if you'd like.'

'Not if *I'd* like, Daniel; do you *want* to hear it?'

Daniel hesitated. He did want to hear it but felt vaguely that things were going too far. At that moment he became aware of what seemed like a woman's voice – muffled and distant but getting increasingly distinct. He knew it was probably someone in one of the neighbouring flats, but it frightened him somehow, and he said abruptly, 'Yes, yes I would.'

Amos took a second to prepare himself. He moistened his lips as if he were about to play a trumpet, then elevated his head and intoned in a breathy voice with the slightest Welsh lilt:

> 'Wild Nights – Wild Nights!
> Were I with thee
> Wild Nights should be
> Our luxury!
>
> Futile – the Winds –
> To a Heart in port –
> Done with the Compass –
> Done with the Chart!
>
> Rowing in Eden –
> Ah, the Sea!
> Might I but moor – Tonight –
> In Thee!'

Daniel didn't say anything for a moment. The poem lingered in his mind and, though he knew he hadn't, it was as if he'd heard it (now *remembered* it) in a woman's voice. More than that, it was as if it were the voice he'd just begun to hear. What was wrong with him? He tried to put this out of his head and said casually, 'Not bad. Not subtle, but not bad.'

'No, not bad,' Amos agreed. 'And more of her poems came after that. Some like that one, full of love and hope:

> *'I love thee to the depth and breadth and height*
> *My soul can reach, when feeling out of sight*
> *For the ends of Being and ideal Grace.*

'But towards the end of my recovery – my physical recovery – they turned darker and more desperate:

> *'You did not come*
> *And marching Time drew on, and wore me numb.*
> *Yet less for loss of your dear presence there*
> *Than that I thus found lacking in your make*
> *That high compassion which can overbear*
> *Reluctance for pure loving kindness' sake.*
> *Grieved I, when, as the hope-hour stroked its sum,*
> *You did not come.'*

The woman's voice was returning.

> *'With witness I speak this. But where I say*
> *Hours, I mean years, mean life. And my lament*
> *Is cries countless, cries like dead letters sent*
> *To dearest him that lives alas! away.*

> *Such body lovers have,*
> *Such exacting breath,*
> *That they touch or sigh. Every touch they give,*
> *Love is nearer death. Prove –'*

'You remember *all* of them?' Daniel cut him off, had to, the nerves at the back of his neck raw – these words in *that* voice.

Amos got up, went over to the window, and looked out of it as if he were checking on a sleeping child. 'Not one thing,' Amos said, 'there's not one thing in all the years I don't remember.' He paused, then softly exclaimed, '*Tonio Kröger.*'

'What?'

'That first story she read to me: it was *Tonio Kröger.*'

He returned to the armchair. 'And, of course, if I ever did forget her poems, I could always find them again.'

'Find them?'

'I'm *ashamed* of you, Daniel,' he cried out with sincere disappointment. 'Claiming them to be her own, she was reading me the poems of Dickinson, Browning, Hardy, Yeats, Hopkins –'

'They're not her poems?'

'Of *course* not. I admit I didn't know it at the time either, but I was an illiterate bloody sailor.'

'Why? Why would she lie to you?'

'Why do you think?' Amos replied, his anger directed more at himself than at Daniel. 'She wanted me to love her. And I wanted her to love me. I wanted her to suffer. On one day I'd take her hand, the next I'd act as if she didn't exist. I was trying to rid myself of what remained of my heart. And believe me, Daniel, I'd give anything right now to undo my cruelty – that memory like shrapnel, liable to shift at any moment.

'I never told her I was going to stay, no, but I'd let her chatter on about us being together. And, towards the end of my recovery, she gave herself to me, a virgin –'

'Like you.'

'No, not like me. Not like me.' Amos spoke in a clipped, angry tone. 'I wasn't whole anymore. She was, and she gave herself to me, a simple-hearted girl for whom this was sacred. And I made love to her, made it expertly, sculpting her body, fascinated that I could create the form – the very truth – of desire while feeling nothing. *Nothing*. I felt nothing, Daniel.'

He hesitated, then went on more calmly. 'The work of real love makes the maker. Chloe, lying naked on that bunk as I touched her, *made me*. You understand? But Sylvia could make nothing. I was nothing but a cold ambition: to be as deeply silent as I could, to be a man. You understand *that*, don't you, Daniel?'

This last question seemed direct and accusative, almost cruel. *To be a man*. No, Daniel thought, almost said, *that* I do not understand.

'Sylvia began to look drawn, pale, sleepless. She became accident prone, always had a new cut or bruise, was constantly burning herself on the sterilising equipment. She kept getting sick, the flu, cold sores, eye infections.

'I remember, late one night, she stole into my room. I could smell the gardenia perfume she'd begun to wear all the time – no doubt because I'd once told her it smelled nice, though I actually found it sickeningly sweet. As I listened to her removing her clothes in the darkness – she was extremely shy – a cruel impulse overcame me and I switched on the lamp beside my bed. She threw her hands over her nakedness, hissing at me to turn it off, but I was too horrified to move. She was emaciated.

'She switched off the lamp herself, and her freezing body, as it entered the bed, sent a revolted shiver through mine.'

Daniel shifted on the sofa, having felt that cold touch against his own skin.

'Meanwhile, every day I was getting stronger, healthier . . .

'On one afternoon, a few days before I was to be discharged, Sylvia, who was on duty, came into my room and sat beside my bed.

'There was a long, stitched wound just above her right eye. I didn't ask her directly about it but couldn't stop looking at it, and she volunteered that she'd stood up into the metal edge of the medicine cabinet door. Fifteen stitches.

'I made no comment, and she said, "You're almost better."

'I just nodded.

'Then, in a kind of spasm of desperation, she took my hand and told me that everything was ready at her flat, and that if I found it too cramped we could rent a bigger place.

'I couldn't stand it. I was just about to tell her I had no intention of staying in Pekan when the door opened and who should walk –'

'Hamid,' Daniel cut in, flooded with relief.

Amos gave him a surprised look.

'Who else?' Daniel said.

'Yes, I suppose you're right. Who else.

'Anyway, Sylvia snatched her hand out of mine. Hamid went white at the sight of her. She looked like death.

'"Nurse," he said, "you need a nurse."

'Such *joy* I felt at seeing him, Daniel, as if this nightmare had ended and my life had come back to me. I asked him what the hell he was doing here. He stared at me, baffled, and said, "Well, I was hoping someone might shove a red-hot wire up my urethra – what do you think I'm doing here?"

'Turns out he'd bumped into an old kiwi friend of his in Bangkok, who'd told him about some limey idiot they'd rescued in the Balintang Channel. So he'd hitched a ride here on a shore tramp and only had a few minutes before it was heading back to Bangkok.

'Sylvia made her excuses and left.

'There was a long, grave silence between us until, at last, he said it: "What happened to Chloe?"

'"She's dead," I said.

'Another long silence then, before he said, "What about this nurse? She seems to care for you."

'"I'm in such a mess," I told him. "I'm torturing her and I can't stop myself. In three days I'm leaving, and she just won't believe it."

'"To go where?" he said.

'I admitted I didn't know, and that's when he told me that, if I wanted it, he'd got me a job on the *Prince of Scots,* South America bound, leaving Bangkok in a week. I told him I'd see him onboard.

'On the day before I was to leave, Sylvia entered my room together with a man and two of the other nurses, who were done up to the nines. The man was a missionary. Looked like a sick rabbit. Sylvia was wearing a hat with a small veil, through which I could still see the scar on her forehead.

'One of the nurses chided me for not wearing a tie. The other suggested we stand by the window, as it was such a beautiful day. I didn't move. The atmosphere soured. Sylvia reached down and pressed a gold ring into my hand. By this time a few curious patients had gathered at the door in their pyjamas. I let the ring sit in my open palm. The missionary cracked his fingers. Finally, he mumbled that he ought perhaps to come back another time. One of the nurses let out a sob and left the room. The other shot me a murderous look and ushered Sylvia away.

'The next day I didn't see her as I got ready to leave, but when I stepped out of the hospital into the blazing sun, there she stood, waiting for me in the street. For a few minutes we talked, of all things, about the weather. Then there was a long silence. She kept trying to catch my eye. Finally, she shoved a piece of paper into my hand, saying she'd written it for me, and that she'd *really* written it. I asked her what she meant, and she said I'd probably know one day. Without looking, I took it and left. Just before I turned the corner, I glanced back. She was smiling, Daniel. Smiling.'

Amos sighed, slapped his knees, stood and walked sombrely into Daniel's bedroom. Daniel – surprised by his own impulse – picked up the plait of hair. Coarse and heavy, it smelled faintly rank. The cut end was held together with wax. Suddenly, it seemed to writhe in his hands. He dropped it on the table.

A moment later, Amos returned, holding a piece of yellowed paper. He handed it to Daniel, whose heart was still pounding. Daniel felt afraid. Numbly, his fingers unfolded the brittle sheet.

The words were ruined. Blue smudges. Sea, sweat, and years. He released his breath, smiled, and looked at Amos.

Amos was squatting with his feet up on the chair, his toes hooked over the edge of the cushion, his arms wrapped around his knees. He looked like a gargoyle, staring at Daniel with an expression that might have been sinister if it weren't so confused.

After refolding the sheet, Daniel put it down on the coffee table.

'Did you ever read it?' he asked.

Clearly surprised that he'd been addressed, Amos seemed, all at once, to become aware of himself and slid down into the seat.

'No.' He took a moment to regain his poise and dignity. 'No. I was going to throw it away as soon as I'd turned the corner. I suppose I can count keeping it as the one remnant of humanity in my behaviour towards her. Behaviour that probably led Sylvia to revenge herself on someone, and that someone to revenge himself and so on. But here it is, this poem that I kept.' He paused. 'Did you know that Michelangelo could never continue a sculpture, no matter how long or hard he'd worked on it, if he discovered a flaw in the stone? The first version of the *David*, apparently, had a flaw right at the knee. The smile on her face, on Sylvia Brandreth's face, Daniel, as I walked away, I think of now as the flaw that smiled at Michelangelo after all his work. It was God's smile. It said: Don't forget me.'

15

AMOS STOOD UP, frowned, seemed restless. Daniel too had begun to feel a kind of restlessness, all this regret invoking a desire in him to make things somehow right – in Amos's life, in his own. Amos walked over to the rain-streaked window again and looked out.

'The world changes,' he said. He pointed down at something outside. 'I remember on top of those garages almost five years ago, someone painted, "You are the damned," in huge red letters. It seemed so personal. The years passed. In autumn, it was hushed by the leaves, reiterated by the wind; in winter, it was silenced by the snow, repeated at each thaw. The years passed and it faded, was spoken to me more and more quietly, under the breath, so to speak, until it finally reached that subtlety available to those who've been together a long time. Now, for me, those barren roofs intimate it. They'll never be rid of it.'

Rain began to fall harder against the window. Amos stood for a long time staring out. Daniel felt alone, a voyeur, forgotten.

'So when did you learn to read?' he said, finding it hard to bear this man's back, his silence.

'I didn't,' Amos said.

'You didn't?'

'Never had time.'

'You mean you *can't* read.'

'I can't read.'

'And you can't write.'

'I can't write.'

'Then who wrote the letters to us?'

'Sarah. She lives on the fifth floor. She helps me. She reads to me when she has time. I have lots of people who read to me.'

'You *can't* write?'

'Not even enough for my own epitaph, my mighty oak.' Amos turned around.

'But . . .' Was this man just making a fool of him? He remembered why he'd come here, remembered the man's claims. *I have great work ahead of me, Daniel.* He stared at Amos, that scar on his exposed shin, those terrible eyes – a lie, a lie that had lived so long, had become so layered and aspected, that it had attracted, been inhabited by, some naked spirit. Did that then make it – *Amos* – true? No, no, there was no truth here, nothing but a con man, a soulless savant playing a shell game. Daniel wondered if this were real anger he was feeling, or if he were just trying to find an excuse to act upon this increasing restlessness in him, this sense, urgent now, that he had to do something. He stood up. *This is – this was – my home.* He'd missed it, that moment it might have been said. But there was something else in him now, something else to be said. He could feel it, hear it – a voice.

'Look, Mr Radcliff, I'm going to say that there were extenuating circumstances, all right. I'll do as much as I can to try to make sure there are no criminal charges brought against you. But the cheques will stop. You must get yourself a job.'

'A job,' Amos replied wistfully, turning back to stare out of the window. 'I've had so many jobs. You know, I even spent some time as a gigolo in Blackpool. I was paid to dance with single women at the Ritz.'

He turned back to Daniel. In the dim light, there seemed something vaguely malevolent about his look.

'The waltzes were my favourite. You must have danced with your wife?'

'My wife?' It was as if Amos had just provided a focus for all Daniel's nervous energy, a recipient for that inchoate voice.

'Yes,' Amos said, 'you must have danced with her?'

'What?' Daniel didn't want to speak. He needed to go, and he now knew where. 'No,' he replied distractedly, 'no, not ballroom.'

'Pity.' Amos's tone became oddly pedantic. 'It's a nice way of touching someone, a nice way of moving with someone. You're cleaved. The constraints are simple: the music and another person. To be a good dancer, you have to remember both. But if you must yield, my friend' – he wagged a wry finger – 'you must yield to the latter. Why? Because you don't dance to forget, but to remember. Let me show you something. Listen to this.'

He went to the record player, fumbled about with the

records beneath it, pulled one from its cover, and set it on. The music began in a haze of scratches, sounding like the sea. Amos took hold of one end of the coffee table.

'Help me with this, will you.'

'Help you?'

'Let's get it out of the way.'

'What? Why?'

'Come on.'

Reluctantly, Daniel took the other end of the table, and they shifted it over towards the window. He needed to get out of here.

'Now, let me show you something.'

'Mr Radcliff –'

'Five minutes, then you can go. Give me your hand.'

Amos snatched up Daniel's left hand and wrapped Daniel's right arm behind him.

'Now, slowly, one, two, three. It's easy. When you get back you can dance with your wife. It'll surprise her. Stop being so inert. It's worse than dancing with a sack of bloody potatoes.'

'Mr Radcliff, let go of me.' Daniel could hardly believe how strong Amos was. They were spinning around in the small space between the shifted sofa and the armchair. He tried to stop a few times and pull himself away, but Amos quite literally carried him through the motions.

'Where's your life? Where's your rhythm? Yield a little; we're not fighting.'

'Let go of me, Mr Radcliff.'

'Laaa two three, daaa, two three, la da da da two three.'

'Amos, please!'

'No, no, we can't stop. The intimation of a dance is that it will last forever.'

'Damn you. Let me go!'

Daniel tore himself away. Amos regarded him darkly. He seemed all at once a very different man. Daniel felt afraid, afraid of this man's strength, his smile, his bleak eyes. Amos pulled the needle off the record. He walked back to the window and looked out as if nothing had happened.

'I need time,' he said. 'I need time to think. I've never had time. My life came in a rush. I need to look down upon this, and it needs me to look down upon it. Do you understand? All of this that I see needs to be resolved in me. My job is to see. To feel. All you have to do, my friend, is to forget me.'

'Is that all, Mr Radcliff?'

'That is all.'

'Before I leave, would you like me to help you move this back?' Daniel placed his hand on the edge of the table.

'No . . . No, this way I can remember that I danced with you here.'

An ambiguous smile touched the corner of Amos's lips.

'Good-bye, Mr Radcliff.'

He walked over to Amos and put out his hand.

'How glibly people offer their hands,' Amos said as he turned around.

He took Daniel's hand in his own. Again, Daniel felt that profound strength.

'I killed a man with this hand.'

'Are you trying to scare me?'

'Scare *you*?' Amos seemed amazed. 'No, I'm on my knees. I'm at my last stand, my friend.'

'What?'

'I'm giving myself up to you. After thirty years, I'm –'

'No, what did you say? What did you just say?'

'That I killed –'

'Good-bye, Mr Radcliff.'

Daniel freed his hand, turned, and took a step towards the short hallway that led to the door. He felt a little afraid to have his back to this man. Though he needed to go, it didn't seem possible somehow that he could leave – not now. He kept thinking, *Don't turn around* but, at the door, he did. The room shocked him. The shifted table made it seem bereft. Not only bereft but ruined somehow, like a room many years after the disturbance of life. A dark aura had gathered about the coil of hair, the chestnut, the spectacles, the tin of tobacco, the old dictionary, the pieces of the pipe, and the yellowed note on the coffee table. Amos stood at the window, clasping his hands behind his back, staring out. The pyjama leg he'd pulled up in order to show Daniel his scar was still hoisted above his muscular calf. Just beside Amos on the wall hung the Matisse. The sun had drowned completely in the black clouds, and the room was now etched by a grainy luminance, as of dust motes in moonlight. Amos cast no shadow. Daniel's vertigo, which he'd been struggling to subdue, intensified as he approached the door: sixteen stories to the street; nothing but sky. He took firm hold of the door handle to steady himself, his head spinning. Finally, shutting his eyes, Daniel opened the door and stepped out.

16

I N T H E S T R E E T, an impatient breeze, the rain
spattering down as if spilling over the edges of the full
clouds. Daniel walked quickly to consume his nervous
energy. At the end of Walnut Street, he looked back at
the towers of the Windsor Estate. *I killed a man* – Amos
hadn't finished. This troubled him, but he'd started now
and had to have faith in that emergent voice. He thought
of Sally among the daffodils: if he could have said
something then. But he hadn't had it then, had now – or
almost – the thing to be said. Daniel knew there was
something a little crazy about this, but he'd been filled in
these last few hours with the conviction that he mustn't
allow it to be too late again. He had to talk to Sally.

He joined a nun in full habit at the bus stop. When
she turned to smile at him, he was confronted by a pretty
face covered in acne. He reached for his cigarettes, but
the 33 arrived; it would take him right to Palm Court.

He sat towards the front. As the bus moved on, to ease
his nervousness, he tried to imagine his wife listening to
him as he spoke these words, words that were just
sounds right now, like the baffled rhythm of that
woman's voice just before Amos had recited Sylvia's
poem. He felt as if he were about to go onstage to deliver
lines learned in dreams, terrified, though some part of

him knew it was a role merely, a character developed from one of Amos's remembrances: *Let me tell you, my friend, about a man called Daniel Mulvaugh who, one day, tried to say everything to his wife.*

On the seat before him was a man wearing a tiny fawn-coloured cap on his fat, bald head. It made Daniel think, for some reason, of pork in muslin. At the back of the bus, on one of the seats facing the aisle, sat a woman who struck him as an impeccably maintained cul-de-sac of feeling, her beauty as unimpeachable as it was bland. Opposite her another woman – no, a man, a young man with long hair, trying not to fall asleep, his hands interwoven, his head nodding into the cowl of his hair as if he were making devotions of some kind. It reminded him of Galvin, which troubled him because the words, which had been focussed on his wife, seemed to want to speak to this also. *Ashamed of you, Galv, of your letters, fidelity, and confused love.* Stop. He had to stop this. This wasn't for Galvin. Galvin was dead. To distract himself, he looked across at the acned nun with her nun smile.

The bus halted outside the senior centre. A half-dozen old men and women staggered on. They seemed to Daniel like the remnants of an army, routed again, bearing their blue-rinse hair and liver-spotted hands, their wounds and their shame. Nothing seemed so hard to him now as just living until you are old. Just making it. He thought of what Amos had made it through – had still to make it through.

The bus crossed Richmond Bridge and stopped again.

Two women boarded, a young woman with a baby and an older woman carrying the folded pushchair. They sat on the vacant seat across the aisle from his. The baby lay jerky and boneless in its mother's arms, vagrant expressions flickering across its face. He noticed the grandmother's hands, fused into the semblance of fins by arthritis.

The mother, who seemed still in a kind of postbirth euphoria, had placed her hand under the baby's downy skull, as if she were learning, with an ecstatic intimacy, the word *skull,* as one could only learn it by feeling one bared to the bone, and one, such as this, so recently filled and fleshed. And somewhere deep in him Daniel felt this, the tiny head in her hand, not as something soft but as an edging spur of his crystalline life.

He looked out of the window and up into the clouds, had a strange sense that Amos was watching him; not just a sense but a clear image of Amos, as he'd left him, standing at his window, sixteen stories up, no building around him, just him and the window frame in drifts of cloud, his face almost like that of this child, full of flickering expressions, as if some remembered life were streaming though him. *I killed a man with this hand.* Daniel glanced down at his own hands. They were trembling. Was he feeling poorly? Was this what it was like? This brittleness and awful lucidity? Was he having a breakdown? He mustn't. Mustn't. He became aware that a number of people on the bus were staring at him.

He looked over at the baby again. It seemed to smile, then tried to put its whole fist into its mouth. He felt such tenderness for it, felt that he could regain his equilibrium if he could touch it, touch its foot, hold its foot for just a second.

Easy, though – too easy – to feel for such things. It was when feeling was expected, needed, directed, that something in him refused to respond. It was the specificity of the love his wife had demanded that had been too hard. But, surely, he thought, one had to be allowed to fail sometimes, to murmur a 'sweetheart' that might have gone to anyone, to embrace a body that was merely a body. He thought of how physically close he'd been to his mother, acutely aware of her body – breasts glimpsed through the buttons of her pyjamas. Once, in a handbag, he'd found a photograph of her as a young woman, standing beneath the portrait of a grim patriarch. She'd filled both hands with her thick, curly hair and was holding it away from her neck in mock flirtation. For Daniel, to look into this photograph had been to look into the time about which his mother's silence had been silent. Whenever his mother had looked right through him, as she had sometimes, she'd been looking into this time. It occurred to Daniel that this was also the time of Amos's stories. Was that why they so engaged him? Was it a crazy hope that she would be among them, as if he might find a lost keepsake in a stranger's attic, find it for no better reason than because old things are there, and because he *must* find it. Among the bric-a-brac of another's past he'd recover his mother, forever giving her hair away to her future, the pretty girl whom he could love not just as a son but as a man.

How on earth had this girl ended up shorn, silenced, and pregnant in a London council flat?

Christ, why couldn't she have lied to him, made up a life, made up a father, brave and good, who had died? He'd asked her questions – once whether she had brothers or sisters. In answer (they were both on her bed) she'd said, 'Imagine we're shipwrecked on an island, Danny. Try to think what would be on that island – the good and the bad things.' But he was like her. He longed to give form to everything he was feeling but hadn't that gift, that capacity to imagine gods and monsters into existence. That had been Galvin's gift, and Daniel couldn't conceive of how he would have survived childhood without Galvin's extraordinary imagination. Had that also been why he'd surrendered so utterly to Amos's remembrances – because they'd made sense of feeling, of what he felt, of him?

This thought filled Daniel with a longing for his home and for Amos – for Amos's voice.

The baby made a loud noise and squirmed. The mother and grandmother responded with encouraging sounds. It hurt him to look at the child. Sally had so much wanted a child. He thought of how fearful he would have been to be responsible for something so fragile, felt it in him, that fear, like the bulb of this baby's head, heavy with potential, the bone a membrane yet, crust of this little world closing up about a liquid core that would itself harden into discernment, prejudice, obsession – all the igneous forms of our limitations.

Daniel felt dizzy and grabbed the steel rail over the back of the seat in front of him. Here he was, with this voice inside him, this raw song for his wife. Here he was, in the middle of a teeming city, on a London bus, so moved by this child and full of a panicked longing to make everything right in his life. Here he was, sur-rounded by these little husks of sense – the head of this child (whose feet he wanted to touch), and the fused fingers of the grandmother, and the rolls of fat at the back of the bald man's neck. Christ, he wanted something, wanted to *believe* something. Jill called him a cynic, but that wasn't true. He *was* belief, that verb in a world with no significant subject, no clear object.

He looked over at the baby again, baby with its secret of otherworldly happiness and unassuageable grief, imagined asking the mother if he could hold the child, just for a second. And she lets him, out of politeness, because he looks kind. He rests the child's head in his hand, touches that foot. And after a few moments, he turns his back to the apprehensive women and strangles the child. The two women leap on him, bite and claw, but he's too big, too strong, and in a moment the child is dead.

Daniel shuddered and pulled his clenched hands into his stomach. *I killed a man with this hand. I killed –*

'Are you all right?'

Daniel looked up. It was the nun.

'Are you feeling sick?' she said.

'Oh no – yes, yes, it's nothing, just a little . . . you know.'

'Is it your tummy?'

Everyone was staring at him.

'Tummy?' he said, fixating on her acne, that mask of inflammation. He stared so blatantly, and for so long, she became clearly uncomfortable. Suddenly aware of this, he looked away, at the mother, who was also regarding him with concern. Sickened, ashamed, he wanted to pull this nun a little closer and say, 'I just imagined killing that child. I only wanted to touch it.'

'I haven't eaten,' he said. 'I'm almost home. I'll get a bite soon as I'm home. Thank you.'

She nodded, smiled, and returned to her seat. Then, over his shoulder, it appeared, an ancient hand offering jewels.

'Go on, love, it'll tide you over.'

He looked back at the old woman behind him, one of the lost army, a garish impasto of makeup on her face.

'No, thank you,' he said. 'I'm almost there.'

He straightened up, checked out of the window to see where he was. Just a few more stops.

A moment later, the grandmother remarked to her daughter that the child was looking more like his dad every day. The idea that this baby had, somewhere, the difficulty of a father – *You have a father* – pierced him. He thought of the fathers in the estate when he was growing up: dangerous, strange, they'd seemed to him like rocks in offshore waters, things to be navigated.

A hefty woman in a yellow head scarf got on to the bus and regarded everyone in it as if she were a famous surgeon entering a ward of desperate patients. She bustled up the aisle and pushed herself in beside Daniel. A second later, she took hold of the baby's feet and pistoned its little legs. Daniel smiled to himself. Here he was in all his difficulty, like an inept spider caught in its own web, and this woman, without a thought, had taken into her hands what he'd wanted all this time to touch.

The bus left Daniel just a short walk from Palm Court. The low sun looked like the moon behind the grey clouds. Perhaps it was the moon; he had no sense of what time it was. The rain had abated but would come again; the air was restless for it. The closer he got to the sanitarium, the harder his heart pounded, the beat seeming almost to fall and strike something in him, like a pile driver. It was the same feeling he used to get at school when he had the answer to a teacher's question, and just the thought of getting it out, saying it right, made him so nervous the sweat would drip under his arms and he'd feel his heart in his throat. Mostly he never got it out, but sometimes, if there were a long enough silence and the subject weren't changed, he'd say it and, once it was coming, say it well. And the teacher would look at him, quiet Daniel, delighted and amazed, and would sometimes ask him after class why he didn't speak more. And Daniel would wonder that this person had no sense of how difficult it was to speak, to ever say the right thing.

But he'd say it today. If everything would keep silent, keep still, he'd say it.

After signing in, Daniel made his way through Palm Court's bare corridors with their ammoniac smell and light. He pulled his coat tight around him, protecting himself like a candle flame in a draughty house.

At the entrance to the common room, he checked for his wife. This time the room resounded with the roar of the ocean. On the television, which was being watched by most of the patients, David Attenborough was kneeling on a bare promontory surrounded by iguanas. Eveline, Sally's obsessive-compulsive friend, was rocking back and forth in her chair, clutching a photograph into her stomach – no doubt the one of her dead brother. At the fireplace, the mad Russian was scribbling into his notebook as if he'd never have enough time in his life to get it all down.

'Francis!'

Daniel turned around. At the far end of the corridor stood that old lady he'd encountered two days ago in the garden. This time she was holding a toy tractor. Quickly, Daniel cut across the common room and through the French doors.

Seconds later, the doors were flung open behind him, that old lady in gimpy pursuit.

Feeling too raw to engage with her, he began to run. Just as he glanced back, he barrelled into something and fell, rolling over on the lawn.

'Shit.' He got up, hopping on one leg. It was a deck chair, which he angrily flung aside. He'd hit his injured shin, and it took a second for the shock of pain to ebb.

He hobbled to the cottage and knocked. The door was opened almost immediately.

'Danny!' Jill looked as astonished and dismayed to see him as he was to see her.

The old woman was just yards away. He pushed past Jill and closed the door.

Sally was sitting at the table with Richard and Morgan. Jillybeans, dressed in a purple dragonfly costume, clung, shy and squirmy, to her father.

"Ey up, matey,' Richard stammered, unable to conceal his surprise. 'You all right?'

A knock came at the door.

'It's that old lady,' Daniel said. 'She thinks I'm her son.'

Sally got up, gesturing for him to stay put. Her hair was down past her shoulders. She was looking beautiful.

She opened the door.

'Where's Francis?' he heard the old woman demand.

'He's not here, Consuelo.'

'Not here? I just wanted to tell him he could keep it. It was a naughty thing he did, but I'm going to give them some of his old toys so we can make up for it. He was terribly upset – running, he was.'

'He'll be all right. You should be at the house when he gets back.'

'Should I? Oh, I suppose I should.'

The old woman paused and then said, 'Give him this when you see him.'

After closing the door, Sally put the toy tractor on her sideboard. She returned to her seat and lifted Jillybeans into her lap, clearly feeling the need to place something between herself and Daniel.

'You been a naughty boy, Francis?' Richard teased.

Daniel felt too bewildered to respond – all of them here, his wife looking so lovely, and the terrible pressure of all he needed to say to her inside him.

'I'm out of chairs,' Sally said. 'Why don't you pull up that stool there.'

Jill had already set another place and poured tea for him as he sat. It frightened Daniel that she was here after what had happened last night, but she seemed to be in a good mood. Morgan, slumped in Sally's armchair, looked down at him with concern. Daniel's seat was a footstool; his head was barely above the table.

Laughing at this, Jill called over to Richard, 'Give us some of those books here, Rich.'

Richard pulled a few of the thicker volumes off the bookshelf beside him. He examined one as he handed it over: 'This looks good,' he said. 'Joseph Campbell, *The Myth of Female Orgasm*. I knew it was a myth. That's bloody Hollywood for you.' He looked at another: 'Ooh, Jill, you might want to have a peruse of this – *The Idiot's Guide to Living with an I.Q. of Less Than Sixty-five*.'

Morgan laughed.

'Morgan gets my jokes,' Richard said.

'He's just being polite.' Jill slotted the books under Daniel.

Jillybeans had taken hold of handfuls of Sally's hair and was peeking through it at him. Since his wife wouldn't meet his eyes, some part of the pressure of what Daniel was feeling released itself in a rush of tenderness for Richard's daughter.

'Sally make you that costume?' he said.

Jillybeans nodded, her little antennae waving.

'Did you wear it at your party?'

She nodded again.

'You off to Texas soon?'

'Alabama,' she said quietly.

'Why are you leaving us?'

Pulling free from Sally, Jillybeans went to her father, climbing into his lap.

'I'm sorry,' Daniel said. 'I didn't –'

'That's okay, matey.' Richard cradled her in his arms. 'She's just a bit touchy today.'

Morgan put a friendly hand on Daniel's shoulder. 'Dan-i-el, what on earth happened to you this morning?'

Jill now rested a hand on his other shoulder. 'Did you forget your appointments?'

'Will you two pervs get your mitts off him,' Richard said.

They did so, and Daniel was grateful to Richard. He thought about telling them he was sick, but even such a meaningless lie seemed inconceivable to him right now.

'I went to see Radcliff.'

'The one-legged writer?' Richard said.

Daniel nodded.

Jill explained to Sally: 'It's this real character. He's living in Danny's old flat.'

'My mum's flat,' Daniel quickly added, managing, for the first time, to get Sally to meet his eyes.

'Is this the "etiolated" fellow?' Morgan said.

'That's right.'

Jill seemed dubious. 'So you've been there all day? What's he doing, telling you his life story?'

'Actually he is,' Daniel said. 'Strange stories.' He hadn't taken his eyes off Sally.

Hefting one side of her hair behind her shoulder, she said, 'What are they about?'

'All the things he shouldn't have done . . . mostly.'

'Anything juicy?' Richard said.

'They're odd. He was a sailor. Went through all these things. He was in a typhoon.'

'Sounds as if he's been reading too much Conrad,' Morgan said.

They all fell silent, a heavy silence, which Morgan seemed to feel himself responsible for.

'I went through a Conrad kick a few years ago,' he declared a little too enthusiastically. 'Loved it: three parts testosterone, two parts hysteria – "The horror! The horror!"'

Richard leaned forward. Securing his balled-up daughter in one arm, he crushed his features together to make a simian face and raked the fingers of his free hand through the fleece of his hair. He then spoke slowly, intensely, and as if he were injured and out of breath: 'I remember when I was with Special Forces – seems like a thousand centuries ago. We went into a camp to inoculate little children. We left the camp after we had inoculated the children for polio, and this old man came running after us. He was crying; he couldn't see. We went back there, and they had come and *hacked* off every inoculated arm. There they were in a pile – pile of little arms and . . . and I remember I cried, I wept like some grandmother. I wanted to tear my teeth out, I didn't know what I wanted to do. And I want to remember it. I never want to forget it. I never want to forget. And then I realised, like a shot, like I was shot with a diamond, like a diamond bullet right through my –'

'Stop it, Daddy,' his daughter ordered, frightened by his transformation.

He returned to himself. 'I'm only playing, darling.'

'Oh, you're *so* strange,' Jill said.

'Marlon Brando, *Apocalypse Now*,' Richard explained. 'That's from a Conrad thing, isn't it? I love that speech.'

'Rich,' Jill said, 'has it ever occurred to you that you might have too much time on your hands?'

Sally addressed Morgan: 'Could you read him again?'

'Who, Conrad? Oh, I don't think so. I go through phases. The only thing that's ever lasted is my love of pretty much anything French.'

'Like body odour and having intercourse with animals?'

Slapping Richard's arm, Sally went on. 'It just made me think because, Danny, you told me once that you went through a big Conrad phase just after your mum died. Isn't that right?'

'Don't remember,' Daniel said, though he did – remembered very well how he'd obsessively devoured everything by writers such as Conrad, Melville, and London, how those far-flung adventures had filled all the lonely places of his grief. But he knew Sally, could hear it in her voice – she was leading into one of her theories. He didn't want to be the crux of one of these, the theories of a naïve savant, which always invoked, for him, the spectre of her essential solitude.

She continued without his help: 'I had to close down when I got here – to get better. But it's so important to keep finding ways to make yourself open.'

'So that things can get inside you?' Richard said.

She nodded.

'Do you want to go on a date?'

She cut her eyes at him. 'Things I *choose* to have inside me.'

'So, let me get this right.' Richard spoke like an earnest initiate trying to understand a great master. 'In order to get things inside us, we have to open ourselves up to those things?'

Sally just stared at him.

'And tell me, Sally,' he said, 'is it also true that children are the future and that Wrigley's is the Doublemint Doublemint Doublemint gum?'

'Oh, shut up, you.' Sally broke into a smile. 'I know it sounds obvious, but it isn't really.' She hefted the other side of her hair behind her shoulder. 'I mean, as I said, me being here was about closing things off. When I was getting poorly, *everything* used to get through to me. It was awful, but I really miss it in a way. I remember one time I went to the public lavs in Richmond, and someone had written on the door of one of the cubicles, "King Dick rogered Moira here." And this struck me as being so profound and tragic that I began to cry. And for about a week when I was at my worst, just the thought of "King Dick rogered Moira here" was enough to make me feel that there was mystery and love and beauty in the world. Just to whisper it would make me shiver.'

Richard looked up into the ceiling. 'Moira,' he said. 'Richmond public lavs . . .' He remembered: 'Oh, *God* yes. Big girl she was, made sounds like a tree frog when she got excited.'

Jill, Sally, and Morgan laughed. Daniel tried to smile but felt far away and frustrated. Morgan's presence oppressed him. Sally had asked him here, this man she admired, for whom she was looking so beautiful. Daniel was also aware of the difficulty of his own presence among them. It didn't help that he was still sitting much lower than everyone else. He thought of his home, Amos, and felt a tug of longing.

'On a slightly different tack from "King Dick rogered Moira here" – as lovely as that is,' Morgan took up the slack, 'I've discovered a new passion: medieval poetry.'

'Well, there's something we can all talk about,' Richard muttered.

'Listen to this,' Morgan went on obliviously, reciting:

> *'Mirie it is while sumer ilast*
> *With fugheles song,*
> *Oc nu necheth windes blast*
> *And weder strong.*
> *Ai! Ai! that this nicht is long*
> *And ich wid wel michel wrong*
> *Soregh and murne and fast.'*

'What language is that?' Jill said.

'Middle English. It's called "Now Comes the Blast of Winter." I've only just memorised it, so it's a little rough.'

'It's lovely,' Sally said, smiling at Morgan.

'A man who memorises poetry' – Jill held up a sage finger – 'can have any woman he wants.'

'I've got a good one,' Richard declared. 'Middling English. Twentieth-century Twickenham:

> *'There was a young woman from Sussex*
> *Known for the size of her –'*

'Rich,' Jill warned, glancing down at Jillybeans.

'You can't hear, can you, darling?' Richard said.

Jillybeans shook her antennae.

'Do you have another one?' Sally asked Morgan.

Morgan pondered for a moment. 'Here's one I think you'll like.'

Daniel couldn't stand it. As Morgan was about to begin, he turned to him and said, 'Was it classics you studied at Oxford?'

Morgan's good-humoured expression seized. 'No,' he said.

This surprised Daniel. He hadn't meant it to be an actual question.

'Give us the poem,' Jill demanded.

Morgan smiled at Jill but clearly felt he should respond to Daniel first: 'I didn't go to Oxford.'

'Here,' Jill declared, 'how many Oxford dons does it take to change a lightbulb?'

'I re-sat my O levels at a small college there.'

Jill imitated a wheezy and outraged old professor: 'Change? Change?'

Now he'd begun, Morgan seemed to feel he had to explain everything: 'The college actually called itself Christchurch – CES, Christchurch Educational Services – but it didn't have anything to do with the university.'

Richard cut in with simple curiosity: 'Where'd you do your degree, then?'

'Brighton Polytechnic.' Morgan's face had gone scarlet.

'Right on.' Richard pumped his fist into the air.

They all fell silent. Daniel had actually heard Morgan

say something about Oxford yesterday and now caught a glimpse of the Christchurch scarf Morgan often wore hanging on Sally's coatrack. It occurred to him that Jill probably knew most things about Morgan from their relationship, and that was why Morgan hadn't been able to dodge the question or to lie.

'I love Brighton,' Sally said. 'How long were you there?'

'About ten years in the end.'

'Jillybeans,' Jill called, 'show Danny how your wings work.'

Jillybeans shook her head.

'Yes, come on, darling,' Richard encouraged. 'I'll hold you up so you can fly around the room.'

He tried to lift her, but she made an early-tantrum-warning sound. Richard shrugged.

Sally now addressed Daniel, her tone careful, almost formal. 'Was it strange to be in your mum's flat?'

'Very strange,' he replied. It was so painful. He had to speak to her but didn't know how to begin with this audience between them.

Jill broke in: 'What kinds of things did this man regret?'

'Oh, the usual things,' he replied a little sharply.

There was an awkward silence, which Morgan rushed to fill. 'Well, how about you, Sally? What do *you* regret most?'

Sally was staring at Daniel, lost in thought, and it took her a moment to respond. 'Me? Oh, I'm not the regretting kind. But if I had to choose, it would be the way I treated my friend Moira at boarding school.'

'Of rogering fame?' Richard said.

'That's definitely another reason that graffiti touched me so much.'

'In what way did you treat her badly?' Morgan pursued.

'Well, she was one of my closest friends when I first went to boarding school. Sweetest girl, totally gorgeous, breasts like Uma Thurman. I had no boobs and this nose' – she tapped her nose – 'I looked like a baby vulture.

'And one night the two of us were in my room and, I can't remember why, but I ended up showing her the burn scar on my back.'

'Burn scar?' Morgan said.

'Oh, I pulled something off the stove when I was a kid. Anyway, she then told me she'd been involved in a terrible car accident some years ago, and that the whole front of her body was badly scarred – not just from the accident but also from all the operations she'd had to have afterwards. And she showed them to me. And of course every girl in the house had caught glimpses of these scars – we'd all been in the same dorm for years – but she'd been pretty discreet about them, and it seemed a tremendous privilege to be shown them and to be allowed even to touch them. There were a half-dozen long scars on her stomach, and there was quite a little chunk taken out of one of her breasts.'

'I love scars,' Richard cut in. Then he shook his

head as if he'd made a Freudian slip. 'I mean breasts.'

'Rich,' Jill said, 'you need a good, long, cold shower.'

'I need a good, long something.' Richard winked at her. Jill smiled.

Sally now hefted all her hair forward over one shoulder and toyed with it as she spoke. 'So, a few weeks later, a bunch of us are having a secret little party in my room, and this girl, Rebecca Gunn-Russell, who was utterly vicious, and her monstrous sidekick, Tara Pratts, had managed to sneak in two boys. I don't know where they dug them up. Two townies – absolute troglodytes, but we wanted to eat them alive.

'And of course the boys were just mad about Moira, who seemed to have no interest in them at all, while there was I, reeking of desperation, flinging myself at these creatures.'

Morgan was incredulous. 'Reeking of desperation?'

'Oh, I've done my fair share of reeking,' Sally said.

'Doesn't seem possible.' Morgan was shaking his head.

Shying from this, which was too direct a compliment, Sally forged on. 'So I resented her for this. And the other girls did too. I mean, those boys were thin gruel, to say the least, but they were all we had.

'I'll tell you something revolting. One of the boys, who was leaning back against my bed, had incredibly greasy hair, and actually left a sort of smear on my sheet. And for days after that, I'd sit on the floor in spasms of longing, sniffing the grease.'

A general cry of revulsion went up.

'There's a child in here,' Jill exclaimed, laughing.

'That's all right.' Richard rocked his daughter. 'She'll sniff the grease soon enough.'

Jillybeans fiercely shook her head.

'So,' Sally went on, 'we all played some drinking games and got pretty blotto – except for Moira, who was looking bored. And then she got up to leave, and I didn't want this to happen, because it was like an announcement of how desperate we all were. So I begged her not to go, and she said she had to trot to the loo but would come back and stay a little while longer. And as soon as she'd left the room, I asked if anyone had any interesting scars. And when Moira came back –' Sally hesitated. The memory was upsetting her. 'I could see she was troubled because one of the boys was showing us his appendix scar – giving us a good deal more of his groin than he needed to. And I knew I didn't have to do much more. I could count on Rebecca and Tara. And as soon as Moira sits down, sure enough, Rebecca asks her to show the boys her scars. And Moira says no. And this turns into a bit of an argument, so Moira gets up to go, but Rebecca and Tara take hold of her, and then the other girls and those two boys join in.' Sally faltered again. 'I actually held down one of her ankles. She never spoke to me again.'

After a moment of silence, Sally took a deep breath, recovering herself, and declared, 'Now, I'm absolutely sure Jill has never done anything awful.'

'She must have done,' Richard said.

Jill fluttered her eyes. 'I'm just an angel.'

'It's true.' Sally regarded her sister with slightly baffled admiration. 'Jill is constitutionally incapable of hurting anyone.'

It was Jill's turn to flush a little. Daniel wondered if he and Jill would ever talk about what had happened last night.

Morgan pointed at Richard. 'What about you?' he said playfully. 'I bet you've done some things you regret.'

Daniel noticed a tentativeness in both Jill's and Sally's reactions to this. He wondered if Jill had told Sally, or if Sally, who was so acute about such things, had long ago intuited that Richard should never be asked such a question. Everyone seemed to have forgotten Jillybeans, tightly balled in her father's arms, but her presence frightened Daniel – the little girl, suspended here in this amnion of place, people, and father, all of which she was soon to leave. Daniel sensed himself in her consciousness as something half-remembered, dreamed, the perplexing image of a man whose head was barely above the table, a man from that time before she knew her father had done something unforgivable. He wondered if Richard would ever get the chance to explain.

Amos had also done something unforgivable. *I killed a man with this hand.* Thinking of him now caused the pain and frustration Daniel was feeling to recede a little – in part, perhaps, because there was a way in which he could conceive of this all being told. Told by that strange man in his home: *But Daniel Mulvaugh, desperate to say everything to his wife, discovered that she was not alone.*

Richard had been talking for a little while, and Daniel now attended again.

' – things the Cubs had to do every year was bob-a-job. So I used to go around knocking on people's doors and washing people's cars and stuff. And there was this old lady, Sybil Nuttall, right, who lived a couple of doors down from us. So I tried her, and she had me weed her garden all day, and at the end of it gave me twenty pence. I didn't want to go back, but she got my phone number and began to call all the time to get me to do all these jobs for her. And she was very deaf and a bit batty, and was always mislaying things. So a couple times a week at least, she'd call my house and scream down the phone at my parents, "'As 'e got my rake? 'As 'e got my shovel?"

'Anyway, so, during the summer holidays, she gets me to uproot these old privet bushes in her garden. It was like a weeklong job – backbreaking. And every morning she heads off to volunteer at the Oxfam shop. And while she was gone I'd go into her house and have some milk and she'd leave me some cake or something. So, of course, there was I, a healthily curious eleven-year-old, in this house alone. What would anyone do?'

'Eat the cake, drink the milk, and return to work?' Jill suggested.

'That's right,' Richard said. 'Pop upstairs and have a good shifty around. And on the dresser in her bedroom, there's this sort of shrine to some bloke, right – it's covered in photographs of him, mostly in uniform. And at the back of one of her cupboards –'

'You're digging around in her cupboards?' Jill said.

'Is there a dimmer switch on your halo, perchance? I'm getting a bit of a headache here. So I find this wooden trunk. And in this trunk is a uniform and a whole bunch of other stuff belonging to this bloke – Gaylord Nuttall – including a medal and a telegram saying he died bravely in battle blah, blah, blah.'

'I'm going to cry,' Sally warned.

'It gets better. So me and my mate Steve are absolutely crazy about anything to do with the war, and I was convinced that this medal was the Victoria Cross, and I wanted to show Steve the medal and the telegram. So not dreaming that she ever looked at these things on any regular basis, I took them to show my mate, right. I was going to put them back the next day. But ten minutes after I get home that night, there's this hammering on the door and Sybil comes in frantic, and there's this nightmare scene. My mum and dad don't have a clue what's going on. And she keeps grabbing hold of both my wrists and shaking me and telling me to give them back. And I know my dad will beat the living daylights out of me, so I did what any kid would do.'

'You admitted what you'd done and returned her things,' Jill said.

'*Exactly*. I swore on my mum's life that I had no idea what the old bat was talking about.

'And, of course, my mum and dad already knew she wasn't playing with a full deck, so my dad ends up almost pushing her out of the house, saying he's going to call the police, and she falls over and she's screaming and it's just this horrendous scene.

'So, after she's gone, I did what any eleven-year-old in fear of his life would do. I flushed the telegram down the toilet –'

'Rich!' Jill shouted.

'– and, using my dad's wire cutters, I broke up the medal into little pieces, and the next day I chucked all the pieces into the river.'

Richard sighed and sat back, combing his fingers through his daughter's hair. He wore the disappointed but ultimately indulgent face of a kindly priest who has just heard an eleven-year-old confess this. This was one of those stories, Daniel realised, told not to link the teller to his past but to separate him from it, to make him invulnerable. Had a similar mixture of curiosity, longing, and fear resulted in the act Richard had kept secret for all these years, the act that was sending his wife and daughter to another man and another country?

Jill again tried to persuade Jillybeans to show Daniel how her wings worked, but she just clung to her father. Daniel noticed, on the draining board, a big bouquet of lilies and irises, which he suspected Morgan had brought for Sally. For the first time, Daniel looked at the food on the table and realised that some of it – the fruitcake, cheeses, and julienned vegetables – had been recycled from the tea she'd made for him two days ago. This seemed terribly wrong, wrong that Morgan should be eating this food that had inaugurated the end of Sally's relationship to him.

'Thrift,' Daniel muttered.

No one responded, and there was an awkward silence.

Daniel looked at Sally, but she was staring down at the table. He was going to lose her. He wouldn't have another chance.

'I have three things.' Daniel made his declaration.

'You what, matey?' Richard said.

'Three things I regret,' Daniel said. 'Apart from the main one, I mean. Apart from my mum dying.'

No one responded. Sally seemed to be checking her hair for split ends. Daniel felt, and it relieved him, that, even if no one else was listening, Amos somehow was, up there in his drift of cloud.

'Enough regrets for one day,' Jill said tenderly, rubbing Daniel's arm. 'Shall we play charades?'

'What are the other choices, Satan?' Richard said. 'Rolling a big rock up a hill? Feeding each other our own entrails?'

She threw her napkin at him.

Daniel knew he was being a bit strange, but he had to tell her. 'I wrote you lots of letters.'

'Danny, let's talk later.' Sally was still not looking at him.

'I need to tell you now.'

Jill leaned across and put her hand on Sally's thigh. 'We should all head off.'

'No,' Sally almost shouted, snatching up her sister's hand.

Daniel said it: 'Not speaking to you that night in the park.'

Sally frowned, confused: she clearly had no idea what he was talking about.

'Just before you had your breakdown, don't you remember? You got me up in the middle of the night and dragged me to that little park in Wapping.'

'You mean the little square?' Sally said. 'With the old tree and the pond?'

Daniel, aware that the others were uncomfortable, addressed them. 'It was a place I used to play on as a kid. Near the estate. Before Sally's dad moved them all to Dulwich, she used to walk past it every week with him on her way to her violin lessons. Jillybeans's age; maybe a bit older. So Sally and I used always to say that we must have seen each other as kids. Me and my mate Galvin were always in that tree watching people and making up stories about them.'

Jillybeans had emerged slightly from her little chrysalis and had fixed her gaze on Daniel.

'Do you remember bringing me there that night?' Daniel said.

Sally was kneading her forehead. 'I wasn't well.'

'You knelt down by the water –'

Sally seemed to wince, and Daniel quickly directed what he was saying to the others.

'It was a paddling pool when I was a kid; it's just been a pond for years now.' But he needed to say this to Sally, and he addressed her again, speaking as quickly as he could. 'And you were touching the water and I was just standing under the tree. And you wanted me to come and kneel down there with you, but I wouldn't. And you told me that every time you passed it as a kid, you always wanted to play in the paddling pool with the other kids, but your dad wouldn't let you. And he turned out to be right because drunks kept throwing beer bottles into the paddling pool and kids were always cutting their feet open.'

Sally hadn't stopped him. He went on more calmly. 'And that night, you kept asking me to come over and speak to you, but I wouldn't. That's what I really remember. I wouldn't move and I wouldn't say a word. I bet you couldn't even see my face, could you?'

Morgan shifted in his seat, and Daniel glanced at him. He was examining his fingernails, embarrassed.

'It wasn't your fault,' Sally insisted. 'I was being unreasonable.'

'That *wasn't* unreasonable. You wanted me to speak to you. You kept asking me if I were going to say anything, and I didn't say anything.'

Sally snatched up Richard's and Jill's plates – Morgan handed over his – and she took them to the sink. Jill went to her. She put her arm around Sally's shoulders, and the two sisters whispered for a moment.

Daniel hadn't managed to say what he'd wanted to. How bothered he'd been by the streetlight shining in his polished shoes, no matter how close to the tree he'd stood. Hateful. And how his wife had stroked the water and said, 'It has teeth and blood, and when nothing's touching it, it can see so clearly.' It had taken him a moment to realise she was talking about the pool – the blood of the children and the broken glass. Why hadn't he gone to her and acknowledged that filthy pool as a sacred monster? Why hadn't he asked her to look up into the horse chestnut at the two boys lying in the branches? Why hadn't he told her that he would believe anything she wanted him to?

Jill came back to the table and dealt out the plates again. Sally lingered a moment at the sink before returning to her seat.

'I threw those shoes away, Sally,' Daniel said.

'It's not your fault.' Sally sank her chin into her hands and covered her mouth with her fingers.

'It's not about fault,' Daniel said.

'What's the second one?' Jill spoke formally, as if she'd determined to take on the roll of mediator.

After a moment, he said, 'Well, one night a few months after I'd first arrived at university, I was in my room with a bunch of my friends and some bloke –'

'Where was this?' Morgan cut in gently.

'Nottingham. And some bloke puts his head in and tells me my mum's on the phone. I hadn't been in touch with her for three months. We had no phones in our rooms, and I have no idea how she got the number to the pay phone.'

Sally spoke from behind her fingers: 'Why didn't you call her?'

'I don't know. I was so glad to be away.'

'Were you not close to your mother?' Morgan asked.

'Too close,' Daniel said.

'Anyway, so I went to the entranceway and picked up the phone, and she must have heard me because as soon as I put it to my ear she began to sing – some old song. It made me feel so awful. I just let the receiver hang down – didn't even hang it up. I could still hear her singing as I was walking away.'

'That's pretty bad,' Richard said.

Daniel nodded. Again he'd left out so much: how drunk she'd been; how thick her Scottish accent; the words of that song – the ballad of an abandoned woman; that spatter of fresh vomit in one corner of the bleak entranceway; going that night to the room of a sweet girl who liked him, sleeping with her, telling her cruelly that it meant nothing, leaving her and walking for hours, and how bright and clean the moon had been; how it had seemed to him that there had to be a God.

'What's the third?' Jill asked with more genuine interest.

'Well, I had this good friend – Galvin.'

'He's the one who lived with you, right?' Richard said.

'Just about. And he always used to write to me when I

first went to university. His letters were almost illegible. They embarrassed me.'

'The writing?' Morgan said.

'No. It was just that he was still writing about these games we'd played as kids. He'd make up all these adventures and monsters and things. He had an amazing imagination.' Daniel thought about Galvin for a moment. 'You know, I think he was really a girl.'

'You mean like a girl in a boy's body?' Jill said.

Daniel scowled. 'That's too . . . clinical. Anyway, the sad thing is that he got hit by puberty so hard and so early. He was shaving at thirteen. Ended up being this six-foot-six monster of a man.'

'That's like me,' Richard admitted. 'I'm a lesbian inside a frighteningly masculine body.' He covered Jillybeans's ears. 'That's why I'm such a spectacular lover.'

Jill snorted.

'You ask Moira,' Richard said.

'I think he was dyslexic,' Daniel continued, 'and because we went to a crappy comprehensive, he never got any help, ended up dropping out and going to work for a roofing company. Spent pretty much every night at the pub.

'Anyway, by the time Christmas holiday rolled round, I'd run out of money and I had to go home. And it was just dire being in the flat with my mum. We never talked about the phone call. She seemed so lonely. She didn't seem to know anyone.'

'Didn't she have any family?' Morgan asked.

'Not that I knew of. And no friends really. She was so private.'

'And your father died?' Morgan tapped his temple as if trying to remember.

'Don't know. My mum never said anything about him.'

'Weren't you curious?'

'In the estate a lot of the kids didn't have dads.'

'Wasn't there –'

'So, anyway' – he cut Morgan off – 'that Christmas it seemed as if my mum had maybe decided she was going to tell me some things. I could feel it, and for some reason it just frightened me. And one time when we were having tea she said my name, and I knew she was going to . . . I don't know, tell me something. And I looked at her and I just said "Don't."'

'It wasn't fair of her,' Jill said. 'That's too much.'

Daniel was staring straight at Sally, whose face was almost completely hidden behind her fingers and her hair. She seemed to be remembering or thinking about something else and he wanted desperately to get through to her. Jill's hand was on his shoulder again. He couldn't stand it that she was trying to make him feel better. He wasn't telling it for that.

'I don't know if it was fair or not,' he said, more harshly than he'd intended. 'I didn't know what she'd gone through. I didn't know anything about her. And she'd probably done the right thing. There are a lot of things a child shouldn't know. But the thing is, I knew them anyway.' He glanced at Jillybeans. 'You can't grow up with someone and not know. You might not be able to say what it is exactly, but you do know it. You know it in your body. You know it in *everything*.' He wished Jill would take her hand off his shoulder. 'And I also don't know if what she was going to tell me was that she was ill. I just wanted to get back to university. I –' Daniel broke off because Richard was trying very hard to stop himself laughing.

'I'm so sorry, matey.' Richard flushed bright red. 'I'm so sorry, it's a mental problem. You know me. It's just that you're so low down there, Danny boy. It's like having a very grave ten-year-old at the table.'

'Rich!' Jill was seriously angry at him. 'Pass us some more of those books.'

Richard, now mortified, did this, and Jill slotted more books under Daniel until he came up to something close to their level.

'So you didn't want to be with your mum?' Jill prompted.

She didn't mean it, but her condescension was beginning to infuriate Daniel. She also seemed so connected to Richard, teasing and upbraiding him – while Morgan's heavy, mute discomfort connected him with Sally. Again, Daniel found refuge in the thought of Amos, listening, and in Jillybeans, who was still staring at him with frank innocence.

'No.' Daniel looked back at his wife. 'And to get out of the flat, I'd go for long walks. I was always afraid I'd bump into Galv. A couple of times I did. And I'd feel guilty because he'd be so overjoyed to see me, never said anything about me not answering his letters, and would drag me to the pub. And he'd go on and on about our childhood until he was too drunk to speak.

'And one time he said he wanted to show me something in the beer garden. And when we were out there, he fell to his knees and took hold of my hand and said he loved me, told me there wasn't a minute in the day he didn't think about me.'

'What did you do?' Richard said.

'Walked off. Left him kneeling there. Didn't see him again before I went back.

'Then, a few weeks before the summer holidays, I got a letter from my mum. She told me that Galvin's mum had died – she'd been sick for as long as I'd ever known her.

'I was so sad for him. Couldn't sleep thinking about him. I spent the whole night imagining I was talking with him, saying things, all the right things. I wish I'd written him a letter, a note, something. But I did nothing.'

'Why?' Sally said.

'I don't know,' he said. 'It was as if some part of me wanted to see what would *happen* if I did nothing.'

Daniel stared at his wife, feeling helpless.

'When I got home for the summer holidays, I should have gone straight to Galvin. I just tried to avoid him. But a couple of days after I arrived, I walked past a pub near the estate and the door opened and there he was. And I said I was sorry about his mum, and he said thanks and asked me to come in for a pint. I could see he was desperate to talk to me. God, I could hardly recognise him, this big drunken bloke. And I said, "No." I said, "No, thank you," and I walked away.

'I didn't want to stay with my mum, so I hitchhiked with a friend of mine across Europe. And I got back to London five days after my mum had died.'

'How?'

'Cancer,' he answered Morgan. 'Ovarian cancer. It had metastasised all over her body. Killed her in the three months I was away. The only thing I got out of that old bastard of a doctor was that my mum thought she had something wrong with her stomach.

'And I couldn't face the flat, so I stayed in a bed and breakfast. On my way to the church on the day of the funeral, I bumped into our next-door neighbour, Maggie. She asked me why I hadn't been to Galvin's funeral.'

'You didn't know he was dead?' Richard said.

Daniel shook his head. 'And when she said this, do you know what my first feeling was?'

Sally just stared back at him, her hand so firmly across her mouth it was as if someone else were holding it there.

'Relief,' Daniel said. 'That it was all gone. I'd been so afraid for some reason that Galv would be at my mum's funeral. I don't know why.

'And Maggie told me that Galv had *fallen* . . . fallen off a roof on to a foundation bed. She knew as well as I did that he hadn't fallen. And poor Maggie, she was a lonely old woman, and she was so desperate for me to break down, so she could have something to tell people at the centre. But I just made some joke about it being bad form to be late to my own mum's funeral and wandered off.

'Sally, I just wanted you to –'

'Please don't say any more.' Sally had closed her eyes. '*Please* don't say any more.'

Morgan shifted in his chair. 'I should go,' he said.

'No.' Sally's clogged voice broke into a high pitch, so that it came out almost like a cry.

'What you're doing isn't fair,' she said to Daniel.

'Sally, be reasonable,' Jill said.

'It's not fair,' Sally repeated.

'I didn't mean to –'

'You can't do this.'

Jill was kneeling beside her sister now, holding her arms and whispering.

It had gone wrong. Daniel looked at Jillybeans. He couldn't think what to do.

'So you're going to become a Yank,' he said gently. He wanted to touch her. As he went to stand, the spine of books on which he was sitting gave out, and he tumbled backwards on to the floor.

Morgan helped him up. Daniel felt confused and embarrassed. All he could focus on was saying good-bye to Jillybeans. It seemed all at once terribly important that she should remember him in a good way. He went around Morgan, but as he approached her, she pushed herself back into her father's arms.

'It's all right, sweetheart,' Richard reassured her. 'Hug Danny good-bye.'

Richard tried to lift her off his lap, but she struggled and cried out.

'I just want to say good-bye,' Daniel said. 'I won't see you again for –'

Jillybeans tore herself free from her father and got behind his chair.

'Stop it, darling,' Richard said. 'It's just Daniel. What's wrong with you?'

Daniel tried to go around the back of Richard's chair, but the little girl, now utterly seized with terror, screamed.

'Daniel,' Sally shouted. 'Please. Please just go away. Please.'

It had all gone wrong. He stared at Sally. Hair, skin, veins, bones, a few memories, a few gestures – how could it be so hard to stop loving her?

Daniel left the cottage. As he approached the sanitarium, he saw that old lady waiting at the French doors.

'Francis,' she shouted and set off in his direction. He couldn't face her and cut across the lawn to a stone section of the garden wall, which he thought he could make it over. He wanted to get back to Amos, to his home. He felt he was going crazy.

But just as he got to the wall, someone took hold of his arm and pulled him around. It was Sally. Her face streaming with tears, she looked fierce and desperate, but she took hold of his hands and held them tightly against her stomach. The old woman was still lurching across the lawn towards him, and this frightened Daniel.

'Stay, Danny, stay here,' she said.

'I'm going to make you poorly again.'

'Danny, you don't seem well.'

'I feel strange,' he said. 'I killed a baby.'

'What?'

'It's not me, it's him, it's Amos. I laughed at a woman the other day – an Indian woman. Her life was ruined. He's in my home. I've thought about you every minute of every day for these past three years.'

'Did you hurt someone, Danny?'

'I slept with Jill. I slept with Jill last night. I thought –'

'What's this baby? Did you hurt someone?'

'Francis!' the old woman shouted. She was just yards away.

'Go away, Consuelo,' Sally screamed at her. 'Go away.'

The old lady froze.

Sally put her hand against his cheek. 'Did you hurt someone?'

'It's not me, it's Amos. He's in my home. I think it has something to do with me. I've got to go.' He stared at his wife. He loved her. He couldn't understand it – why a person couldn't just stop loving. He pulled away from her, ran and vaulted himself awkwardly over the stone wall, tearing the shoulder of his coat. He could hear Sally calling for him to come back, but he was in the alley now and running for home.

17

THE DOOR TO THE FLAT was open. Hadn't he shut it? Gently, he did so as he went in.

Amos still stood at the window, looking out. Everything was just as Daniel had left it. He breathed in the smell of his home. Inside him, like a sailor's trick, a knot slipped free.

'Mr Radcliff.'

Amos spun around. He clearly hadn't heard Daniel enter.

'You came back,' Amos declared, as if amazed, breaking into a broad smile.

Daniel nodded.

Neither moved or spoke for a moment. Then Amos made a tentative gesture towards the sofa, and Daniel sat. Amos also returned to his seat.

With the coffee table still pushed off to the side, the space between them, Daniel felt, was at once too bare and too wide. As if sensing his discomfort, Amos got up and took hold of one side of the table. Daniel then helped him shift it and its little freight of objects back between them.

As they returned to their seats, Amos's gaze snagged on the rip at the shoulder of Daniel's coat, and he said again, 'You came back.' More of a question this time.

Daniel nodded.

'You were gone for quite a while.'

A faint panic stirred in Daniel. It hadn't occurred to him that he would have to explain anything. It was then that he saw it, leaned up against the side of the sofa, and blurted out, 'My briefcase. I forgot my briefcase.'

Another flood of relief, those words, that contingency, pushed down like a keel, righting him. He couldn't stop himself smiling, as if he'd just pulled out a last-minute victory, and saw now that Amos was smiling also. Absurd, he knew, to be feeling such relief, even joy at saying those words. But he did, the joy swelling, his smile widening. Amos's smile broadened in reflection, then he began to laugh. This set Daniel off; the two of them tried to stifle it at first, like schoolboys in a class. Finally they couldn't hold it and broke down completely, Amos howling and slapping his leg, Daniel pressing his face into his hands, trying to stop himself.

At last it came to a hitchy halt, Amos wiping his eyes, Daniel trying to catch his breath.

Pulling out a hankie, Amos blew his nose, and the seriousness settled, washing back into the dim room over the two men as the soft reverberations of their laughter rippled away into the silence.

They sat quiet for a while, until Amos, with a last sigh, said, 'Tea? Let me get you some fresh tea.'

'No, thank you,' Daniel said.

Another long silence ensued, in which Amos seemed finally to accept that Daniel wasn't going to say anything more than that he'd forgotten his briefcase. He brought his hands together, interlocking his fingers.

'His name,' Amos said, 'was Andrew Scofield. He was my cabin mate on the *Prince of Scots*.'

Amos paused, not reluctantly, Daniel felt, but as if a little daunted by the difficulty of any beginning.

'Funny-looking lad, he was, at once broodingly handsome and pathetic – imagine Heathcliff on heroin. Every day he wore the same oversized and old-fashioned blue serge jacket with fat brass buttons. And he always reeked of a eucalyptus-cinnamon chest rub his mother had concocted to alleviate his asthma.'

'This is the man you killed?' Daniel said.

Amos nodded. 'And I need you to understand –' Amos broke off frustrated, and renewed with intensity, 'to understand why I became so *involved* with him.'

Though Amos looked as if he wanted some response to this, Daniel just waited.

Amos continued. 'Well, of course, his sister was the obvious reason, but there were others. One in particular that had to do with my past.

'You see, I once had a brother – not Toby, a younger brother. His name was Jimmy, and I think that my relationship to him gave my connection to Andrew some of its strange chemistry.

'Jimmy had been born more than a month premature. My mum had taken to drinking a little bit while she was pregnant, which might have accounted for it. When he was young, he threw up almost everything he ate. He was just tiny, frail, and would cling to our mum as if he were drowning.

'When I was ten and he was seven, I decided he'd live, that I'd take him under my wing.

'It was hard for him to break his attachment to our mum, but I was insistent. The truth was that she didn't want him near her. She couldn't bring herself to love him. She actually told me this when I was older. I like to think it was because she couldn't stand being in constant fear for his life, that her dislike stemmed from love overtaxed – from love. But I think the truth was that she was simply repulsed by his weakness. What she loved about the rest of us – me, Eileen, and Toby – was our strength, our vigour, our rapid independence from her.'

'What about your father?' Daniel asked.

'We didn't have –' He broke off. 'I mean, we never knew him.'

'Not even Toby? You said he was older.'

'Both he and Eileen were older, but no. No, you see, my mother would go away every now and then for a few weeks – leaving our grandmother to look after us – and from those absences she'd returned pregnant four times – six actually. There were two miscarriages.'

'You don't have any idea who it was?'

'Far as any of us knew, Daniel, she'd bared her backside to the wind.'

'Was it the same man?'

'I think so. You could see him if you put all us kids together – his features – and there was a brief period in my teens when I kept trying to draw him. I was making a composite, as if he were a criminal, from the evidence he'd left in his children. I kept this project secret until it was completed, then I put it on my bedroom wall. And I must have been close, because when my mum came in one day and saw it, she let out the strangest sound. I remember it still, Daniel – not like a cry, but as if someone had torn the cry right out of her throat.'

'Did she let you keep it?'

'No. She ripped it down, threw it away.'

Daniel went to ask more but stopped himself. Though calmer, he still felt brittle, his energy limited. He wanted just to listen. He'd pushed his hand into the gap between the arm and cushion of the sofa, and while Amos talked was running his fingers through dried-out bits of tangerine skin, the broken limbs of toy soldiers, and the little balls of spit-dampened sweet wrappers he and Galvin would flick at each other.

'She was a hard and independent woman, Daniel. She'd rarely provide comfort if we hurt ourselves, unless it was serious. She refused to act as peacemaker in our bickering. But it wasn't cruelty or neglect.' A defensive loyalty flared in Amos. 'It wasn't. She loved our health, our appetites, our vigour, our loud voices – everything that was vital. I heard her say to Gran once that Jimmy was perhaps inevitable. That he was the chaff.' Amos paused, holding his hands out in front of him, as if he were trying to express, in sign language, a paradox.

He gave up.

'Strange really, because he was so much her son. A number of times, while I was growing up, she fell apart. Saw rats in the shadows, maggots in her skin. A hysterectomy was the first thing. Then they used electroshock. I remember seeing her after one of these treatments in the sanitarium, lying in bed –' Amos stopped. 'But that's another story.

'So I decided Jimmy would live. I dragged him away from her, and he soon became extremely attached to me. I led him through the mortal perils that are the bread and mead of children at that age – Oh mothers, if they only knew.'

'Not your mother,' Daniel said.

'Even mine, I think. We walked out on narrow jetties during storms; we climbed sluice gates above torrential waters; we hung in the steel arches beneath railway bridges.

'For years, I was plucking his small hands from my body. I felt he was lucky enough as it was. After all, I led our gang of boys. This protected him at first, but soon the other boys learned that, if a confrontation did occur, he was on his own.

'Now, you have to understand, I believed I was changing him. I *believed* he was changing. And to all appearances he was becoming tougher, hardier, braver. It seemed he ate more, and with gusto. I discovered only later, from my sister, that he'd been vomiting in secret. I think he'd developed a kind of fatalism that took the place of bravery. Whatever the case, his hands were no more upon me. And, honestly, I think I missed that as much as he did.

'But Mum was happy. She'd pinch at his little muscles, would pile his plate, not noticing his flickers of despair, and smile encouragingly at the stories he told that he was going to work his way from port to port around the world, that he'd make for himself a new life in some distant land, and would return to us altered beyond all recognition.

'Signs of internal breakage began to appear: a slight stutter, a constant trembling of the muscle below his right eye. Then there were those sudden bouts of the most terrifying foolhardiness. One time – and I beat the living shite out of him when I found out – he'd lain between the rails on the train track while a train had passed over him.

'But these bouts were balanced by periods of the most extreme weakness, when he'd hide himself like an ailing animal, vomiting, incontinent, nights of sweating and crying out. He also began to succumb to a strange condition, a kind of epilepsy, I think. He'd freeze and stare into space, stock-still for sometimes half an hour. I remember seeing him in the middle of the yard one time, holding a sack of grain, the chickens pecking fruitlessly at his feet.

'But what was most awful, I think, was his suggestibility during these periods. I remember one time Mum shouted across the yard at me to go and milk the cows. When I arrived at the barn, there sat Jimmy, pistoning the teats of a cow, squirting milk all over his legs, all over the floor, all over the howling, delirious cats.

'As I broke the hold of his stiff hands, I wanted to say to him, Be weak again, be sick again, take hold of me again. But, of course, it was too late.

'The two of us got jobs at the docks in Dublin. It was hard work, and I was constantly worried about him. But the dockers were good to Jimmy. He was like a child, even looked like a child, his eyes so large in his gaunt face. He'd stand at the fringe of things, laughing appropriately, smoking badly.

'When he was working, he seemed to be able to feel those periods of complete withdrawal coming on, and would go somewhere to succumb to it. I'd search for him and find him perhaps squatting on a great coil of rope, staring down into the river.

'Then one day – it was almost as dark as night, black clouds, pouring with rain. On that day, Jimmy walked over to the open hold of the ship to which he'd been assigned as part of the loading crew, and must have had one of his seizures right there at the lip. Kelly, who was operating the derrick, didn't see him as he hauled across the deck two tons of tweed. Jimmy was knocked into the hold, and those two tons were lowered expertly on to his body.

'They found what remained of him in America . . . Do you have any brothers or sisters, Daniel?'

'No.' Daniel didn't want to speak.

'An only child: did your mum dote on you?'

'Not really.'

'What happened to your dad?'

'I told you, I never knew him.' Daniel was becoming irritated. He didn't want to remember, just to listen.

'Dead?'

'Worse' – Daniel's response was angrily flippant – 'he was never mentioned.'

'And your mum?'

Anger still, but there was no joke here: 'She's dead too.'

Daniel felt a catch in his throat as he said this. She seemed suddenly so close. He could smell her, the cold cream on her face, the tea on her breath as she kissed him good night. While he'd been away at university trying to shed the inexplicable shame of his home and her love, she'd been here alone. Now Daniel felt as if he'd give his life to be no more than her tender and sustaining gestures towards herself – ironing her clothes, shaving her legs, using a pumice on the hard skin of her feet, drinking sherry from a lead crystal glass, which made it seem somehow as if she weren't drinking alone, weren't finishing the entire bottle as she lay here on this sofa in the twilight from that window. This was the image of his soul: a room in which what little light remained was pooling in such a way as to suggest the limbs of a woman.

'You all right?' Amos said.

'What? Yes . . . yes. Anyway, so this Andrew, you're saying he reminded you of your brother?'

Amos stared at Daniel with a strange, speculative intensity for a few seconds and finally said, 'He did – though "reminded" doesn't seem quite the right way to put it. There were moments when he *was* my brother – it's difficult to explain.

'I remember the first time I met him. I'd just boarded the *Prince of Scots* and had found Hamid. He'd managed to get a cabin to himself, full of his beasts and his books.

'Just as we embraced, Hamid spotted Andrew walking by on the deck and called him over.' Amos sighed. 'And there he was. *There he was.* God, I can still see him, the man I would murder, standing in Hamid's doorway, wearing that oversized jacket, the reek of his chest rub overwhelming even the smell of Hamid's animals.

'Hamid invited him in, but Andrew said he was fine where he was. I detected a slight Scottish accent.'

'Scottish?'

'Yes. Turns out he was from a little village called Lochbroom. His mother – a snob – had tried to purge him and his sister of the accent, but you could still hear it.

'So, I said to him, "Don't you like animals?"

'"Some animals I don't like," he said, looking at me as if I were something he'd stepped in.

'Not knowing what else to say, I said I liked his jacket. He told me gravely that it had belonged to his father.

'Just then, one of Hamid's birds squawked and Andrew actually staggered backwards out of the door, mumbled something, and disappeared.

'I threw my friend a perplexed look, but he just

shrugged. I asked if Andrew always wore that ridiculous jacket. Hamid nodded, then told me he was surprised that Andrew had even approached his door. The first time he'd entered the cabin, he'd almost had a seizure on seeing Hamid's chameleon. Andrew suffered, it turned out, from a serious phobia of lizards. Hamid had had to get rid of it.

"'He's from bloody Scotland,'" I said. "How can he be afraid of lizards?"

'I expected Hamid to agree – the one thing he had absolutely no sense of humour about was his animals – but he looked at me as if I were completely dense and said, "Dragons."

"'Oh, I forgot about the dragons," I said.

"'Yes, everyone has,' he said. He was *deadly* serious, Daniel. Then he beckons me over.' Amos did this to Daniel in earnest, and Daniel leaned across the table. 'And he whispers . . .' Daniel felt Amos's warm breath, then something else – his tongue. Daniel flung himself back into the sofa. Amos laughed.

Daniel was stunned, wiping his neck. Amos clearly just thought it a tremendous joke.

As his laughter tapered off, Amos picked up the stem of his pipe, which he began to clean again, and said casually, 'Do you have any phobias, Daniel?'

'What?'

'Phobias – do you have any?'

'Being licked by strange men is right up there, oddly enough,' he said.

Amos laughed again, and waited for Daniel's answer.

Finally Daniel said, 'No, not really.'

'Nothing?'

'Well, heights. I've always been bothered by heights.'

Amos seemed unimpressed.

'What about you?'

'Me? I do have an odd one, yes: mirrors.'

'Mirrors,' Daniel repeated, flatly at first. But then it surged back, like a word he'd been trying to remember for hours. 'Mirrors,' he exclaimed. 'The mirror.' He pointed. 'There was a mirror above the mantelpiece.' *That* was why the room had seemed so much smaller.

Amos arched his eyebrows. 'You remember this flat very well.'

'It was an antique mirror,' Daniel hastily explained, 'a huge thing.'

'Ah.'

'So you don't have any mirrors anywhere?'

'Not one.'

'What are you afraid of?'

'Isn't it obvious?'

Neither of them spoke for a moment.

Daniel remembered something: 'My mum used to say that if you stared too long into a mirror, you'd see the devil.'

Amos smiled and remained silent.

Daniel shifted in the sofa. Amos's continued silence was like an intimation of falling, like moving closer to the edge. 'Dragons,' he blurted.

Amos looked confused.

'Hamid was talking about dragons.'

'Oh, yes – yes, of course. So I ask him how Daniel had ever landed this job.'

'Andrew.'

'What?'

'You called him Daniel.'

'Did I? Andrew. Yes, Andrew. Anyway, turns out that Andrew has a twin sister, Vivian, who's engaged to the ship's captain. For her sake, the captain had agreed to take Andrew under his wing. I rolled my eyes, but Hamid told me to give the boy a chance, that he'd never been out of his godforsaken village and was trying desperately to make a man of himself, had dreams of being at the wheel of a ship one day, like his own father.

'It was then that Hamid took me to meet the captain.

'But before that, I should give you some idea of the world in which I lived and worked in those days. I assume you're not familiar with the merchant marine?'

Daniel shook his head. The hand he'd pushed between the sofa's arm and cushion had disinterred a chewed-up piece of Lego, which Daniel rolled around in his fingers as Amos continued.

'Well, the *Prince of Scots* was pretty typical of those times, I'd say – a real hulk, most of the crew picked up in the South Seas, where the ship had been used for years in the copra trade. At any moment onboard you could hear a dozen languages. The two cooks were Chinese, but one spoke Cantonese, the other Mandarin, and they hated each other. A good number of the crew were from the East Indies and spoke to each other using a very simple bazaar Malay. The English sailors would communicate with the natives in pidgin – a wonderfully raw language in which emphasis and superlative are created by repetition, where "to find" also means "to seek," and where a single word can unite an almost infinite range of connected concepts. *Su-su* is a great example. It's plural, as in a woman's breasts, and seems to include everything associated with those captivating appendages: milk, to suck, to drink, to smoke; it can refer to mountains, ocean swells, even to nipplelike objects, such as the lugs left as handgrips when a bag of copra is sewn up at the top. It's the language of a frontier, the kind we used before we all settled, for the rest of our civilisations, into our sitting rooms. Of course, it was a language that could also lead to a lot of misunderstandings. Hamid once told me the story of a wealthy Englishwoman who was a passenger aboard a ship he'd crewed in the South Seas. Having tea on the upper deck with a number of the other passengers, she called to one of the Malay boys to bring a cover for her milk jug: "Calico belong su-su," she kept demanding, despite the boy's astonished look. Finally, he runs off, returning a second later with one of her bras.'

Amos let out a snort of a laugh. Daniel smiled but sensed that, with these digressions, Amos was just delaying the inevitable. It then occurred to Daniel that Amos might also be trying to judge how much the spine of this confession could bear – what of even the things of merely sentimental value it might carry for him to the end.

'You seem fascinated by language,' Daniel said.

'Yes, I suppose I am,' Amos replied. 'Perhaps because it's been, in some ways, so unavailable to me.'

Amos went quiet, looking into his own lap. Once more the years accrued, the shadows seeming to curl and char him like paper in a fire. He was, in moments, an old man, seventy, a veteran of the wars, a shell of fled memories.

'The crew,' Daniel prompted, a little frightened by this.

'Ah yes.' Amos straightened himself and took a deep breath, his smile strained as if he were covering up physical pain or incapacity. 'Yes, the crew.

'Actually, talking about language makes me think of Ay Yam. He was from Singapore. Been on the *Prince of Scots* forever. For some reason, we developed an affinity for each other – one of those inexplicable connections, a kindred soul, I suppose. We couldn't speak a word of each other's language but would smoke together on deck for hours at a time. Then one day he began to speak to me in his native Mandarin, softly, seriously, and I got the sense that he was confessing something. When he stopped, I spoke to him in English, told him everything that had happened with Chloe – everything. And this became a habit of ours, these confessions.

'But the truth is that there was a kind of apartheid on the ship. The whites and natives had separate messes and kept to themselves. Ay Yam, since he'd been so long on the ship, was one of the two exceptions, the honourary whites. The other was a bloke called Joseph Christian.

'Joseph had native features and very dark skin, but dazzling green eyes. He claimed he was a Pitcairner, directly descended from Mr Christian himself. To back it up he had an old naval rating's cap from the *Bounty* that looked genuine enough.

'Our first mate was a florid Scotsman named Boyd Wallace, who'd sunk a ship while trying to get it into Sydney Harbor. He blamed his Malay quartermaster for this, which had lost him his pilot's certificate. As a result, he hated the natives. He always carried a hankie, which he'd hold up to his nose every now and then. I thought this an odd delicacy in him until I realised, by his constantly bloodshot eyes and the careful rigidity of his poise, that it was soaked with something a little more heady than lavender water.

'But the most remarkable thing about him was that – because of either some injury of the larynx or the effect of whatever he was inhaling on his throat – he was so quietly spoken he'd had to hire a native boy as his . . . well, his amplifier, I suppose. The kid followed Boyd everywhere, and since he couldn't speak English would simply phonetically repeat – invariably at the top of his lungs – the first mate's orders. Boyd, though generally pretty taciturn, would also sometimes have brief, actual, ordinary conversations *through* the boy, whose tone and facial expressions were always comically incongruous with what was being conveyed in English.

'Then there was the supercargo, Doolan McDaid – Daidy – who'd lost his right eye and most of his right arm ten years before while geligniting fish in the Jordan River in Santo. Whenever Daidy got drunk, he'd always tell the same story, about a Dutchman he knew who also used to gelignite fish there. A delicate business. You had to throw the gelignite at exactly the right moment so that it would explode just as it touched the surface of the water. One day Daidy went down to the river and arrived right as this Dutchman was lighting the fuse of his gelignite with a match pulled from a box. The sight of Daidy distracted him – or perhaps he was just muddleheaded that day, or a little drunk, who knows. Whatever the case, he gave Daidy a friendly smile as he slipped the gelignite back into his top pocket and threw the box of matches out over the water. A second later, still smiling at Daidy, he was blown to kingdom come.'

Amos was getting animated, his youthfulness returning as he filled with the fond memory of these men and tried to do them justice. 'At this point in the story, Daidy would always ease himself back into his chair in the mess' – Amos imitated this – 'and he'd say, "I'll never forget it, that smile, then *Bam*, nothing left . . . nothing but a mist of blood, hitting me like spindrift. And I was left there" – he'd end his story always in exactly the same way, Daniel – "I was left there, covered from head to toe, red as an Arubi Indian." And I, Daniel, I could see Daidy standing there on the bank, that one-armed, one-eyed man in the kingdom of those who'd smiled and evaporated.

'And invariably, at the end of this story, Nigel Claiborne – good old Nige – would tell him he was a bloody liar. Nige was from Liverpool. Catholic, he was, and holy as shite. I'd often see him kneeling at the prow of the ship – scrawny little sod – fingering his rosary and mumbling his Hail Marys so bitterly it was as if he were cursing God. But you certainly couldn't fault him for not going forth and multiplying. Turns out he had a wife in Liverpool, a wife in London, a native Aoba wife in the Pacific New Hebrides and, between them all, two dozen children.

'And finally there was Jonas and his son, Larry. At least that's how we referred to them – as father and son – and that's how they talked of and, in public, acted towards each other. No one but the sprogs questioned the fact that Larry was an enormous West Indian lad from Brixton no more than ten years younger than Jonas, who was a dyed-in-the-wool Geordie. Calling them father and son was how their relationship had been incorporated into the world of the ship. It allowed them to be affectionate with one another outside the cabin they shared, protected by these euphemisms, which had become more than that, had become one of a number of shibboleths that delineated all of the ship's crew as part of one definable experience. It was a kind of initiatory moment when any sailor new to the ship referred unconsciously to "Jonas's son" or "Larry's father." That's ever the truth, isn't it, Daniel, that it's the nuances of a language that give the strongest sense of a cultural identity. And many of the crew, being abandoned men, lost men, men far from home, longed for that – though onshore they'd have beaten up a "bloody pouf" at the drop of a hat.

'So, there you have it, a few in the cast of characters. But you haven't yet met the captain and his familiar, towards whom Hamid was, at this very moment, leading me on my first day aboard.'

18

A MOS STOOD. 'Got to see a man about a dog,' he said, and shuffled off towards the bathroom.

Daniel sat up. Looking around at his shadowed home, he felt as if he'd been here, listening to Amos, forever, that *this*, not his life, had come first. Releasing the piece of Lego he'd been toying with, he lifted the hand he'd had between the sofa's arm and cushion to his nose, anticipating the smell: wood, wax, apples, plastic, stale biscuits, graphite, chalk, and rubbers. He flinched: it was sickening, like sour milk and old urine.

Amos returned, still tugging up his fly, sat, sighed, and continued with renewed energy.

'As we walked, Hamid explained that Captain Miles Morris was the last surviving member of some ancient aristocratic family that had lost its fortune somehow, though he still retained a kind of servant-cum-companion who was from a family that had always served his own. This man's name was Jean Perrot, but the crew had dubbed him Parrot.

'We came upon them on the upper deck, a comical sight together. The captain was a huge, burly man with the face of a decadent Roman senator. Parrot, on the other hand, was a diminutive fellow, aptly named, not only because it was easy to visualise him perched on the captain's shoulder but because of his superb Gallic nose, which, for size, rivalled even Hamid's.

'Hamid made the introductions. The captain, casting me a shrewdly speculative look, asked me whence I'd hailed. He spoke with old-fashioned grandiloquence, a slight, struggling pause before each utterance. I got the impression he'd once had a terrible stutter, and was so good at speaking for the same reason great writers are so good at writing – because speaking had always been the thing most difficult for him.

'I answered London and asked where he was from.

'"You're standing on it," he replied, "my brief home at least. My long home is out there somewhere."

'"Long home, sir?" I said.

'"It's from something no one reads anymore," he drawled as if exhausted – he *always* seemed exhausted – and after that slight struggle at his lips, intoned: '"Because man goeth to his Long Home and the mourners go about the streets."'

'I was still baffled, as you could imagine, until Parrot put in with irritated condescension, "Shakespeare."

'"Yes, Amos," Hamid took up, resting a hand on my shoulder, "it's from *King James,* one of Shakespeare's longer and more . . . diasporadic plays."

'The captain laughed at this, I remember, his eyes lingering appreciatively on Hamid. Though I didn't understand the joke, I knew that Parrot was its butt, and that Hamid had come to my rescue again.

'So that was my introduction to the captain and

Parrot. I couldn't imagine what had incited any woman to a desire for a man so pompous and phlegmatic. I assumed that Andrew's sister was either very plain or very naïve.

'But I have to admit,' Amos said, almost with reluctance, 'he was a brilliant man, self-taught, though a little morbid. He seemed to me like a kind of cursed Jeremiah, all his profundities echoed to obscurity in the little hollow of Parrot's mind. He was –'

Daniel interrupted. 'You're making them both sound a bit absurd.' He didn't want Amos to venture too much further off track.

'Am I?' Amos paused. 'Yes, you're right.' He sighed. 'It's amazing that I can still feel jealous of the captain despite . . . despite what was to happen to him.'

19

AFTER THAT MEETING, I went to the cabin I was to share with Andrew, entered it for the first time. He was sitting on his bunk, I remember, reading a letter, which he quickly shoved into his jacket pocket. The whole room reeked of his chest rub.

'"We'll be off in a few hours," I said.

'He didn't respond, seemed angry, his whole body in a kind of feral crouch.

'"Hamid tells me you don't like lizards," I said, just to say something.

'He shot me a defensive look. I think he suspected I was making fun of him, but I did nothing to justify this, and after a while he said no.

'"Where did that come from?" I said. "Can't imagine you saw many of those in Scotland."

'He didn't respond for a moment, but some kind of change seemed to come over him, his whole body easing up. Then he told me he thought it was from a funeral he went to one time.

'"There were lizards?" I said.

'"Oh no," he replied. And now, Daniel, he gave me a look that betrayed the most appalling innocence. "No" he said, "it was an open coffin, an older man – my father, I believe."

'Strange, the way he said this – "my father, I believe." His whole manner had altered. He was now lounging upon his bed, and his body had about it that disturbing, unconscious sensuality you sometimes see in young children. Astonishing, how quickly he'd transformed from that bitter, clenched young man of just moments ago to this. Though I felt a scruple at taking advantage of his vulnerable state, my curiosity got the better of me.

'"Your father?" I said.

'After another long pause, he replied that he believed so, that though he didn't know how he remembered it – he'd been just a few years old – he remembered him and Viv being brought up to the coffin.

'"Viv's your sister?" I said.

'"Vivian," he corrected me, that slightly paranoid expression of his surfacing. I looked as abashed as I could, and he soon calmed and continued.

'"We were brought up to the coffin," he said, "and told to kiss . . . to kiss him good-bye. And we were being held up by someone – my mother, I suppose – because we were so little. And Viv quickly bent over and kissed his hands. And I went to do the same, but I could smell something, something awful, and as I went to kiss those old hands, they seemed to flinch."

'"Like two lizards," I said.

'He didn't answer this, just gave me a despairing look, as if stupidity were the one thing against which there was no defence. Then, all at once, he seemed to remember himself, where he was, and that I was a stranger.

Instantly, he became that nervous, scowling young man I'd first encountered.

'Feeling awkward, I lit my pipe, but he began to clear his throat as if he were choking.

'I asked if my pipe were bothering him, and he told me rather rudely that he suffered from asthma.

'So I put it out – which was a real hardship for me.'

Amos lifted the stem of his pipe between the pinch of two fingers and examined it. 'No one smokes a pipe anymore, do they?'

'I've always liked the smell of a pipe,' Daniel said.

'Do you smoke?'

'Yes. In fact' – Daniel pulled out his cigarettes – 'do you mind?' He'd been dying for one.

'Not at all. I'm about to have a smoke myself.' Amos got up and retrieved an ashtray from the sideboard. It was the misshapen clay one Daniel had made for his mother in school.

Daniel lit up and drew the smoke in as deeply as he could.

'That's an impressive lighter,' Amos said.

'I've had it forever.'

Amos reached out. 'Let's have a look.'

Daniel yielded it to him, but felt a reluctance to do so – a reluctance that deepened to regret as Amos weighed the lighter acquisitively in the palm of his hand.

'Don't make them like this anymore, do they?' he said.

'No.' Daniel wanted it back. He reached for it, but

Amos, indicating towards the pieces of his pipe, said, 'Do you mind if I use it to . . ?'

Daniel wanted to tell him that he'd give it to him when he needed it but just nodded.

Putting the lighter down between the horse chestnut and the yellowing note, Amos continued. 'Anyway, so I looked for something to empty my pipe into, and that's when I first saw them, in a little porcelain bowl on top of the clothes chest – three large ball bearings. I took one in my hand and hefted it.' To illustrate this, Amos picked up the lighter again. Daniel flushed and wondered if Amos had seen him, from the kitchen, doing this with the ball bearing on the mantelpiece.

'I said, "What do you have these for?"

'He told me he'd found them among his father's effects, and believed they were bearings from the engine of one of the ships his father had captained. He added shyly that he didn't quite know why his father had kept them or, indeed, why he himself had kept them.

'Though I didn't say anything, I think I did understand. There they were, these steel atoms of a vast machine, the dream of men such as his father – that the Earth itself would be a huge vessel one day, which they would pilot through space.

'But my understanding was more innocent and personal also, because I'd owned one of these as a child. It had championed my marbling, won me the largest collection in school. It had been a *Merrimack* among wooden battleships, often shattering precious chinas into fragments. With Ned, the son of a hospital orderly, I'd traded one shilling, a snakeskin wallet, and a rabbit skull for it; and I'd loved more than anything in the world that pure, smooth sphere with its unnatural heft.'

Amos got up, went over to the mantelpiece, and returned with the ball bearing, which he put down next to the lighter. All at once, it seemed to absorb the dying light from the window, and the whole room appeared to dim perceptibly. Daniel could see his own distorted image in it.

'But not all bearings,' Amos went on, 'are created equal. The three Andrew owned were once perfect, used for the purpose for which they'd been made, while mine, I later found out from Ned, was one of those that hadn't passed the final quality control. These were sold to hospitals and used to fill bags that acted as counter-weights, keeping people's broken arms and legs at the correct elevation and tension. His and my ball bearings were as distinct from each other as the same object in the dreams of two different people, as distinct as power is from frailty. They were –'

'Ball bearings,' Daniel interrupted, a little restless, wanting Amos to get back to the stem of the story.

'Yes, they were ball bearings,' Amos conceded. 'After putting the ball bearing back down, I idly picked up a framed photograph that was facing his bunk. And *that*, Daniel' – Amos hesitated, as if astonished even now – 'that was the first time I ever saw her. Beautiful . . . beautiful, she was. But it was more than her beauty.

How can I explain? How the life manifested in those features, those limbs, spoke to me not in the manner of infatuation or lust but as if . . . Well, as if my whole being, for as long as I could remember, had been struggling to utter some word. And here it was, in *her*, her form – not spoken, it could never be spoken, but all-but-spoken, as if I'd woken at the very moment I'd dreamed the word complete. Can you believe it, Daniel, that that's how – *where* – I felt her when I first saw her: in my throat and my mouth, on my tongue. And what was even stranger about the strength of my response to her was that she was the *image* of her brother. But, while she fairly pulsed with life, in him something seemed to have died at the root, the word uttered, unmoored, and meaningless.

'This difference in their vitalities was expressed most strikingly by their hair: his was close shorn, coarse, and already greying at the temples, though he was barely twenty-four, while hers was a dense profusion of coppery curls, tumbling down about her shoulders.

'"Your sweetheart?" I asked, though I knew full well it wasn't.

'"My sister," he replied, horrified.

'"Oh, of course," I said, wanting, for some reason – who can explain these things? – to be cruel. "Lord, you're the spit, aren't you."

'"Except that she's beautiful," he said, reading my mind and almost as if jealous – or at once jealous and protective.

'"Well, a man wouldn't want to be too beautiful, would he?" I said. "But she is beautiful and has such a lovely –"

'He was off his bed in a second, snatched the photograph out of my hand, and threw it into a drawer.

'I apologised, though I felt no conviction in my voice or heart, as he returned to his bunk, only that unwonted cruelty that prompted me now to ask him if he had a sweetheart.

'He shook his head. I wondered if he'd ever had one. I couldn't imagine it.

'"What do you think of her marrying the captain?" I asked.

'He winced, again seeming to lose all awareness of his manner and bearing.

'Suddenly, speaking fifteen to the dozen, he blurts out, "I told her it's a mistake. She'll ruin her life. Ruin it. Why does she need to get married anyway? She doesn't care for him. She *can't* care for him. She's got enough as it is with Mother –"

'"But I'm sure she wants a husband, children," I cut in, still possessed by that cruelty, which had been further provoked by his emotional transparency.

'He became so agitated he stood up again. "Can we not talk about this," he said. Then, once more, he seemed to lose all sense of my presence, that angry, internal monologue resurfacing. "Touching her," he was muttering, his Scottish brogue broadening. "I mean look at him, a vile old man, touching her."

'"Well, none of us," I interjected, "would have been here without people touching each other, would we. I mean, your father –"

'"I never knew my father," he shouts, staring at me fiercely and with horror, as if I were in danger of transgressing even more sacred ground.

'"I never knew mine either," I countered, and was about to go on when – thank God – the door opened and from it emerged the gleaming dome of Hamid's head.

'Aware right away of the tension in the cabin, Hamid surveyed us over the tops of his little spectacles for a moment before announcing that we'd all been invited to the captain's cabin for dinner tonight. Andrew, still agitated, pushed past him, out on to the deck.

'Hamid asked me what was going on.

'"Very touchy about his sister, isn't he,' I said, retrieving her photograph from the drawer.

'"Stunner, isn't she," Hamid said. "Looks after her invalid mother in godforsaken Lochbroom, where I doubt there's another soul under seventy."

'"No wonder she fell for the captain," I said.

'Hamid threw me a searching look. He knew it wasn't like me to say such things and let me languish for a moment in his silence, before saying, "Anyway, dress up. We've got a feast tonight."'

20

'WHEN I ENTERED the captain's cabin with Hamid a few hours later, I was utterly astonished. I could have been on the *Titanic*: a chandelier above a gorgeously set table; all the furniture antique; bookshelves packed with leather-bound editions; classical music playing softly; and Parrot, starched with contempt, wearing brown-and-gold servant's livery. On the walls hung portraits of aristocratic-looking men and women, whom I took to be of the captain's family, though none of them bore him the slightest resemblance. And at the far end of the room hung a great coat of arms in silk.

'"It's Lord bloody Muck," I whispered to Hamid.

'"This is how you know," he says to me, "that he was a dockside bastard like the rest of us."

'"He's a fake?" I said.

'"A fake?" Hamid stared at me as if I were either stupid or slightly crazy. "He speaks nine languages, has read all there is to read, lives in one palatial room on a rotting hulk in the middle of the South Pacific: a more genuine article of the human race, my friend, you're not likely ever to meet again."

'It was as we went to take our seats that I noticed the shells – became aware of how many of them there were, scattered throughout this incongruous grandeur: tritons, murex, whelks, conches, helmets, volutes. They struck me somehow, I remember, as both vulnerable and extravagant, their fleshy openings like wounds that had hardened before they'd managed to heal. They seemed –'

'So who was at this dinner?'

Amos looked abashed, and Daniel felt a little guilty for his impatience.

'Ah . . . well, most of the white sailors I've mentioned, as well as the putatively white Joseph Christian. The captain was at the end of the long table. My gilded name card placed me to his immediate right, Andrew to his left, and Hamid was beside Andrew.

'As we sat, Hamid and I exchanged a puzzled glance: while everyone else at the table had a place setting of bone china, heavy silver, and Waterford crystal, Andrew, whose name had been scrawled on to a sheet of greasy newspaper, was confronted by a tin plate, a Swiss Army knife, and an empty pickle jar.

'As Andrew was regarding this anomaly in his anxious and finicky fashion, the captain wrapped one of his huge hands around the nape of Andrew's neck, his manner somewhere between threatening and avuncular, and muttered, "Andrew, my lad, there weren't enough place settings. I would have given those to myself except that as captain one has to keep up appearances, you understand. They're animals, the lot of them, and as I feel you to be almost family . . ."

'It was clear that the captain was more than a little drunk, his eyes watery and bloodshot.

'We began with the most delicious prawn cocktail in crystal bowls, placed sombrely before us by Parrot, who was being aided by a couple of the Malay sailors dressed in traditional garb. But Andrew received a half-coconut husk in which lay just the heads and shells of all our prawn, smothered in ketchup. The captain galvanised conversation and ate with gusto. I could see Andrew's face reddening and flickering with confusion as he dug about through that inedible mess with one of the Swiss Army knife's countless implements.

'As he was doing this, Parrot was serving the wine. He arrived last at Andrew's place, put the bottle down, and from behind a cabinet retrieved an old galosh, from which, solemnly, he poured seawater into Andrew's pickle jar.

'A number of the sailors began to laugh, but the captain returned a look of frowning perplexity, which quelled them. Andrew was completely bewildered. The confused silence became almost unbearable. Suddenly the captain let out a great bellow of laughter, gave Andrew a slap on the back that sent him crashing into the table, and said, "Forgive me, my lad. You know, our lovely Vivian claims that the one thing I lack – *the one thing* – is humour."

'Andrew, wiping ketchup from his father's precious jacket, responded with the most fragile smile I'd ever seen.

'The main course arrived. There was an enormous

ham – apparently one that the captain had had sent all the way from Virginia. "A thirty-dollar ham," he kept saying. "It will melt in your mouths." At that point it didn't appear so appetising. It was surrounded by spongy white fat and looked to my mind like a large, wet scab. There was also a whole tunny fish cooked in garlic butter and covered in a julienne of vegetables.

'The captain insisted on carving. With the ham, he shaved off all the fat down to the pink and succulent meat. The fish he decapitated and neatly boned. He gave us all mountains of food – delivered with dignified celerity by Parrot, beginning at the far end of the table. As he was doing this, he picked up his thread, now addressing the whole table.

'"Yes, no sense of humour, she said. Of course, she's always had a great sense of humour herself. You know what she told me? She told me that, up until their late teens, she and Andrew – they're twins, you know – looked so much alike they'd often dress in each other's clothes – to fool people, you see."

'"That's *not* true," Andrew cut in, appalled and confused.

'"Don't deny it," the captain murmured fondly, giving the top of Andrew's head a bearish pat. "She told me the only reason she'd stopped the whole business is that you looked better in a dress than she did."

'A couple of the sailors laughed.

'"On top of that," the captain continued, "you'd let a few of the village boys take liberties with you."

'The laughter got a little louder.

'"That is a lie. That is a complete lie,"Andrew shouted, staring desperately at me, for some reason.

'"The lady doth protest too much," the captain muttered.

'Just then, pointedly, though with a veneer of playfulness, Jonas interjected, "It's hardly fair, Captain, you've had such a head start with the wine."

'"Indeed I have, my lovely," the captain rejoined, "and *fine* wine it is, squeezed beneath the feet of big, swarthy, gypsy lads. You'd appreciate that, wouldn't you, Jonas – big, swarthy, gypsy lads."

'"I'd appreciate it," Jonas said – and now things were turning very sour – "if we changed the subject."

'Daidy began to clear his throat. I was to learn that he was a man much respected by all aboard, and that his throat clearing was usually enough to dissipate any incipient conflicts. With a glance at Daidy, the captain's combativeness visibly waned. It wasn't just his supercargo's disapproval, I think, but that the captain realised how close he'd come to damaging one of those fictions that helped maintain the integrity of the world over which he presided. The tension caused by this near transgression was evident all around the table: Joseph Christian, clearly refusing to believe that such behaviour could take place between his fellow white men, had gone rigid; old Nige seemed to be mouthing one of his bitter prayers; and Boyd, with his hand jammed into his pocket, was longing, I could see, for one of those brief oblivions his hankie could provide.

'At this point, everyone had been served but Andrew. Now, on to his battered old plate, the captain piled all of the ham's slick, white, wet fat and the fish's head, both of which he garnished with a rose made from the rolled peel of a tomato.

'As Parrot placed this revolting pile in front of Andrew, the captain stage-whispered, "No humour, she said. Pity she's not here to share this feast with us, my lad. Bon appétit!"

'The captain then downed his fourth glass of wine and went carelessly on. "Makes sense your sister dressing as a man, you know; she was so much like a man in other ways. Andrew, are you familiar with the story of Lilith?"

'"Who?" Andrew said.

'"Well," the captain replied, "let's just say that your sister likes to be on top."

'It was only the coarsest sailors who laughed at this. Most didn't know where to look. Daidy sounded as if he were choking. None of us could understand why the captain was talking in this way about his own fiancée.

'Andrew, in his innocence, was still perplexed and made things worse by saying, "On top? On top of what?"

'This caused even some of the more shocked sailors to snort as the captain replied, "My mast, my lad, my stalwart mast."

'Whatever Andrew understood, he understood enough

now to know that his sister was being grievously insulted. His face went completely white. A terrible pressure seemed to be building inside him. He hinged open the Swiss Army knife's largest blade. I'll tell you, Daniel, my body has never been more tense. I noticed Parrot moving into position behind Andrew. The captain, though still flushed with his affected humour, narrowed the focus of his eyes upon the knife.

'And then . . . and then thank God for angels. In a flash, Hamid replaced Andrew's plate with his own and snatched the Swiss Army knife out of his hand. He picked up the fish's head and, using the blade as a tongue depressor, subjected it to a thorough oral examination. For the rest of the evening, with a great deal of help from the fish's head, he played the fool relentlessly. At one stage, I remember, he had it jutting from his crotch and was making lascivious advances towards the easily out-raged Joseph Christian. A little later, he and the fish's head became Ella Fitzgerald and Louis Armstrong, the two of them leading the table in a raucous, sailor's version of "Let's Call the Whole Thing Off."'

Amos went quiet. He picked up the spectacles, unfolding them as if he were spreading the wings of a small bird.

'Are they Hamid's?' Daniel asked, crushing out the stub of his cigarette in the ashtray.

Amos simply smiled as he returned them to the table.

'Where is he now?'

Amos looked around the dim room for a moment, as if

he might just see his friend, not lost, merely discarded and forgotten, like a child's toy.

'He's in the ground,' he said at last.

'Dead?'

'He's in big trouble if he isn't.'

'How'd he die?'

'Hanged himself.'

Before Daniel could ask any more, Amos continued: 'So, the next day we docked at Pernambuco, and the reason for the captain's bizarre behaviour became apparent.'

21

'I WAS ON DECK, smoking my pipe, when Andrew raced up to me, out of breath, holding an opened aerogramme in his hand, saying, "I know why he did it now."

'He'd clearly come straight to me with this news, and I realised, with a throb of pity towards him that, despite our uncomfortable introduction, he considered me a friend.

'He told me he'd just received a letter from his sister. Much to my horror, he thrust it into my hands. I'd kept my illiteracy from everyone but Hamid. Luckily, Andrew was so agitated he needed to speak, and revealed the contents as I pretended to read it. He explained first that his sister had mentioned in previous aerogrammes that the captain's letters to her were getting increasingly morose. So she'd written back to tell him that she was uncomfortable with this; also that he was reacting far too seriously to her more lighthearted comments, that some of her letters were meant in a playful mode, since her life was depressing enough as it was. His response had been furious, telling her that she clearly had no appreciation of the gravity of their approaching union, or of her fitting place in it as the mother of his children – the scions of a great line that could be traced directly back to Charlemagne.

'Andrew stabbed his finger into the aerogramme at this point, crying out, "Charlemagne! Look here, he really says Charlemagne. Our father captained ships that wouldn't have had this pile of junk for a liter. 'Her privilege,' he quoted mockingly, 'appreciate her privilege!' – and tells her he has no more ear for her humour than he'd have for the bantering inanities of a huckster."

'Andrew was shouting. I told him to keep his voice down. To my surprise, he immediately complied, concluding in a harsh whisper that his sister had lost her temper and had written back to break off the engagement.

'"She's broken it off?" I repeated, staring into those meaningless scrawls as if to confirm this for myself.

'"Yes," he said, "it's over."

'I gave him back the letter. There was an expression in his face at that moment that reminded me acutely of my brother – an utterly helpless pain. I told him that the captain didn't seem like a very stable man, but as soon as I began to suggest to Andrew that he should consider leaving the ship, he gave me a look as close to peremptory as anything I ever saw his brittle constitution produce.

'"You don't understand," he says. "It was *my* choice to do this. I *have* to see it through."

'"Andrew," I persisted, "a ship is a closed world. A voyage is like a small lifetime."

'But he was having none of it: "If there's trouble," he said, as if he were repeating some credo by rote, "I have to deal with it – and I will."

'Just then we both flinched as the captain's voice rang out above us. "Mr Scofield!"

'He was standing on the upper deck. I wondered how long he'd been there, how much he'd heard.

'He asked Andrew if he were responsible for the polishing of the brass today. When Andrew said yes, the captain threw down to him a brass bell that was completely blackened and demanded an explanation. I'd seen this before: someone had mixed lemon juice into the cleaning solvent. Andrew said he'd spent all morning polishing and had no idea how this had happened.

'"Well I hope," the captain said, "that you have no special plans for this evening. Even the captain of a pile of junk has to maintain some standards." Then he was gone, and Andrew himself scurried away.'

22

Daniel took out another cigarette – his last. Before he could reach for his lighter, Amos picked it up, lit the cigarette for him, and returned the lighter to its place on the coffee table.

'We were in Pernambuco for almost two months, overhauling the ship. The captain assigned Andrew to clean out the boilers – single-handedly – a job generally given only to the lowest of the coolies. Hamid and I offered to help him, but he refused and worked himself so hard I found him one night collapsed with exhaustion in the sludge at the bottom of one of the boilers.

'Just before we were to head back out to sea, Nige comes to my cabin and tells me there's a letter for me in the mess. I thought he'd made a mistake. Who would write a letter to me? But a letter there was, and I quickly took it to Hamid, who was in his cabin.

'He was sitting beside his fish tank, staring into it, a small net in his hand, a half-drunk bottle of whiskey at his feet. He told me he'd been up all night. Among the last batch of neons he'd bought had been a fish he called a carvoris, which looked exactly like a neon but was a predator. It had already killed one of his angelfish, and he'd been up all night waiting for it to make another move.

'"When I find it," he says to me, "I'm going to build a pyre out of matchsticks and I'm going to roast that bloody little bastard alive."

'I offered my condolences and gave him the letter.

'He examined the stamp and the postmark, taking his time. I felt a little flare of irritation.

'At last, he opened it.

'"Well, well," he declared, "it's from Andrew's sister." He threw me a ribald look, feathering the end of the net up and down his inner thighs. I told him to stop it. He could see I was serious and read the letter without further shenanigans.

'As he read, I began to hear her voice so clearly, could picture her writing it, at a desk in that cottage, her mother asleep in an armchair.

'She began tentatively, saying that she hoped I didn't think it too presumptuous of her to write, that Andrew –'

'The whole letter?' Daniel interrupted with surprise. 'You can remember the whole letter after all these years?'

'I can't read,' Amos replied. 'Just as the captain's eloquence derived from his stutter, my memory, especially of words, derives from my helplessness in this regard. More often it's shame, not talent, that makes us remarkable, Daniel.

'She said that Andrew had written to her about me in glowing terms. I thought this was just politeness on her part, as I'd barely eked more out of Daniel –'

'Andrew.'

'Yes, Andrew – than a sullen frown. She wanted to thank me for being patient with him, and admitted that Andrew had somehow been born in pain, with a wound that had never healed, and which he protected as an injured animal would, snapping even at those who attempted to help him. From this line of revelation, she broke off abruptly, seemed to start the letter again, saying that she didn't know exactly why she was writing to me, that there were so few people she could really talk to. There followed some beautiful passages about the Highlands, the walks she took in the countryside around their cottage, passages imbued exquisitely with the tenor of her own loneliness and sense of wasted life. She talked about how she envied Andrew his opportunity to fashion himself in response to a more importunate reality, that she often tried to imagine what he was experiencing but feared that imagination without substance, without details, hard surfaces, even the tedium of life, would degenerate to fantasy, and that fantasising, in the end, did nothing but rot you from the inside out.

'She then asked me not to let him know that she'd written to me as he was extremely possessive. They'd spent every minute of their childhood together, and what had been traded between them, she said, was not memory but being – isn't that the measure of intimacy, Daniel?'

Caught off guard by the unrhetorical tone of this

question, Daniel took a moment to respond. 'Yes . . . yes, I suppose it is.'

'She went on that since Andrew had been seized by this obsession to make a man of himself, he'd tried to separate her being out of his. He was determined to throw himself into the maw of what he most feared, taking employment aboard Miles's ship as much, she was sure, to reconcile himself to Miles, the man who was to take her away from him, as to encounter a masculine world he'd always longed to be a part of – though it had ever been an alien, even inimical, world to him.

'The letter ended with her lamenting that she always revealed too much, and would regret it.

'You can hardly imagine how this letter – this *voice* – made me feel. I knew for the first time what it was to be inspired. I told Hamid that I had to write to her. He was as excited as I was, striding about his cabin, gathering paper and a pen.

'I said, "Hamid, is it possible to fall in love with a photograph and a letter?"

'Throwing me a canny glance over his spectacles, he told me that he'd once known a man who'd been in the presence of a certain woman when she'd heard news of the sudden death of her sister. She'd issued a single sound, a deeply resonant and strangely inflected moan. The man ended up becoming this woman's lover, and was so for three years before he realised that his desire had never been for *her* but for the particular tenor and music of her grief.

"There's a warning in this, my friend," he concluded, "but I'm half drunk and half in love with her myself."

'So I dictated a letter back to Vivian.'

Amos moaned. 'Even to this day, Daniel, *even to this day*, it makes me sick to think of that letter. Hamid, that weeping romantic, wove into it a few dozen extended metaphors of his own. My God, it reeked of purple prose and thinly disguised ardour, words concerning the vast loneliness of the sea, the yearning cries of the gulls, and so forth. Strange that, despite everything that was to happen, the horror of it, just thinking about her receiving that letter can still make me wince. I can see her reading it in her garden, flushing, laughing, but being ultimately touched, as one might be touched by the sight of a six-year-old earnestly singing Handel's *Messiah*.

'Just as Hamid signed my name to this, I remember, he glanced over at his aquarium and began to utter what were clearly curses in a language I'd never heard him use. Another of his angelfish was swimming askew, a bloody gash at its gills. He threw down everything, took up his net, and stared feverishly into the tank.

'"Where is that *bastard*?" he was shouting, and just as I leaned forward to help him look, the dying angelfish turned towards us . . . turned towards us and opened its mouth, and out of its mouth slid the carvoris.

'Hamid tried to get him with the net, but the aquarium was full of fish and living rock and, after a flurry of activity, we couldn't distinguish our killer from any of the other neons.'

23

'AT VALPARAISO, I received my reply. She described my letter as "hearteningly *enthusiastic*" – a welcome voice in her silent home. She then, of all things, told me what she imagined *me* to be like. It was a sort of playful eulogy, both teasing and tender, and I was amazed by how much she knew – all the minutiae of my habits and mannerisms, which she could only have learned from Andrew.

'After this, she told me she wanted to give me a sense of their life together – hers and Andrew's. Because she knew Andrew wouldn't do it, is what she claimed. She said that their home had always been something of a mausoleum for their dead father. His presence pervaded everything, and their mother, like the single surviving priestess of some lost religion, still, as she had through-out their childhood, revered and mourned him in a way that Vivian was only just beginning to realise was unnatural.

'As a result of their mother's obsessive grief – the guise, perhaps, of a profound depression – they were somewhat neglected as children and, like many twins, I suppose, we lived in a world of our own, even spoke our own language, lived here with a woman we called Mother, but with whom we had no real connection. We could only imagine the object of her grief. And imagine we did. Our culture existed within the ruins of this necrolatrous culture in which we'd found ourselves, the two of us like one being, inseparable in the world of our imaginations, a world in which all the real people with whom we ever had contact were incorporated as gods and monsters.

'It was really the fertility of my brother's imagination that saved us. I was his believer, his zealot, losing myself entirely in the worlds and predicaments he generated, losing myself in a way, I think, that he, as their creator, longed to but never could.

'But our sealed world was breached inevitably by life. Upon us, separating us, grew the bodies of a man and a woman. He became filled with shame at our childhood intimacies, shame at the rawness of his sensitivities and fears, at how unprepared he was to face a world into which his body and time were forcing him. He closed off the world he'd created, and his own imagination took revenge on him: inanimate things came to life; he developed a profound fear of old men, especially of their hands; he saw faces in darkened windows. Madness is having no one believe what you imagine. I would have believed if he'd let me. I would have believed anything.

'So, while I remain here among our father's relics, my brother has journeyed out in the hope, I think, of being possessed by his spirit. But trying always to be open to possession is the very thing that leaves him so vulnerable. This waiting openness is his wound and, I suspect, has something of the shape not of our father's but of *my* absence.

'What a lot to unburden on you, Amos. I'm sorry. I worry about my brother so constantly, and I'm moved by his observations of you, feel as if I know you, in a way, and confess to having spoken to you a few times, softly, alone in my room.

'Please look after him. The last letter he sent me contained such venom against Miles – to whom I've written also, begging him to treat my brother as he would any other member of his crew. I can hardly believe that I felt for Miles as I once did. He was an impressive, worldly presence for me, can speak so beautifully. I felt like such an empty little girl, was overwhelmed when he declared his feelings for me, can still hardly conceive that I have, as he claims in his latest letters – awful, angry, bitter letters – destroyed him.

'I've now slipped from confidence to incontinence, as is my wont, being surrounded by the silence of this place, which sometimes drives my voice so deep I fear I'll never recover it.

'But, looking back over the sprawl of this letter, I clearly don't have too much to worry about at the moment.

'With great regard, Vivian.'

Amos's face had become almost completely obscured by shadow. Daniel, leaning forward, his elbows on his knees, couldn't see Amos's mouth. The tone of his – *her* – voice still percussed the air. A latent voice, it seemed to Daniel, which hadn't been issued but had precipitated from this clear solution of silence, a voice as intimate as the side of his mother's mouth brushing against his five-year-old ear as she'd read to him here on the sofa, his little body bundled in her lap. *Mother, you sang to me. I let your voice bleed out into that filthy place. But you hurt me. Inexplicable woman. Loving me. Inexplicably. You have to understand* – No . . . no, there was no one to reply to. It was his own confused and exhausted mind, nothing more, it was –

'She was a woman' – Amos's voice, clear, unequivocal, broke back in, and Daniel's whole being snatched at it as if he'd lost his footing at the edge of . . . of what? – 'who longed to give herself, to trust, and was, in this regard, naïve. She needed to speak, to be spoken to – to a fault. Like most women, she believed in language. As a result, she revealed many things to me long before she knew enough to trust me. She'd done the same, I think, with the captain.'

'So, at the dinner,' Daniel cut in, 'were some of the things he said –'

'Yes . . . yes, there was some truth to them.'

24

'A FTER VALPARAISO, we headed off to Guayaquil to pick up a group of American biologists that had commissioned us to take them to the Galápagos islands. They and their equipment were to be brought aboard on the shore boat, manned by Hamid, Andrew, and a number of the other sailors, including Larry and Jonas.

'I remember standing nervously on deck beside the captain and Parrot as the shore boat approached. The captain had selected me to direct the biologists to their cabins. I was holding a sheet containing the list of their names and cabin numbers. I'd had Hamid read it to me earlier that morning so that I could memorise it.

'Horrible, Daniel, the fear I felt clutching that indecipherable sheet, the shame. That's another of those moments that haunts me still.

'Anyway, when the shore boat was secured, Hamid was the first aboard, carrying two small cloth-covered cages.

'"More inmates for your menagerie?" the captain called to him.

'"Just a couple of little fellows," Hamid replied. "I couldn't resist." He winked at me and was just about to whisk them off to his cabin when something on the shore boat caught his attention. Andrew was trying to carry aboard, by himself, a heavy movie camera.

'"Use the winch," Hamid shouted. But Andrew was already in trouble, teetering. Putting the cages down, Hamid went to help him.

'As I began to direct the biologists to their cabins, Parrot, curious, lifted the cover off one of the cages. It contained a small parakeet. At that moment, Andrew came aboard, went over to the winch, and began to haul up the camera.

'Just as Hamid returned to the ship, Parrot lifted the cover off the other cage. Hamid shouted at him to stop, which did no more than draw everyone's attention to what was in it.'

'A lizard,' Daniel said.

'What else? – a little goanna lizard.

'Instantly, Andrew fell back against the taffrail, releasing the rope. There was a tremendous crash and shouts from below.

'I snatched the cage from the bewildered Parrot and ordered Hamid to get it off the ship. He took it, his face flushed with frustration and apology, and returned to the shore boat, from which still arose all kinds of panicked noises.

'I ran over to Andrew, who'd slumped down with his hands covering his eyes, and told him that the goanna wasn't on board anymore. Larry appeared on deck from the shore boat, his face livid. Jonas – his "father" – had been hit by the falling camera and was lying almost unconscious, his head covered in blood.

'In a fury, Larry launched himself at Andrew, but I tackled him to the deck. Huge bloke he was. He was trying to get at Andrew, I was desperate to prevent him, and the two of us – we were friends – were equally determined not to hurt each other. So we thrashed about like a pair of landed marlins, the biologists scattering, the captain bellowing at us to stop.'

Amos paused and leaned forward. 'You know, I'll tell you something, Daniel: though that physically con-summated love one man might have for another had ever been strange to me, towards the end of that struggle, when we were both breathing hard and he was close to tears, when my hold on him was no longer a way to prevent him from getting to Andrew, but purely a means for him to physically expend his fears about his lover, I got such a vivid intimation not only of their passion but of their love, and was, for a moment, freed from my own particular predicament by this sudden, transcendent clairvoyance of his.'

'His *predicament*?' Daniel said.

'I don't mean it in a bad way. We're straight, we're bent, we're black, white, beautiful, ugly, intelligent, stupid – none of them to be celebrated or lamented, they're just a predicament – *our* predicament . . . But, of course, I forget that you're a social worker.'

'What's that got to do with it?'

'I mean hardly a stranger to human predicaments.'

'Oh . . . well, no, I suppose not,' Daniel agreed, though he was trying to remember the last time he'd felt anything but hopelessness for or irritation at any one of his clients. He thought of the Indian woman, her grotesque gestures, masklike face, the horror of what had happened to her. He'd laughed. And, just a little while ago, Richard had laughed at him. Daniel took a final drag on his cigarette and stubbed it out.

'Anyway,' Amos continued. 'A chaotic scene: Larry and I lying exhausted on the deck, Andrew still collapsed against the taffrail, the captain screaming blue bloody murder, Jonas lying injured on the shore boat among the broken remains of the camera.

'The result for Larry and me was a week of KP duties. Andrew got it worse, though. Despite the fact that the camera was insured, the captain insisted Andrew pay for it, which cost virtually his whole salary for the voyage. And not only was Andrew now working for nothing but because Jonas, who was very popular among the crew, had been hurt, and Andrew didn't have sufficient social graces to express regret and show penitence – to appear to be anything, indeed, but his sullen and irascible self – a good number of the other sailors now turned against him.

'This, of course, just made him even more withdrawn. But I have a sense he almost wanted this alienation, or needed it – was somehow using the compressive force of the general ill feeling towards him to hold himself together.

'He became the butt of a prankster, or a number of pranksters. Someone replaced his shoe polish with axle grease and his brilliantine with swarfega. Someone smeared butter inside his slippers, which filled them with cockroaches. Someone went to the trouble of sewing razor blades into the pocket of his overcoat. It made a bloody mess of his hands, I'll tell you. He discovered a small, dead rat under a pile of mashed potatoes he was eating and vomited right there and then in the mess. Someone dropped a bucket of excrement on him from the upper deck. Someone even went so far as to procure from one of the Chilean ports a vile-smelling green oil extracted from a chinghui, which is a kind of skunk, and put it into Andrew's chest rub. He stank for days. I really don't think the captain was responsible for most, if any, of this. Certainly his anger never diminished, but he was a phlegmatic man, one who could react cruelly in moments but simply didn't have the kind of energy and careful, petty premeditation required for such an exhaustive campaign. No, the prankster, I would guess, was either Parrot, trying to get rid of Andrew for the captain's sake, or a few of the other sailors getting revenge for the Jonas incident, or perhaps all the men banding together against weakness in the way men tend to. Whatever the case, Andrew himself *believed* the captain was behind it, and this conviction was reinforced by something that happened a week or so after we'd left Guayaquil.

'You see, Andrew had the habit of going down to have

a shower at four-thirty in the morning. There was one large communal shower belowdecks – a long room with a row of spigots. He was very shy about physical things, always left the cabin whenever I was changing. I never once saw him even in his skivvies, despite sharing a cabin the size of a confessional with him for almost a year.

'One morning, on returning from his shower, he woke me up by thundering the door open and switching on the light. Extremely agitated, he paced about the cabin and obviously needed to talk.

'He said that while he'd been having his shower that morning, the captain, stinking like a bloody brewery and singing "There was a young woman from Glasgow," had come in and taken the spigot next to his. After a moment, he began to talk to Andrew, telling him he didn't sleep well, so had often noticed Andrew going down to the shower, and had wondered why he always did so at such an ungodly hour. Andrew had replied that he was a private person.

'"Are you ashamed of your body?" the captain had asked. Andrew had responded, curtly, that he wasn't.

'A few seconds later, the captain had said, "You know, it's uncanny how much you look like your sister . . . even from behind."

'"He never said that," I said, and couldn't stop myself laughing. But, humourless as ever, Andrew insisted he had, and in response he'd turned around to the captain and had demanded he not talk about his sister like that.

'Can't you just see it, Daniel, the captain bathing Andrew in that corrupt look of his, his gaze lingering' – Amos pointed into his own crotch – '"down *there*," as Andrew put it. The captain had then uttered something "filthy" about Andrew's body, adding, as Andrew turned away, that being well-endowed seemed to run in his family.

'A moment later, Andrew, reaching for his towel, had felt the captain's large hands firmly cupping each of his buttocks. He'd almost jumped out of his skin, and as he'd fled the shower room, the captain had finished off that song I knew too well from many a drunken night's singing:

> 'There was a young woman from Glasgow,
> Who wasn't so bad as young slags go.
> She'd get on her knees
> And she'd do what you please . . .

'Incensed myself, as you could imagine, I told Andrew I'd go and see the captain that day, have it out with him. But he just got furious, screaming at me not to butt in, saying that it was his problem to deal with – and deal with it he would. Then he left the cabin.

'I lay there now, angry and frustrated. He'd woken me at five-thirty in the bloody morning to shout at me as if I were the captain himself, had vented his anger as one might vent lust. There are few things more soul-destroying than to be used in this way by someone. What made it worse was the stake I had in my relationship with Andrew. Though my feelings for him were intensely ambivalent, those for his sister weren't. I was afraid he'd come to hate me so violently it would preclude any relationship I might have with her. I was beginning to feel him already as a kind of blockage in my life – my longings.'

Amos went quiet, resting his chin on his interwoven fingers. All Daniel could make out were his lips and those ruined hands. His eyes were the darkness, watching.

'You know,' Amos mused, 'after everything was over, I'd often wonder if what happened to Andrew was inevitable. Wasn't that what he'd come to find, after all – his patrimony?'

'Patrimony?' Daniel was a little shocked. 'You mean his death?'

'Can't you imagine a world where they mean the same thing?'

'The same thing? But you're not talking about death and patrimony, you're talking about death and murder. They are *not* the same.'

Amos, clearly unable to respond for a moment, looked betrayed. Finally, leaning forward, he said in a voice taut with rage, 'Daniel, are you suggesting you've made no violations in your language to live? Are you?'

This barely contained fury unsettled Daniel. It was an intimation of something he now sensed had always existed just below the surface.

'In my –' Daniel lost his words. His voice was still there, but untenable, caught in his throat, giving him the awful sensation that he was choking on silence. This sensation quickly passed, but he remained quiet. What had really frightened him was the thought that Amos might not continue.

Finally, Daniel managed to get out, 'So you were in the cabin . . .'

Amos didn't speak for a moment, but then he released a long breath, as if he were relieved, and went on more calmly:

'Yes . . . yes, and I looked over at Andrew's dishevelled bunk. On its thin mattress he'd placed a varnished wooden board – because he had a bad back, he claimed. Usually, by the time I'd awoken he'd removed his sheets. He had the habit of washing them every day, which I put down to his compulsive nature. But I noticed something now, got out of bed, and pulled back his blankets to discover another reason for his early showers, for his sheet changing, and for that wooden board. He'd wet his bed.

'The sight of this filled me with a tremendous sadness, Daniel, a sense of how precariously he was holding himself together, like someone hiding a terminal sickness from those he loves or fears.'

25

AMOS WENT QUIET. Reaching to the table, he shifted some of the objects just fractionally, as if a millimetre one way or another could make a crucial difference. With the image of Andrew's stained sheets still before him, Daniel fantasised storming through the ship and confronting the captain. Hovering above these lives as he was, it seemed so simple, even in the face of Amos's minute and futile adjustments, to be brave and good, to be a man. Simple to change things, to leave his job and go to South America, to let London's rain become the sweat on his wife's body, which he'd cool with a damp towel as they drank coffee rich as soil. Simple. And this simple love now rested a gentle hand upon the head of its recalcitrant little creation, Amos Radcliff.

Giving up on the objects, Amos sat back, releasing a sigh.

'A few days later,' he continued, 'from the upper deck, where I was having a smoke with Ay Yam and Daidy, I saw Andrew mopping the lower deck. There was quite a crowd around, including most of the biologists, taking in the sun. The captain appeared on the lower deck and stood for a moment staring down at the soapy boards. He was swaying slightly, and had the faraway, underwater look of the drunk. Suddenly he went straight for Andrew, took hold of him by the collar of his shirt, and bellowed into his face, "We have passengers. Where are your signs?"

'Andrew hadn't put up the signs the swabber was meant to use to warn people of a slippery surface. The truth is that none of us ever used them.

'Dozens were witness to this humiliating scene, which got worse as the captain dragged Andrew by his collar to the stern of the ship and opened the locker where the signs were kept, shouting, "What are these, boy? What are they, you bloody useless piece of ullage?"

'Andrew hung limp in the grip of the captain's powerful hands, the collar of his shirt ripped almost clean away.

'We stayed anchored off the Galápagos for a number of months while the biologists conducted their research. Often, when I went out for a smoke, I'd see Andrew alone on the deck somewhere, whispering fiercely to himself. The supply ship would come every week, and I always got a letter from Vivian. The address on the envelope would be typed, the postmark from London, where she must have sent them to a friend to mail on to me – so careful . . . so careful that Andrew shouldn't discover we were corresponding.

'We'd found each other in our loneliness. Our letters fluctuated from the most rarefied expressions of love to something resembling the moans of animals. Love, desire for her possessed me entirely. Like Andrew, I'd often be talking to myself, but not in anger: speaking to her, composing the letters I'd later dictate to Hamid. So, while love dilated me on one side of the ship, hatred contracted Andrew on the other.

'Insidiously, the conflict between Andrew and the captain began to infect my relationship with Vivian. Her fears for her brother made her will herself into my place, my body, to be, as she'd always been, his protector. Such a desire for my limbs, my strength, my sex, my proximity to Andrew was easily conflated with her desire for me. I should have hated the captain for what he was doing, but his vile behaviour was serving my love so well. As you can see, I was becoming increasingly sophisticated, increasingly estranged from my own image in the mirror. Nothing was simple.

'Andrew himself was like some shoddy rope bridge to the thing I most desired, shuddering, falling to bits beneath me as I tried to inch my way across the crevasse he spanned. I had to dissimulate constantly in front of him. So many times I wanted to scream, shake him, craved just a single gesture of recognition for my kindnesses. I was also afflicted every now and then by the whole realm of guilt that associated him with my brother. There were even times, unguarded moments in our cabin, when Andrew's face had slackened, become innocent, that I'd see his sister in him, and would find myself filled with a too-long-repressed desire. I dreamed, a few times, of being in the passionate embrace of a creature that was both of them, sister and brother. This would leave a sour residue in me for the whole day, making me inexplicably angry with him. *Think of it, Daniel, all these mediations, everything contingent. And poor Andrew*' – Amos cried this out, real anguish in his voice – 'trying to escape being merely a mediation, a bridge, the distorted image of someone else, trying *desperately* to exist. But what makes what was to happen truly tragic is that I knew, on some level, that only by discovering what was at the heart of him, only by responding to him not as my brother, not as his sister, not as gestures around a void of being, could I regain my own innocence. I *did* try.' Amos said this as if in response to an accusation. 'I tried to fix them in me, the image of his wet bed, of his lonely, punctilious motions – smoothing down the lapels of his jacket, licking his finger to wipe a scuff from his shoes. I'd try to observe him when he didn't know I was doing so. I wanted to feel it – *feel it* – his predicament, even for a second, as I'd felt Larry's, in a way that would actually change me. Like an –'

'I get the idea, Amos,' Daniel interrupted. 'I understand.'

Amos took a moment. He was clearly moved.

'I'll tell you a funny thing, Daniel,' he continued quietly. 'I began to wash his sheets in the morning. It was a kind of devotion, I suppose. Isn't that strange? And you know what? He never said a word to me about it, never asked me why I did it or thanked me.'

26

'WHEN THE BIOLOGISTS had completed their research, we returned to Guayaquil, arriving a few days after Easter Sunday. In the middle of the day of our arrival, the captain gathered the crew for an Easter service. Just as it was about to begin, an enormous Easter egg was delivered to the ship.

'It was for Andrew, from his sister, bigger than the biggest watermelon you've ever seen, wrapped in silver paper and tied together with a yellow ribbon. One of the sailors had to help the deliveryman on board with it. The sun flashed from its surface. All the crew let out impressed exclamations and, for the first time since almost the journey's start, I saw Andrew smile.

'"You're a lucky man," the captain called down, not unkindly. There seemed a sort of resignation in his voice. "I hope you'll share some of your bounty with us, Andrew." This was the first time he'd called Andrew by his name for months.

'The other sailors urged him to open the egg, and tentatively, taking his time to enjoy his first taste of what it was like to be at the very centre of affable attention, Andrew tugged at the ribbon's bow. But it was tied too tight. We all urged him on as he struggled with it, and he broke into shy laughter. Every now and then he'd glance with filial deference up at the captain, who looked down benevolently. Finally, one of the sailors lent Andrew a knife. With one wrench of his thin frame, the ribbon snapped and the egg fell into two halves. The general cry of triumph was suddenly choked.

'Fortunately, Andrew immediately collapsed into a dead faint. The huge iguana, obviously kidnapped from the Galápagos, sat on that split shell, looking sleepily upon the world.

'Hamid and I instantly started from the now laughing crowd and dragged Andrew's limp body from the proximity of the iguana, which, along with the captain, seemed, almost imperceptibly, to smile.'

'And you still don't think the captain was responsible?' Daniel said.

'Not directly, no,' Amos replied, 'but he didn't condemn any of these pranks, and in that way encouraged the general ill feeling towards Andrew to flourish.

'We carried Andrew back to the cabin. For the next few nights, he slept fitfully, crying out and waking up in a cold sweat. Slowly, he recovered, but stopped working completely, became a ghost on the ship, staring out to sea. Hamid and I convinced Boyd to give him a little more time in return for us doing Andrew's work ourselves.

'Andrew was constantly anxious, would ask me only about the iguana, his questions staggering out as if emerging from a thick fog of something else going on in his mind. What had happened to it? Had I seen it thrown overboard? Who else had seen it? Who had thrown it? He began to develop all kinds of morbid fears. He'd eat only after very carefully examining his food, and would often hang around the galley so he could see what was being cooked. He'd have me check everywhere before he entered our cabin and insisted, even on the most stifling nights, that the door be locked before he could sleep. I remember that eucalyptus-cinnamon smell saturating the room, causing my saliva to taste revoltingly sweet.

'On docking at Callao, I got an aerogramme from his sister in response to the one I'd sent her from Guayaquil – in which I'd told her about the incident with the iguana. It was a long, erratic, and extremely intimate outpouring. You might wonder why she was so open with me, Daniel, given the trouble it had got her into with the captain. Well, as she'd put it herself, she was a zealot, a believer, needed to have faith, and had put that faith in me. But I think that what she was trying to do in that letter was to convey to me not just memory but being – his being. It was a disorderly storming of my heart through my imagination, in that it consisted, for the most part, of stories. Stories about her brother, one coming helter-skelter after another, their connecting theme, it occurs to me now – *just now*, Daniel – transformations, her brother's transformations.

'So few people know the value of a well-told story, my friend. When we're judged by our Maker, I wouldn't be surprised if he demanded not a confession of our sins but a story that expresses, with just the right details, the singular predicament of our lives.

'In that letter, there was one particular story that haunted me, an incident that had occurred when their uncle Hamish had come to visit . . . Uncle Hamish, a man with T-bone hands and a head that should have been served on a platter with an apple in its mouth. Twice a year he came to try to persuade their mother to get married again so that her "wee bairns" might have the benefit of a father. Andrew and Vivian called him the Megathere. He was one of a specific species of demon inhabiting their version of the Underworld. We'd seen what he'd done to his own children with his crushing obtuseness, hollowing them out into high-pitched chambers to echo the half-dozen clichés he'd use to disguise his existence as that of a human being. Each time he visited us he would institute some oppressive change. After one trip, we could no longer run about in bare feet. After another, we had to always wear clothes clearly indicative of our sex. On the last visit he'd forced our mother to put us into separate bedrooms. Up until then, we'd shared the same room; indeed, the same bed.

'During the second night of this latest visit, I'd snuck back into my brother's room, as I did every night, and he and I were enacting some scene in the ongoing drama of our imaginary world. I won't explain the scene, but it was one derived from his imagination by the intrusion of the Megathere. We were naked, had painted each other's bodies with burnt cork and a lipstick I'd stolen from my mother.

'Perhaps he smelled the burnt cork or heard our whispering, for the door opened and there he stood, bellowing as a beast should, ordering me out. I refused, placing myself between him and my brother. My mother arrived at this moment to see her two children naked and painted like savages. Immediately, she obeyed her brother's order and dragged me downstairs.

'Struggling fiercely in my mother's arms, I could hear my uncle's strident voice above us, the floor creaking beneath his pacing feet. Something was smashed. All of a sudden the noise stopped. Moments later a door slammed and I heard that creature returning to his room.

'I broke from my mother and ran upstairs, back into the bedroom, to be confronted by an image I'll never forget: my brother standing beside the bed, still naked, a graffitied Donatello David, all the make-up on his body smeared, his right cheek raw and bleeding as if he'd fallen into gravel, and on his face a look of exaltation – his eyes as if irrecoverably dilated by the sight of something divine. Never had I felt so jealous or seen him as so separate from me.

'He told me later that our uncle – he refused to call him the Megathere – had acted as if he were in an uncontrollable rage, screaming, breaking one of the lamps, knocking chairs to the ground. Suddenly he took hold of my brother and lifted him into his arms. To my brother's surprise, our uncle held him as if he were terribly fragile and precious for a moment before laying him on the bed. He then tented his own body over my brother's and kneaded his forehead into my brother's chest, uttering sobs and strange, murmuring supplications as he did so. At last, he broke down completely.

'My brother, to comfort him, took hold of our uncle by his head – that massive, coarse, grotesque head, which smelled of tobacco and carious teeth. Cradling it as if it were a creature in itself, he placed his smooth cheek against those unshaven jowls. After a little while, without knowing why, he began to rub his face against that of this man, helpless in his arms, rubbing harder and harder until his own soft cheek began to chafe, to burn, and finally to bleed. Pressing his palm to this cheek, my brother then placed a bloody imprint of his small hand upon our uncle's broad forehead.'

Her voice vanished. Amos's hand broke from the shadows of his body and settled between the dictionary and Chloe's plait, a boneless creature, like something one might find on the seabed.

'I remember,' Amos said, 'wishing she hadn't told me this, as if I had some prescient fear, as if, despite my ostensible efforts to make him human, I knew already what I was going to do to him, knew already the end of the narrative I'd begun. That is the human condition: to see so much and stagger so blindly. I knew it, somehow, and didn't want to be afflicted by the ghost of that painted and smeared boy-girl, with the bleeding, ecstatic face. I don't want it still, but it's here, as are the ghosts of every one of these stories, *mine*, inhabiting these flats, wandering these stairwells and those streets.

'Dozens of pages long, that letter gave me such sense of the world in which the two of them had grown up, in which their ageless father looked down upon them from every wall and their mother was an echo, existing only to sound the hollow silence of her dead husband. You know, our mother would actually put food out for him on big holidays, like Christmas. When I was twelve, my brother said to me, "Let's see what she does if we eat from his plate." During the dinner, at his signal, we both reached over and snatched a strip of turkey from our father's plate. But my brother couldn't put it into his mouth. I did, though, ate it as my mother went wild, took hold of me, tried to make me throw it up, as if I'd eaten his flesh. Which is how I felt, as if I'd eaten his flesh, and I felt wonderful, with the power to scream the roof off that house. Do I sound mad to you?'

'No.'

'Do I, Danny?'

'No, Mum. You –'

'Not mad enough. But I felt it sometimes, looking at my mother sleeping in her armchair, thinking, She's nothing, nothing inside her, that we have no connection, none. And none with my father, for I searched him out when I was fifteen, broke my way into her cupboards and suitcases, into his relics. I tried to rout him from the darkness. I found a dank smell; I found his vicious, petty voice in letters he'd written her – lifeless, lifeless letters, in which he showed a passion for nothing but his position and the cubic capacity of the engines in the ships he commanded. I never told this to my brother, for in the world he'd created, our father was the source of life, and my brother wanted to be heir to his mystery, while I had come to wonder if the greatest thing our father had ever done for us, at least for our imaginations, was to die. I feel, feel truly, that only in his death was our life, that in his death is my longing and my brother's imagination. I just wish I'd been a man, Danny. I wish I'd been a man. I wish I'd found a way into my brother's body besides –'

'Stop.' Daniel stood up, that voice throbbing in his limbs. He felt suddenly dizzy, staggered and knocked his shin against the table, causing a sharp, disproportionate pain. But he was almost glad for the pain, because it allowed him to orient himself a little in a room that had lost definition and dimension, the play of light and shadow vertiginous. He still felt as if he might lose his balance and was momentarily panicked by the notion that if he fell, he'd fall into – *through* – Amos, through that shadowed form into darkness. To steady himself, Daniel bent over, put his hands on the table, and fixed his eyes on the steel lighter and ball bearing, in which had pooled some of the receded light.

Amos's voice seemed to emanate from all around him in the darkness: 'Are you all right?'

'Just a little dizzy. I stood up too quickly. I haven't eaten since lunch.' Daniel's own voice sounded strange to him, like her voice, as if her voice had come from him, as if his voice were emerging from hers. He cleared his throat. 'I have to go to the toilet.' He straightened up.

'Why don't I make you a bite to eat, eh?'

'Please don't. I have to leave soon. I have to go.' Daniel was calling this back as he made his way over to the narrow hall that led to the bathroom.

27

After locking it, Daniel leaned back against the bathroom door and tried to centre himself, to understand what had just happened – his mother's voice, so clear. He felt exhausted and confused, as if he'd suffered a seizure. He tried to remember Amos's voice, to take hold of it, as if that were the thread that could lead him back through these stories, out of these lives, but it eluded him. Just voices – voices from his own past, suddenly rising, like startled birds. He couldn't sense that man in the flat at all, could hear, beyond the spongy throb of his heart, only her silence.

He looked around the bathroom. Daniel had never imagined he'd be in this room again, the only room with a lock in this flat. In here, as a child, he'd hidden his wrongness. In here he'd cried at his humiliations, dreamed of retribution, asked for forgiveness. In here he'd explored his changing body.

He shivered. A desperate feeling in him now: sun sinking, shadows able only to reach in a direction opposite to the light that had made them, reach only for what they already were.

A pulse of pain at his leg focussed him again. He lifted the turn-up of his trousers to expose his shin, which was streaked with semi-congealed blood. Surely he hadn't hit the coffee table that hard. He was confused, then remembered the fox – his shin being hit by that iron bar – and recently running into that deck chair. The sight of this wound made him feel even more like a child. He went to the sink, wanting, he realised, to see, in the mirror above it, a man, a grown man. But the mirror had been removed. This room was as blind as the rest. *To see so much and stagger so blindly.*

He pulled out his pack of cigarettes. It was empty. After flushing the toilet he returned to the sitting room.

28

AMOS WASN'T IN THERE. As Daniel called for him, he saw that the front door was wide open. Where would he have gone?

Daniel needed to get cigarettes anyway, so after calling for Amos a couple more times he left the flat, got the lift down, and hurried through the rain to the Derby Arms.

At the bar sat a woman, mid-forties, drunk and ravaged, her right arm moving in front of her like a charmed snake in time to 'Sexual Healing,' which was blasting from the jukebox. A half-dozen plasterers and painters, still in their overalls, were playing pool and darts. Here and there a few old men read the paper over their pints.

Galvin had spent every night in here drinking. How many times had Daniel looked into Galvin's ruined face across one of these tables? Physically, nothing had remained of the sensitive, pretty child. *Do you remember, Danny, how we would . . . Do you remember when . . . Do you remember?* His hands, calloused and scarred from roofing, seemed like creatures even upon this huge man, who sat in here, day after day, trying to kill his imagination with drink before it killed him. A man on his knees in the beer garden: *Not a minute of the day, Danny,*

I don't think of you. A man who was – is still – Sally, squatting by the pool: *Speak to me, Danny. Say anything.* A man who is his mother singing, softly Scottish, into the phone:

> *Defiant she waited*
> *For word from her man.*
> *The English she hated . . .*

Clear to him now: how worlds end, as they begin, with a song.

Daniel got cigarettes from the machine. Putting one between his lips, he patted his pockets for a moment before remembering that his lighter was still in the flat. He got a pint and a light from the barman and sat down at a booth near the door.

The sight of his own face reflected in the darkened window made Daniel wonder what Galvin had felt when he'd seen him in the street from this pub at their last encounter. What he'd felt when Daniel had turned down his invitation for a drink. Daniel wished he could explain it to someone, derive from that moment as many stories as it took to reveal something so simple it's blinding: saying 'No, thank you' because you're afraid of everything, because your curious gift is to sever your life and still remain alive.

He thought of his disastrous attempts to explain things at Sally's today, how you imagine the story coming out of you like a song, people being moved beyond understanding. Instead they laugh, are embarrassed, ashamed, annoyed, bored.

One story before God.

One story: Amos wasn't doing so badly. Daniel could feel the unforgivable act as if it were gathering in his own limbs, an act that would be a negation of everything Amos had ever been or could be. And yet, for the sake of that act's survival, Amos was trying to find a way to make it live in Daniel. Moreover, to make it live, not as an isolated act but as the darkness at the heart of love. What a task. Daniel found himself filled now with a sense of Amos's fortitude – and more, with an expansive sensation like pride, which Daniel quickly smothered. It was just – and this deserved acknowledgment – that Amos, rather than turning, as most did, to beer, television, self-pity, recrimination, had chosen to attempt, again and again, to give life to – to draw life from – what had destroyed him.

In the pub, one of the workmen, who had a lion rampant shaved into the back of his crew cut, was trying his luck with the woman at the bar. This saddened Daniel. She was so drunk she could barely keep herself on the stool. Daniel wanted to return to the flat now, yet leaving this place seemed like leaving Galvin again. He could almost see Galvin, sitting across from him. But it was a hybrid memory, the face of the sweet and girlish child, the body of the man, the hulks of his hands beached upon the table. And there, along his right forearm, that pattern of small scars. Another place to begin perhaps, another story, a day written in those scars, Daniel's eleventh birthday, his new bike.

Daniel's mother had saved a full year for that bike. Even now, in this pub, stirred the echo of that percussion of pleasure in his nerves at waking to see the silver Raleigh racer propped against his bed. He loved it as he'd loved only his air rifle, which he'd bought secretly with money he'd saved from his paper round, and which his mother had taken away before he'd even had a chance to fire it. They were possessions that made him real. A gun and a bike: what more does any boy need to be a boy who would be a man? And pleasure also in that his joy had unravelled his mother, her hand pressed to her flushed neck as if she were the shy twin of the defiant girl posing in the old photograph. He'd fetched Galvin immediately because Daniel's joy, no matter how extreme, had never been more than conditional until he could share it with Galvin.

They spent an hour as if they were blind, running their hands across its flanks and withers, over its proudly mute, single-minded form, talking about all the things they were going to add to it – dynamos, reflectors, a mile gauge and, of course, a strong rack so they could be on it together. Finally, they took it down to the towpath.

While Daniel was riding it for the first time, Galvin saw something glitter from the riverbank. He'd been obsessed with Roman artefacts since reading that a sword had been found near Hammersmith Bridge, and ran down to check what it was. As he pulled an old wing

mirror out of the bank, three boys appeared from behind
a sewer outlet. They were a few years older than Daniel
or Galvin, thirteen, fourteen perhaps, all smoking. They
went up to Galvin and stood around him. Galvin cradled
his slender body in his arms and looked into the mud.
The boys asked him for money for their bus fare. When
he told them he didn't have any, they checked his
pockets. Then one of the boys, a wiry kid with a gold
hoop earring, called up to Daniel to ask if he had any
money. Daniel, congealed with fear, shook his head.
Taking a few steps towards Daniel, this boy then asked
if he could have a go on his bike. Again Daniel shook his
head. He knew these boys would steal it. He couldn't
imagine what his mother would do after a year of saving
if he came home without it. The boy began to walk
towards Daniel, repeating that he just wanted to have a
go. Paralysed, Daniel didn't know what to do until Galvin
looked up and screamed, 'Don't let them get the bike,
Danny.' At which Daniel rode off as fast as he could.

He waited for Galvin at the entrance to the estate.
When his friend's small figure appeared at the end of
Walnut, Daniel ran down and told him immediately that
the bike was his, that he could have it whenever he
wanted. Galvin was bent over, hugging himself as if he
were cold. Daniel saw them then, the cigarette burns all
down his right arm.

They went to the little park and climbed into the horse
chestnut. Daniel didn't know what to say.

After a while, Galvin spoke. 'It was a trap,' he said

softly. 'They were Bavens, river demons, those boys. They knew, right, that if they could get you near the water, you'd lose your powers. They –' But he began to cry, rubbing his burned arm. The tree sighed, as if it wanted to be free of them.

'We have to stay away from the river,' Daniel took up, 'make a trap for them here in the park.' He wanted Galvin to take over, to weave this story into one of retribution, in which Daniel would hack those boys to pieces. But Galvin was still crying.

Daniel climbed closer and put his arm around his friend. 'We'll make a trap,' he urged softly.

In the pub an old man a few tables away glanced over, and Daniel realised he'd said this out loud.

Daniel got up. His heart felt saturated. He wanted to approach those workmen and ask them where his friend was.

But instantly he knew. He *was* Galvin – a sensation so strong he became afraid that if he looked down he'd see Galvin's steel-capped work boots. He raised his hand and forced himself to look at it. It was his own, and the feeling dissolved into a confused mix of relief and regret.

He went to the pay phone. He wanted to hear a voice he knew from someone who knew him. Sally had no phone in her cottage. He tried Richard, but he wasn't home. He called Jill.

She picked up as soon as Daniel began to speak into her answering machine.

'Danny, are you all right?'

It was wonderful to hear her voice – his *name* in her voice. He was instantly overwhelmed by a desire to see her, to touch her and make sure that she was real, to say sorry for what had happened. In his head flashed the image of her clutching her naked body in the kitchen.

'Danny, are you –'

'I'm fine,' he said. 'I'm just going to come round for a little while. I thought –'

'No, Danny. I don't think that would be a good idea.'

'I just want a quick word. I've got to be back here soon anyway. I've got some other things to do here.'

'Have you been drinking, Danny?'

'No. I just –'

'It's not really a good time.'

In the background, he heard a voice.

'Is someone there?'

She was silent for a moment. 'Danny, I'll tell you what, I'll come down and meet you. Where are you?'

'I'm all right,' he said.

'No, Danny, please I want to –'

'I'll see you tomorrow.' He put down the phone.

The woman at the bar was even more lost in the music now, her arm flailing wildly. The workman, whispering something into her ear, was pushing his body against hers. Abruptly, she shoved him away with her dancing hand, canted her head back, and said, like an East End

Joan Crawford, 'You stink like a cheap slag's fanny rag, you animal. Fuck off.'

The man skulked back to his mates, she returned to her wild and lonely dance, and Daniel left the pub.

I T W A S A R E L I E F to get back to the flat. The door was still open and he called for Amos as he entered, but there was no reply. He wanted to check in the kitchen, and took a few steps towards it, but a faint panic fluttered in his chest. He was afraid to look in, could imagine only a derelict space opening out into the sky. He returned to the sofa. Moonlight or perhaps some artificial light from a balcony shone into the window beside the Matisse. Strange shadows writhed on the ceiling.

'Amos,' he called.

There was no reply, no sounds in the flat at all.

Those shadows had stilled and now began to roil again, like flames, and he realised that it had to be something outside. But, as he went to investigate, his vertigo returned. His stomach felt as if it were dissolving. He shut his eyes as he got to the window, trying to calm down, but then became afraid to open them, convinced that, if he did, he'd find himself in the sky, falling, falling, falling.

'Shit,' he hissed, trapped in his own fear.

'What's wrong?'

The voice was right at his ear. Daniel flung himself back against the Matisse, almost knocking it off the wall, and opened his eyes.

Amos was staring at him. 'You all right?'

'Where the blazes did you come from?'

'Been down on the ground floor in Mrs Almond's. I hope you appreciate what I had to go through to get this for your bloody cheese on toast.' Amos shook the half-dozen slices of bread in his right hand. 'I'll tell you, that woman's had every ailment known to man.' He sighed. 'But she's a sweet old thing at heart, and I think I just insulted her.'

Despite the shock, it was good to see Amos, to hear his voice again. Amos turned to go to the kitchen, but Daniel wanted him to remain a little longer. 'You insulted her?'

Amos turned back. 'What?'

'What do you mean you insulted her?' Daniel became aware again of the shadows on the ceiling.

'Oh, well, see, she has an electric wheelchair,' Amos explained, 'and she has to drive it through the back passage downstairs because that exit has the automatic door. But kids leave their bikes in the corridor, and people dump rubbish down there. So she has trouble getting it through.

'Anyway, long story short, she's always getting on at the council to clear it out. So I was just down there to borrow this bread, and I'm trying not to ask her how she is. Last time I did, I was in there all day listening to the saga of the mystery lump in her breast. Anyway, I could see she wasn't going to get round to letting me have anything unless I did ask her. So I did, but I wasn't really listening, and she said something about an absolute miracle, and she was feeling much better, and about the back passage being cleared out this morning. So I told her that's great, you know, and that if it ever happened again she should just let me know and I'd clear it out myself. Anyway, she points up to her bread bin, and she's looking at me a bit queer, and after I get the bread, she leans forward, all confidential-like, and she says, "Mr Radcliff . . . Mr Radcliff, I'm sure that's a very kind offer, but I think enemas are best administered by medical professionals."'

Amos made a grimace and shivered.

Daniel smiled, but those shadows on the ceiling began to flicker again. He forced himself to look out of the window. A pigeon had caught one of its legs in a makeshift clothesline stretched across the side of the building.

'Oh, no,' Daniel groaned.

'What is it?'

'There's a pigeon. It's trapped out there. Do you know your neighbour?'

'Yeah, but he was doing three months for postal fraud. Don't think he's out yet.' Amos opened the window.

With the raw feel of the cool air, Daniel had to put his hands against the wall and close his eyes. Almost immediately he heard cooing noises, as if the pigeon were at the sill. He opened his eyes, and it took him a second to realise that these sounds were coming from Amos.

'We've got to help it,' Daniel said.

Amos stopped cooing, put the bread down on to the coffee table, and ran into Daniel's bedroom. He returned a few moments later holding an air rifle. The shock of this was confused by the shock of Daniel's recognition: it was *his* air rifle, the one his mother had found and taken away before he'd even had a chance to use it. His first love, first grief, before the bicycle. It looked brand new.

Amos loaded the little feathered dart, pumped the handle, knelt down before the window, and aimed the rifle.

Daniel pulled the barrel up. 'What are you doing?'

'I'm putting it out of its misery.'

'Are you insane?'

'Oh, come on,' Amos whined. 'Haven't had a chance to use it yet.'

'You're not going to kill it. We just need a coat hanger or something. We can unhook its leg.'

'Ain't got nothing like that.' Snatching the barrel out of Daniel's hand, Amos tried to fire again.

Daniel pushed the barrel down. 'You must have something.'

'I hate bloody pigeons.'

Amos pondered a moment. 'Tell you what, I'll cut you a deal. If I find you a coat hanger, you have to let me have just one shot when it's free. One shot – when it's flying, mind. That's fair odds; moving target. I'll even keep my eyes shut. Deal?'

'Just get the coat hanger,' Daniel said.

'Deal.' Amos got up and went back to the bedroom.

He returned with the hanger and handed it to Daniel. He then hunkered down, hugging the rifle. It hadn't occurred to Daniel that *he* would have to free the bird. The window yawned: livid sky; nothing but nothing. The air in his lungs congealed as he unwound and stretched out the hanger. For some reason he didn't want to show Amos, who looked a little dreamy and was clearly embracing his inner predator, that he was afraid.

On his knees, Daniel took hold of the ledge, cold rain blowing in on his face. The whole sky began to gyre above him. He made a pathetic attempt to reach the pigeon with the wire in his left hand while he clutched the ledge with his right, his head barely out of the window. It was clear he'd have to lean out more and use his right hand. He pulled himself up, his legs trembling, and reached for the pigeon. The bird became frantic, but Daniel finally managed to get the hook of his stretched-out hanger into the loop in which the bird was caught. He tugged a few times, periodically freezing with fear as the ghost of his body was hurled out into the air. The bird almost freed itself a couple of times, and he could hear Amos shifting around behind him, clearly anxious to get a good shot. Suddenly, Daniel's tugging caused the wire to pull away from the old masonry. A second later the pigeon was hanging upside down by its leg, like a chicken trussed for market. It fluttered wildly.

'Damn.' Daniel fell back into the room.

'I'm never going to get a clean shot now,' Amos complained, leaning out of the window and trying to get a bead on the bird.

Daniel pulled Amos in and forced himself back to the ledge. Now he had to look down.

Leaning out, he closed his eyes at first. When he opened them, sixteen stories shimmered like the world behind a haze of heat. The building was a stalk on the top of which he was swaying. 'Jesus, Jesus,' he whispered. 'Jesus, Jesus.' But he stretched down, reaching with his little hook for the hanging bird, flapping and pendulating, everything in him crying out that this was his death, for a bloody pigeon. He *hated* pigeons. But finally, with all the muscles in his arm burning, he managed to lodge the hook in the eye of the line. He tugged and tugged, and suddenly, impossibly, it happened. The filthy bird scurried off up into the air. Daniel flung himself back into the room. Amos aimed the rifle and fired. The dart hit the bottom of the raised window and rebounded at Amos, who covered his face and tumbled back on to the floor.

The two of them just sat there on the carpet for a while, Amos dejected, Daniel happy – so happy he'd done it. He looked up at the ceiling. No shadows.

'I hate pigeons.' Amos leaned the rifle against the edge of the coffee table.

'Not as much as I do,' Daniel said.

They laughed.

Amos hauled himself to his feet, picked up the bread, and went into the kitchen.

Daniel remained where he was for a little while, leaning against the wall, listening to Amos clattering about. There. Amos was in there. Finally, Daniel got up and returned to the sofa.

30

A LITTLE WHILE LATER, Amos entered carrying a tray on which were crisps, jam tarts, a half-dozen slices of cheese on toast, and a fresh pot of tea.

'Tuck in, son,' he urged, as he put the tray down on the coffee table.

'I'm all right, thanks,' Daniel said, though the smell of the cheese on toast was making him light-headed with hunger. This had been his favourite meal as a child.

'Won't bite you.'

Still Daniel hesitated, troubled by the same trepidation he used to feel when offered food at the institution.

Amos picked up the plate of cheese on toast and thrust it towards him. 'Go on. I made it for you.'

Daniel took a slice and ate. It nearly brought him to tears – just the taste of it. He could almost feel her behind him, his mum, gently rubbing his neck. Galvin was sitting on the floor with his back against the sofa. All of them were watching *Fawlty Towers,* eating cheese on toast and crisps and jam tarts, drinking tea. Happiness: his mother laughing with such abandon, Galvin glancing up at them, his joy in theirs. While Daniel's joy had been in his mother's laughter because it had seemed free from her past.

But this feeling had been infused even then for him with the sense that this happiness would, too soon, end. And, as he got older, this sense grew stronger, until every joy seemed over before it had begun. And every grief. His life was the comet's tail, and he the comet itself, a blind velocity though time.

Daniel glanced at Amos and was shocked by his expression. He looked like a starving man watching someone eat, though he was staring not at the food, but at Daniel.

'Aren't you going to have some?' Daniel asked.

Amos shook his head.

Daniel ate the rest of the cheese on toast, finished the crisps, and had two of the jam tarts.

Finally, he put his plate down. He felt much calmer, and strong enough now to return to it, even to have it end: 'Did Andrew get better?'

31

'Yes,' amos said after a moment, 'yes, Andrew did get a little better. But then, a week or so after Vivian's strange letter, he and I were walking around the deck late one evening and he said he wanted to go into the sailors' mess.

'We were close by it and could hear their raucous voices. I told him I didn't think it was such a good idea right now, but he drew himself up in that fiercely brittle manner of his, and said he didn't want them to think they'd got to him.

'Parrot was playing darts with a whole bunch of the men, and I noticed him, as we entered, throwing a significant glance at a new bloke – Ian Gambel. We joined Hamid, who was in the middle of a poker hand with Ay Yam and Joseph Christian.

'Gambel was an East End lad we'd picked up in Guayaquil. I had a sense he'd been in the navy because he talked about serving *in* a ship rather than on it. Didn't much like him. Too familiar by half. Big bloke, he was, good-looking, but undermined somehow, as if he'd been bullied as a kid. He sought out weakness.

'Just as we sit, Gambel thrusts out his loins, begins to scratch his crotch wildly, and calls to Andrew, "Ay, mate, 'ow's your sister?"

'A few of the sailors laughed. Andrew went rigid.

'Parrot, as he threw a couple of darts at the board, muttered, "She's like her brother. The sea's in her blood."

'The laughter got a little louder.

'I wasn't sure what was going on, but I knew it wasn't good. I went to stand up, but Hamid put a restraining hand on the belt of my trousers.

'I called out, "What are you talking about?"

'Parrot, who was accustomed to arrogating his own power from others, obviously felt safe among his confederate sailors, and replied, "Oh, the captain was going on and on about Vivian this morning. He's just had a relapse."

'"A relapse?' I said. "Of what?"

'"Well, Andrew, apparently," he replied, 'isn't the only one who got a gift from the beach.' This set off an uproar of laughter, and as it abated Parrot added, "Nothing a little powdered DDT and a thorough boiling of his linens won't take care of, but a tad . . . irritating nevertheless."

'I felt sick, Daniel, my anger making me breathless. Hamid tried to restrain me again, but I pushed his hand away and stood.

'Andrew asked me what they were talking about. I told him to go back to the cabin. I thought he'd say no, and I was actually ready to manhandle him out of the mess, but he seemed to go blank somehow. Hard to explain. He looked as if he'd been struck by a migraine. I said again, firmly, "Go back to the cabin," at which he got up and walked out.

'As soon as the door closed behind him, I went straight over to Parrot, paying no heed to the gauntlet of sailors who halfheartedly bristled around him. Most were my friends, respected me and, if not, they knew I wasn't someone to be intimidated.

'You should have seen Parrot's eyes, getting wider as I approached. He lifted his arms to protect his face, but I thrust my hand into his crotch, took firm purchase on his family jewels and, with my other hand at his neck, I lifted his body off the ground and pinned it against the dartboard. I held him like this for a long while, his face puce as he tried to pry my fist from his crotch. Finally, I asked him if he had anything more to say. Unable to speak, he shook his head, at which I released him. He crumpled to the ground and curled up like a maggot.

'Jonas, who was among the sailors surrounding Parrot, said, "It's only a joke, Amos."

'Well, I let rip. *God,* the thought of these men talking about Vivian as if she were a port whore . . . And deeper than that was the awful spectre of the captain's intimacy with her.

'I can't recall exactly what I said, but after telling them that they'd all have holy fucking fury to deal with if I heard any one of them mention Vivian again, I started abusing the captain, calling him every name I could lay my tongue to, saying some things about what I was going to do when I got my hands on him that would later return to haunt me.

'They were stunned. None of them knew about my

relationship with Vivian, so this must have seemed an insane reaction. A few started to talk back, and I'll tell you I was ready to take every one of them on. I wanted desperately to fight, to get all of this poisoning mediation and sophistication out of my head. I didn't care if I got the living shite kicked out of me; I wanted things to be simple again.

'It was at this point that Gambel, that damn scaramouche, confident that the tide was turning against me, said, "What the fuck is this slag to you?"

'Before he knew what was happening, I'd taken him by his shirt and had flung him clear across the room. He came up hard against the bulwark. Recovering himself, he took hold of a steel marlinespike that was hanging on a wall rack with a bunch of old tools. But as we went for each other, a table was flung between us with a tremendous crash, cards flying everywhere. It was Hamid, on his feet, in a fury. I'd never seen him like this – no one had – screaming . . . at *me*. Filthy stuff, mostly about what had fathered me: mangy dogs, leprous dwarfs, syphilitic cretins. If it howled, lurched, or oozed pus, it had had a hand in my conception. He looked as if he wanted to kill me, and demanded the marlinespike from Gambel; he intended to use it (he put it more colourfully) to eye-splice my own rectal passage and then hang me with it. Gambel, now more frightened of Hamid than he was of me, gave it up. Though shocked by what was happening, I was still so angry and desperate to fight that I was about to attack Hamid, who was now confronting me with that spike in his hand. A couple of the sailors had already tried to take hold of me, but I'd thrown them off. Abruptly, Hamid went absolutely quiet and still. It happened almost imperceptibly then, the fury in Hamid's face refined to a finicky disdain, his ranging limbs drawn back into the supple, central line of his body, the marlinespike going limp in his hand. Approaching to within inches of me, he stares into my eyes for a moment with languorous contempt, then, like a fey Olivier, whispers, "Look at you, bristling up your crest of youth 'gainst my dignity."'

'What?' Daniel said.

'What indeed. I was flummoxed, so deft had the transition been from a man who looked *genuinely* as if he were going to murder me to this mincing Malvolio, who now fluttered the marlinespike in my direction and declared to the other sailors, "This here, my valiants, is the most omnipotent villain that ever cried stand to a true man. I' faith, the devil take him or I'm the veriest varlet that ever chewed with a tooth. Why look at him – *look at him* – I am whipped and scourged with rods, nettled and stung with pismire – a plague, I say, a plague upon his House." And now this creature, becoming offended at the sailors' incipient laughter, held the marlinespike erect and warned them all against rousing the puissant wrath of his big bare bodkin . . .

'Of course, most of these men wouldn't know Shakespeare from a good shag, but this creature had appeared so unexpectedly from an atmosphere of murderous intention, was so disjunctive, so brilliantly performed that even the notion of violence had become inconceivable. Everyone was laughing, even Ay Yam, who couldn't understand a word of English.

'In a matter of minutes, Hamid had rendered my aggression absurd, robbing my fury of anything to take hold of. But I needed it to take hold of something, Daniel. Despite the fact that I knew these rumours about Vivian were lies, they'd invoked in me the poisonous image of the captain's intimacy with her. With all the tensions of these past months now loose in my limbs, I had to do something. I had to.

'I flung my way out on to the deck. I didn't see Hamid pursuing me, so I was caught completely off guard when he threw me up against the taffrail. Forcing him off, I told him it had gone too far, that I was going to have it out with the captain and didn't give a damn what happened to me.

'Hamid looked so sad. I remember him cupping my cheek with his hand' – Amos put out his hand in this gesture, and Daniel could almost feel it against his own cheek – 'saying, "Listen, if you're too angry about this he'll know what's going on between you and Vivian, and that's going to make everything worse. You have a fine imagination, Amos, so use it. Think of losing what he's lost. You *have* what he's lost."

'I pushed his hand away from my face, desperate to retain what remained of my anger, and said, "What makes you so fucking wise?"

'For a moment, he just stares at me with despair, then he whispers, "Because, Amos, I've lost everything." And what was worse than these words, Daniel, which seemed a revelation even to himself, was that I saw, at that moment, something in him subside, a visible miscarriage of memory, and he seemed, all at once, hardly to know who I was. I saw the face of the man who was to hang himself three years later in a boarding house in Brighton. As he walked away, the afterimage of this unrecognising expression robbed me of what little was left of my anger.'

Amos paused, pensive for a moment, and then said, 'Daniel, I have a sense that in his youth Hamid had done something unforgivable. He was a man in exile – what's more, a man who didn't know how to condemn anyone, was more humble, more multifold, wiser than you could ever get by being only the victim of injustice. When I think of Christ, the god of the fatherless, I think of the essential thing his adherents leave out of his life: that terrible act he must have committed in his youth to have developed his cult of forgiveness.'

Amos picked up the spectacles in that gentle way again, as if they were a small bird. He confronted the empty lenses and seemed incredulous.

'Poor Hamid,' he whispered. 'I loved him, Daniel, a man of . . .' He shook his head sadly. 'A rare man.'

Returning them to the table, he went on. 'But though the anger had gone, I determined to resolve what was happening and continued on to the captain's cabin.'

32

'I KNOCKED AT THE DOOR, not knowing any longer what I was going to say or even what I was feeling.

'The captain called "Enter," and I stepped into the gilt and crystal of his realm, this illusion, the subtlest impeachment of which would, I'm sure, have caused that ship to fold immediately into the ocean. Everywhere, those shells, those awful openings.

'He was sitting below his armorial bearings in an armchair, his hands flat in his lap. On a pedestal table to his left stood a half-empty decanter and a full tumbler of whisky. To his right, an antique lamp, the only light, threw a ghastly cast over his heavy features. The air seemed saturated with his sadness, but, to my surprise, the sight of me caused an almost childish look of joy to enliven his face, and he called my name with an effusion that startled me.

'I just wanted to say what I'd come to say and get out, but before I could speak, he told me to sit down, his voice still full of that eager affection. As I sat opposite him, I realised that his hands were lying across two books – an old hardcover and what appeared to be a notebook, with a pen slotted between its pages. The sight of these – and then all those books, crowding the shelves around him – made me feel stupid, ashamed.

'As I tried to speak again, he leaned over, slapped a heavy hand against my thigh, and asked me if I could smell it.

'"Smell what?" I said.

'"That stench?" he said.

'I was baffled.

'Letting his head fall heavily forwards, he recited in his rich, deep voice:

> *Her legs were spread like a lecherous whore,*
> *Sweating out poisonous fumes,*
> *Who opened in slick invitational style*
> *Her stinking and festering womb.*

'He laughed to himself, sopping drunk.

'This rekindled my anger. Of course I felt he was saying this somehow in reference to Vivian. Coldly, I told him I didn't understand.

'He smiled, as at my naïveté, and asked me if I were a reader like Hamid.

'I considered lying, but this was a direct question, and I'd never directly lied about my illiteracy. "I don't read, sir," I said.

'"Don't?" he said.

'"Can't."

'"Ah," he said, pursing his lips and regarding me for a moment with kindly speculation before he leaned over and whispered, "The man who's stinking up this cabin is a French poet. But he can't help it – being French, that is – and he did at least have the decency to die. But, *God*, what a reek, eh?"

'Still perplexed, I told him the cabin smelled fine.

'He smiled for a moment, then frowned and sank back into his sadness. "No," he said, speaking almost to himself, "it smells of books."

'"Do you write?" I asked, glancing down at the notebook.

'"Oh, I would write," he said, suddenly animated again: "Poems like Baudelaire's, stories like Chekhov's, novels like Tolstoy's, plays like Shakespeare's . . . but the talent I have is too commonplace. My talent, you see, is for loving what I can't possess."

'"Isn't that a writer's talent?" I said, thinking back to all those books and poems Sylvia had read to me.

'"No," he said, "no, a real writer's talent is to find himself in full and terrifying possession of what he can't love."

'He looked right through me for a moment, then asked why I'd never learned to read.

'"Never had time," I said, then I remembered how I'd feigned to read off that sheet as the biologists had come aboard.

'He must have seen the flush in my face, because he said, "It's not a shame not to be able to read. I'd be happy to teach you." And after one of those struggling moments at his lips, he added, "There's a good in you, Amos. Like an ore. You should enter this company." He indicated towards the books. "They'll mine it out for you all right." He smiled bitterly. "They'll mine it out and then you can fashion the good into the beautiful." He laughed. "Wouldn't you like that?" He began to cough, and this gave him an excuse to drain the whiskey in his glass.

'"I'm not really understanding you," I said, becoming frustrated with his abstruseness.

'"It's called equivocation," he replied, "the curse and prerogative of an overeducated mind. Let me bring you into this world, Amos. It would be a father's privilege, and I have a sense you never knew your father."

'"How do you know that?" I said.

'"Because I never knew mine."

'"I seized this opportunity: "The same is true of Andrew," I said.

'The kindness drained out of his face. "Ah," he says, "so, we have a whole ship full of bastards."

'"I'm here," I said, "because of Andrew, because of what's happening with him."

'"It's quite amazing," he said, "how much they look alike, you know, he and his sister."

'"He's not strong – his nerves," I persisted. "If things keep going as they are –"

'He cut me off with an impatient gesture. "It's just a little fun," he said. "Can't he take a joke?"

'"Why," I demanded, "are you spreading these filthy rumours about his sister?"

'As soon as I mentioned Vivian, I witnessed, for the second time that night, a man utterly transform. I'll never forget that grotesque distortion of his face, that brutish thing he became.

'He shouted, "She made a promise to me. She had a responsibility. I was calm here. Why do you think I'm here? Do you think a man would *choose* to spend his life here?" The alcohol seemed to be drowning him, his face, by turns, utterly slack and full of vagrant twitches.

'And though I sensed it only vaguely then, I feel now that there was a way in which he was right, that Vivian had indeed done something unforgivable: she'd brought him to life.'

33

'AS I REENTERED MY CABIN after that strange encounter, Andrew, who'd obviously been waiting for me, got up from where he was sitting on his bunk and began to rail at me as if I were the object of his fury, though he couldn't meet my eyes.

'He was screaming, "He's telling everyone she's a slut. You knew what he was saying about her. Infested, diseased. She'd *never* have let that filthy bastard touch her."

'I just stared at him as he jerked about like a little puppet, his face wild, spittle flying from his lips. I was so sick of this whole business, Daniel, disgusted at my own mendacity, caught between two men who were causing each other such pain over a woman who now loved me.

'I stood absolutely still, but his fury began to feed on itself, and his invective became insane – *literally* – like the stuff that comes out of a schizophrenic. Obscene images: his sister's womb stripped out and hanging in a bloody clot between her legs; her nipples cut off and pushed into the sockets –'

'I get the idea,' Daniel said.

Amos paused, calmed himself. 'And worse things, Daniel, much worse, the products of a powerful but diseased imagination. I took hold of him by his shoulders, shook him, shouted at him to calm down.

'Instantly, as if I'd removed the source of his animation, he went limp and silent, hanging there in front of me as if from the scaffold of his own body. His eyes were blank, his breathing shallow.

'I wanted to get him out of the stifling atmosphere of the cabin, so I suggested we go for a walk, get some air and talk about this.

'He didn't respond or move; his face kept twitching. I became terrified that he was having a nervous breakdown. I told him to put his coat on. Like a robot, he obeyed. I threw on my own yellow sou'wester, opened the door, and made to leave. But Andrew didn't follow, just stood there in his coat, his eyes still vacant.

'"Come with me," I said. As he began to follow me out on to the deck, I noticed he had no shoes on.

'"Your shoes," I said.

'Helplessly, he stared down at his stockinged feet.

'"Put your shoes on," I said. He did so, and it was at this point that I realised he was responding only to imperatives. Like my brother, he was so emotionally drained that he'd lost his will, was now in a completely suggestible state. Without the strength to take the responsibility for his own life, he'd given himself up to my strong voice. I remember, at that moment, thinking, I could tell him to step right over the edge of this ship and he would do it.'

'Were you tempted?'

Amos took a moment to respond. 'I must have been, I suppose. Why else would I have thought that?

'Anyway, we went out on to the deck. I told him just to breathe deeply and look at the ocean. For a long time, we stared out at those dark swells. The rain and the sea brought him back to himself. I watched, as one watches the dawn, his will, his life, returning to his eyes.

'We started to walk. Very gently, I said to him, "Look, everyone knows the captain's lying. Everyone knows she jilted him."

'"What everyone knows," he said, with a knotted frown, still struggling for his breath, "is that she's a filthy whore."

'"For Christ's sake," I said, "what does it matter what these men think? In another week they'll have forgotten it."

'"And you can just as well say," he snapped back at me, "that in another hundred years we'll all be long dead. What's happening *now* matters."

'Then he began to go on about how his father would never have let this happen and what his father would have done, but I cut him off. "You didn't even know your father," I said.

'"I know a man doesn't run away from things," he said.

'Awful, Daniel, to hear this received idea issuing from him. I've always had a horror of such ideas, which infect us at moments of weakness in our lives and break out when our resistance is low. I once knew –'

'Amos,' Daniel admonished softly.

Amos smiled. 'I'm sorry.'

He continued: '"My father was in the Great War,"
Andrew said. "He was awarded the Victoria Cross. He
killed lots —"

'"What?" I said, not hiding my contempt. '"He did
what?"

'Andrew then went quiet for a moment before saying,
"He told my mother once that he felt pity for those who
hadn't been through a war because they'd never be men."'

'I'd been in the more recent war, Daniel, in the thick
of it. I'd seen exactly what it had done to most of the boys
who'd come to it, but I said nothing.

'It was now pouring rain. The decks were deserted.
We walked past the lighted portholes of cabins, with
their breath of tobacco, their soft murmurs and occa-
sional laughter. I talked to him paternally, reminding
him of how little time we had left aboard, telling him
stories of my past conflicts. He listened, or seemed to be
listening. I remember the rain clinging in beads to his
close-shorn hair, forming a kind of aura. As we turned
the corner at the stern of the ship, he pulled up. There
stood the captain, leaning on the taffrail and staring into
the ship's wake, which churned the reflection of a full
yellow moon.

'He didn't see us. Andrew about-faced and returned
swiftly to our cabin, with me in tow. He got on to his
bunk and just lay there like an exhausted child, curled in
towards the steel wall, his clothes soaking wet. I tried to
get him to change, told him he'd catch his death, but he

didn't respond. I felt hopeless, angry. Gathering up my pipe and tobacco I left.'

Amos's voice became soft, imploring: 'And I would have been free of this, Daniel, free of everything . . .' He struggled to lean forward, his face only half-emerging from the coarse net of shadow in which he was caught. Again, he seemed terribly old, his body bent and tremulous. 'I would have been free of this' – he picked up Daniel's lighter – 'if my lighter had worked that night.' He flicked the lid open. 'But it was out of butane.' He closed it and put it back on the table. 'So I returned to the cabin to get matches.

'When I entered, he was no longer there. I felt a strong sense of foreboding, and retraced our walk around the deck. As I approached the stern again, I heard low voices. It was the gentleness of these voices that prevented me from revealing myself. I also felt foolish, prowling about like this, and didn't want to make myself apparent unless absolutely necessary. It even occurred to me that some private confrontation between the two men might bring it to an end once and for all.

'I could tell that the captain, looking down at Andrew with sleepy condescension, was even more drunk than when I'd last seen him. He almost lost his balance a few times and kept clutching for the gunwale. Andrew stood directly in front of him, very close, and spoke in a quick, rhythmic whisper. This continued for a few moments until the captain suddenly took hold of

Andrew's nape, pulled Andrew's head towards him, and began to rub his coarse cheek against the side of Andrew's face.'

'Vivian,' Daniel exclaimed.

'Yes. In her innocence, she must have told him everything.

'Andrew tried to pull free, frantic, furious, but the captain, who was twice his size held him there for a few moments longer, then released him with a laugh. It was then that I saw Andrew reach into the right pocket of his coat, take his hand out and hold it fisted behind his back. Something slowly unravelled from his hand and hung pale against his dark clothes.'

'Why didn't you –'

'Don't ask me why. I don't know.

'It was over in a moment. Andrew swung that thing, hammered it with a dull thud against the captain's temple.

'I heard the soft sound of it. It was like the falling of an apple on to –'

'Amos.'

'But it's true,' Amos defended himself. 'I remember it. I want you to feel it. To see a man die . . . The captain didn't lift his hand to his head, just stood there, so drunk it took him a while to realise he was dead. And then, like some . . . Well, he fell. He collapsed.

'Let me just say that nothing went through my mind. I stepped out. I took the weapon – a heavily weighted sock – from Andrew and placed it calmly into the pocket of my sou'wester. I lifted the captain's body into my arms, my actions quickened by the blood I saw now leaking from his mouth. I was determined not to get it either on me or the deck. I took the erstwhile captain by the hand and lowered his body as far down as I could to minimise the splash. Then he was gone, lost in our wake.

'I told Andrew, who was staring at me very strangely, to go quietly back to our cabin. Mechanically, he obeyed. Then I leaned against the taffrail as the captain had been doing and tried to smoke my pipe so that I could have some measure of time. But my hands were shaking too much to prepare it; besides that I still had no matches. So I stood with the dry pipe in my mouth, my back to the jaundiced moon. The rain had ceased. I girded myself. I'm not an actor. I can't fake things. It doesn't agree with me. Perhaps a minute, perhaps twenty minutes later, I cried out "Man overboard" as loud as I could.'

'Why didn't you –'

'It wasn't as if this were a situation I'd had much experience with.' Amos cut him off fiercely. 'Blind panic has its own logic. I had the sense that if I were quick enough, I could plug this breach and hold the whole dike of truth intact with some plausible lie.'

'I'm sorry.' Daniel did feel sorry now for his impatience.

Amos took a moment to regather himself. 'Anyway, nothing happened. Then I realised, by the unbroken seal of my dry throat, that I hadn't shouted at all. I coughed, and this time I did call out.

'The ship quickened with voices. I shouted again, and those voices rapidly approached. Suddenly, it struck me how casually I was standing, holding my pipe, my legs crossed as if I were leaning on the bar in a pub on a Sunday afternoon. I stuffed the pipe into my pocket and turned around so that I would be looking down into the water. I shouted again. The voices and footsteps were almost upon me when another realisation struck: I'd not attempted to cast a life buoy or fire a flare over the water. When the crew arrived, I was pulling the buoy free. As they crowded around me, I felt panicked. The weapon was in my pocket. Why had I put it in my pocket? I was convinced that even in the midst of all this furore someone would ask me what was weighing down the side of my sou'wester so much. So, of all things, right there and then, I began to pull it off. Instantly, everyone grabbed me. They knew, I thought. Something had given me away. I yielded to their arrest, then I heard a gentle voice, Hamid's voice: "He's gone," he said. "He's gone." I realised then that those hands held me to restrain me from foolhardy heroism.

'So, incapable of dissimulation, my fear had made me dissimulate perfectly. It had introduced me, like the devil himself, into the world of falsehood. I told them all that I'd seen the drunken captain stagger at a sudden swell, lose his footing, and tumble into the water. Hadn't I called? Hadn't I thrown the buoy? Hadn't I even been willing to risk my own life?

'Had all of this not fallen into place, had I been a man less liked, less respected for my honesty and integrity – my moral simplicity, if you like – the accusations, I'm sure, would have begun immediately.'

34

'I REMEMBER STANDING with Hamid at the funeral service. Parrot, right at the front, looked so shrunken and bereft. Every now and then one of the sailors would glance back at me.

'I whispered to Hamid, "They think I killed him, don't they?"

'"Sailors are like old women," he said. "'It'll blow over."

'"They all heard what I said I was going to do to him in the mess the other night. They all saw how crazy I was."

'Hamid then looked at me directly, and said, "Did you kill him?"

'"No," I said.

'"Let them think what they like then."

'In place of the captain's body, that silk rendering of his coat of arms was cast on to the sea.

'In the next few days, Gambel began to accuse me openly of murdering the captain, and a number of the sailors started to avoid me. No one, even Ay Yam, my co-confessor, seemed able to look me in the eyes.

'What had happened remained unspoken between Andrew and me. In fact, we barely spoke at all. But every now and then, I'd find him staring at me very queerly, as if trying to work something out. It was a black look that very much disquieted me. Not that I expected gratitude

–' Amos paused, reconsidering. 'No, perhaps I did. I think, at the very least, I expected a sense of communion, of common fate. We'd become, for better or worse, irrevocably joined by what had happened.

'I decided that I'd broach the subject when we were onshore and alone together, away from the laden atmosphere of the ship.'

35

'OUR NEXT STOP WAS ARICA, a small harbour town at the base of a towering sandstone cliff called the Morro. The moment we docked, he tried to slip off the boat without me, but I hurried down after him. At the bottom of the gangplank, he pulled up. There, on the dock, stood Vivian.

'He was as surprised as I was. As she embraced her brother her eyes flickered over to me. He was crying, had succumbed to her like a child. You couldn't conceive, Daniel, of what it was like for me to see her. Here were Andrew's very features, but centred and serene, as if she were not only the one I loved but a way for me to love him. And, God, that hair, the colour of sunlit mahogany, falling about her face and down to her shoulders in wild curls.

'"Dr Livingstone, I presume," she said, holding out one hand to me, the other rubbing her brother's back. Deeply disappointed, I took her hand and told her I was Amos. She laughed in the most delightful way. I didn't even bother to ask what her joke had been. To touch her after all that time. She smiled at me – oh, the most wonderful smile – and our eyes were locked, the thread of our silence pulled taut between us, our hands not releasing. That I remember as one of the most profound and happy moments of my life.

'But Andrew soon recovered himself, looked back at me savagely, his face puffy and red from the tears. Taking his sister's arm, he tried to drag her away. She resisted and asked me to join them, whereupon her brother wrenched at her again and whispered some harsh words. Her face flushed crimson, and I quickly said that it would be better perhaps if we met up later, considering how long it had been since she'd last seen her brother. They left me at the base of the gangplank.

'I didn't move for a long while. I felt as if a cold steel coulter were being eased through my heart. How extremely one feels in youth. At that moment, I couldn't conceive of my life without her. The thoughts of what he might be telling her tortured me . . . Can you imagine?

'Andrew returned to the cabin late. For the full ten hours of his absence, I'd lain on my bunk just waiting, waiting.

'"She's gone," he said. "She's on her way back to Scotland."

'There was a silence between us like one I'd never experienced and wish never to experience again, a silence of such murderous intensity. To have had her so close. I've never wanted anything like that. Now, as I looked at this cringing man, this blockage, this clot, my gaze burned his humanity away. He must have sensed this because, when I pulled myself off my bunk, he flinched back, and responded with the pitiful barking of his voice, like a little dog recoiling from a huge one trapped behind a fence. And I'll tell you, we must have both felt how flimsy that fence was.

'And do you know what he said? He said, "If you think I'd let my sister marry a murderer . . ."

'He stared feverishly at me. I didn't respond. "Why did you kill him?" he said, but I barely heard his question because I was suddenly euphoric. Marriage. She'd talked of marrying me. But close upon the rush of this, I realised what he was saying.

'"*You* killed him," I said.

'At this, he seemed genuinely amazed. "You threw him into the ocean."

'"But he was already dead," I said. "Anybody could have seen that. There was blood coming from his mouth. I did it to save you. I *did* save you."

'"Oh no," he said, "there wasn't any blood. He wasn't dead."

'We argued for hours, like two people arguing over whose fault it was that the dinner had been burned. But the argument itself was a kind of trap. I persisted because I could sense that there was some doubt in him – the way he kept turning away from me. And yet, after a while, I realised that those fleeting indications of self-doubt were being used subconsciously to bait me. The increase in the intensity of my attestations and protestations allowed him then to intensify his own. I realised that he was using the very heat of the argument to anneal what he was saying, that he was mirroring my absolute faith in my innocence. What I began to see in front of me was the reflection – his imitation – of my amazement and fury. From the outside in, he was imbuing himself with a conviction of his innocence derived from the expression of the conviction I had in mine, convincing himself that, from sheer capriciousness, I'd killed the captain before his eyes, that a debt was not owed from him to me, but from me to him – for his silence. It was a true horror, Daniel, to watch this man taking in the image of my innocence in order to derive from it, by some psychic alchemy, the essence of his own.'

Amos had become very animated and was almost shouting. Pausing, he took some deep breaths, rubbed his face, and went on more calmly.

'As soon as I realised that this was an argument I could only lose, and became aware of the fact that it just needed a word from this unstable man and I'd be hanged, given that a good number of sailors already suspected something, I became afraid of what my fury and frustration might lead me to do. Snatching up my jacket, I left the cabin and went ashore.

'As I walked, every muscle in me was taut with his image, every muscle wanted to extinguish him, his ignoble weakness, his cowering, feverish, and distorted face. The firm ground felt so good under my feet. I entered a maze of squat buildings, pungent with cooking, and it was then . . . then that I felt a hand – her hand – take mine.'

Again Amos struggled to break out of the shadows, his

head half-emerging. He stared at the objects on the table as if he'd just cast them down for auger and was desperate to read a different future this time in their configuration.

Not succeeding, he looked up at Daniel. 'And where is she now?' he said. 'I mean *she*, that moment of her that took my hand and kissed me. That place, where is it, that young man I was, that kiss? I want the damp collision of her skin, the flush of blood in her neck, the ripe smell of her body in that heat, vying with the odours of the marketplace and the harbour. I want her laughter as I took those curls of her hair into my mouth, as I fed on her face, its sanity and strength. Its beauty. I wanted to put all of her into my mouth, like a child.' He paused and became suddenly angry: 'How can we be judged, Daniel, without evidence? Fish, kerosene, rust, hemp, tar, sweat, talc, perfume.' His voice softened, though it was no less passionate. 'Does our son ever wake up as a man with the residue of that smell in him, the smell of her and of the dock? If he ever finds himself on that dock in Arica, will he feel, for a moment, as if his body had taken root?'

'Son?' Daniel murmured.

'In short,' Amos continued, 'love. We decided we'd marry as soon as I returned, and that I'd somehow break the news to Andrew. I asked her what he'd told her, but she said only that it had been mostly incoherent, and that now the captain was dead, Daniel would calm down. I, of course, knew he would not.'

'Andrew,' Daniel corrected.

'What?'

'You called him Daniel again.'

'Did I?'

'Do I remind you of him?'

Amos took a moment to reply. 'Physically – a little. But I should perhaps be honest and admit what I'm sure you already suspect: you have his name.'

'You mean his name's Daniel? Then why are you calling him Andrew?'

'I just thought it would be confusing otherwise, and for me, using his real name makes the story more difficult to tell.'

And Vivian's name? The question was there, but Daniel didn't – couldn't – ask it. (Vivian: he'd heard that name somewhere before.) He now regretted his interjection, felt something like what he'd felt as a child when his mother would stare through him into her past. There are some things one can't look at directly, and in this place there were no mirrors.

After waiting as if to be sure of Daniel's silence, Amos went on. 'When I entered the cloying atmosphere of the cabin some hours later, Andrew was still sitting on his bunk. He seemed feverish, gave me the strangest look of both yearning and fear. Here was the distorted image of the face I'd kissed. It was as if I'd returned to my real life after an encounter with the way things should have been.

'I said, "Listen, we have to talk. Off the ship. It'll clear our heads."

'He told me he didn't have anything to say to me. Confronted by his tenacious weakness, all my despair and fury returned.

'I said, "Andrew, you know you killed him. Somewhere in that crazy head you know you did it."

'Before he could deny it I screamed at him, "You know you did it. You did it because you wanted to be a man and now look at you." I was on the verge of smashing everything up.

'I calmed myself. "Listen," I said, "listen, even if it's true that I threw him in while he was still alive, I did it not believing that. I did it for you."

'"So you're admitting it," he says.

'"I'm not admitting anything."

'"You just said you killed him." He was shouting now. "You just said you killed him. You just said it."

'There were voices outside the cabin, and I pushed my hand over his mouth. I expected him to struggle, but he went completely still and quiet. We were like two children involved in some game of deadly seriousness to us, but which we had to keep secret from the adults around us. I was frightened. Andrew had already brought me to a position I'd never been in, in which I was universally distrusted by the men around me. He was the end of my relationship to his sister, which seemed, at that time, almost worse than the fact that he could also be the end of my life. I mean, who would ever believe that this cringing, helpless man had killed the captain? I was trapped. I couldn't leave the ship, or tell him to leave for fear of what he might say when free from my proximity. I'd also promised Vivian that I'd talk to him about our relationship. She seemed, inexplicably, despite Andrew's behaviour on the dock, to have the impression that Andrew and I were close, that he loved and trusted me.'

Amos paused, a little breathless; began again more quietly.

'One night, some years later, on the anniversary of his death, Vivian read me all the letters he'd written to her from the *Prince of Scots*. Inconceivable, Daniel, that they were by this shivering husk of a man. Beautiful letters, gentle and full of humour. Certainly, parts of them were angry, even senseless, but all of this ire was focussed on the captain. Otherwise, the letters were clearly the product of a profound and loving sensibility of which I'd never once been aware. The letters also made it obvious that he was deeply enamoured of me. Not unlike love letters, in fact, with my every gesture and expression minutely described. There was a whole letter on the qualities of my voice, and one, I remember, so tender and funny, about the spectacle of me clumsily trying to sew a button on to one of my shirts. On that night, Vivian admitted that it had been *his* as much as my own letters that had made her fall in love with me. And, in truth, she was reading those letters not so much in remembrance of her brother, but because things were not going well between us at the time, and she needed a way to express what she felt for me, which she did by putting his words into her own voice. We even made love there, ending up, in our hasty coupling, upon the letters themselves, crumpling, even tearing some of them.'

Amos closed his eyes, dipped his head, and let out a low, pained moan. 'Poor Andrew,' he said, in barely a whisper. 'Poor Andrew, who never, in this world, became anything more than a medium, the very print of his letters transferred to the damp skin of our bodies.

'Vivian was quite unaware that he'd not given me any sense of how he felt about me, and I never knew that his fury over my relationship with his sister was as much because *he* loved me as because she did.

'To think of him giving such meticulous life to me, Daniel, while I was trying to strip him of his humanity, regarding him in the same way my mother had regarded my brother, as chaff – Vivian's chaff. Of course, in truth, he and Vivian were complete only together. He made the world in which she believed, but she was no mere zealot. If he were the librettist of their world, she was its music. There was such a purity in her, so clear a sense of what was right and wrong. What was right was to trust, to abandon yourself, to take the risks required to achieve real intimacy. For her, to live was to be intimate. She had taken me for what Andrew had made me: the object of love in their world. What a gift from the gods Andrew's imagination was, as was her faith, but all such gifts come with their cruel caveats. To maintain such intoxicating imagination, Daniel, requires that one never undergo that merciful truncation and stereotyping of the mind that turns a boy into a man. Andrew had to endure a world in flux. Without the strength to suffer this, he found himself ultimately clinging to a wreckage, to the pieces of what it means to be a man. As for Vivian's faith, it led her to need to believe in me, a man whose very essence was to become the deepest lie. In all innocence, I, the Most Beloved, became the Dissembler, the end of their world. And that, Daniel, is a story we all know.'

Amos paused.

'My hand remained over his mouth,' he continued, 'until the voices outside were gone. Andrew had crumpled, his face twitching.

'I whispered, "All right, listen, we have to share a cabin for the next three months. Look at you. You're going to say something and we're both going to be bloody hanged."

'He didn't reply, just stared at me with that brittle, helpless fierceness.

'"We've got to talk about this," I said. "We're *going* to talk about this."

'I told him we couldn't do it in the cabin because people might hear us, and we needed to get away from the atmosphere of the ship to clear our heads. I spoke softly but deeply, resonantly, staring straight into his eyes, relentlessly pursuing the suggestibility I could sense in him.

'That, Daniel, was one of the most iniquitous moments of my life, playing the advantage of his help-lessness, insinuating my voice into the very seat of his volition, aware of what I was doing and desperate to do it, desperate also because I knew that he might not remain in this acquiescent state for long, that he had a remarkable capacity to reconcentrate himself. Far from the weakest, he was, perhaps, the strongest, certainly the most tenacious man, I'd ever encountered.

'I spoke in imperatives, telling him to get up and get his shoes on. He obeyed. Again that thought: I could tell him to step right over the edge of this ship. But I subdued it.

'When I opened the cabin door, I saw that it had started to rain. Oh, Daniel, if it hadn't been for the rain. Just a light rain, but because of it I put on my sou'wester, which I hadn't worn since the night Andrew had killed the captain. And when I put it on, I felt the weight of that forgotten weapon against my thigh.

'I told him to follow me and he obeyed.

'Almost everyone was already ashore. The few aboard were playing cards at the prow in the last rays of the sun, a small hub of cursing and laughter. I heard Hamid's voice among them, and in my mind I said good-bye to him.

'We skirted the shore and followed a path that climbed the lip of the cliff, he walking a little way in front of me, moving like a man condemned. I'd been so anxious to get off the ship I'd forgotten to tell him to put a coat on. He was wearing only a white shirt. I remember the harsh cries of the birds. They were like coarse hands tearing the dark silk of the sky. The day's soft eye closed, a last moment of consciousness stretched at the rim of the world. At the base of the cliff, far, far down, I could see flecks of white water.

'I stopped walking, and he stopped, turning to face me, his back to the ocean. Some life seemed to have returned to his eyes. I said to him reasonably, "You don't really believe I killed the captain, do you?"

'He said, "Are you telling me not to believe it?" and I realised that he was almost back inside himself.

'"I'm going to marry your sister," I said. "We're going to be brothers."

'"No no," he said; then, I remember, he laughed. A bitter, shallow laugh. He said, "I've decided. I'm going to tell them, and I'm going to tell my sister. I've already started a letter to her . . ." And so he went on. I stopped listening. I felt a pressure in my lungs. My head was swimming.

'I interrupted him: "We're going to be brothers," I said, and reached up to touch his shoulder. He recoiled, and that recoil seemed so inhuman to me, as when you touch the eye of a snail. Where is that moment, too, the weight of his life in my pocket, that fine coating of red dust on his polished shoes? He'd polished his shoes. Can you understand, Daniel, how that can make someone hate you enough to kill you?'

'Amos –'

'So, he'd recoiled at my touch. I'd touched him with my left hand. Only at that point did I realise that my right hand was in my pocket and holding firmly on to the sock.

'I turned slightly away from him, looking up the path that led further along the cliff. I removed the weighted sock and held it behind my right thigh.

'He seemed to realise something; his face became anxious, but some impulse made him turn his head almost full around to look upon the sea. He frowned – at the night, at the ocean, at the wind? I don't know what he frowned at. Then he looked back at me. The weighted sock now hung at my side. He saw it, and his face contorted in a way I . . . My left hand, the hand from which he'd recoiled, took hold of his shirt. He tried to wrench himself free. The buttons flew off as the shirt tore open. I took hold of his collar, grasping the shirt together around his neck. The rest of it flapped up about his naked midriff. He made the strangest sounds, indescribable sounds. He wasn't looking at me but down the path, as if he were watching himself running away. All his strength had left him. He was limp. He reached up and took hold of my hand, the hand that clasped him at his throat. His hands were so cold. I pulled back the weighted sock, held him stiffly at arm's length . . .

'The sound was sickening. The sock tore and –'

'The ball bearings,' Daniel cut in.

'Yes . . . yes, those three bearings fell out. I dropped the torn sock. I walked a little way down the path, sat upon a large rock I'd seen on the way up, and looked back at him. He'd crumpled into a kneeling position, his upper body listing profoundly, his head swaying just above the ground. He looked as if he were davening, a believer, freed at last from the burden of creation. I watched dark blood from his broken temple collect in the socket of his eye, spread down and across his nose, dripping. The three steel balls lay bright and hard before his startled vision in a neat triangle.

'I had jarred from myself completely. Everything seemed to have a supernatural aura. Things-in-them-selves, nameless and unconnected, everywhere. I could smell the tea on my mother's breath. I became a little boy. You say, You were not innocent, you were a murderer. I say, I was a murderer and I couldn't have been more innocent.

'This wasn't my story, Daniel. Do you understand? It wasn't mine. I was a cipher, and the horror of this moment was its simple truth: that a civilisation – even that of a single person – is destroyed by the cipher it creates. What destroys is Nothing – bare idiom clutched around a void.'

'*You* killed him,' Daniel said.

Amos didn't respond for a few seconds. Then he said, 'I did kill him, Daniel, but even in killing there are other truths. There are.'

Something in Daniel gave way just slightly, but he needed to say it again: 'You killed him.'

After a moment, Amos continued. 'I don't know how long I sat there and looked. It became profoundly night. Finally, I returned to him, picked him up as if he were a sleeping child, held him in my arms, and cast him over the cliff. Then I retrieved the bearings and threw two of them as far as I could . . . Strange, when I picked them up, their weight and their smoothness still brought back to me that proud joy of my childhood.

'I made no attempt to skulk back or sneak aboard. As I climbed the gangplank, I heard them still, the laughter, the cards, the curses. I went to my cabin and lay down on my bed. My sleepless eyes alighted restlessly upon all his things. I breathed in his odour. He was gone. In my stomach I felt the nervousness of the actor who is about to make his debut in a great role before a packed theatre. I remembered, once, during the war, going to the house of the mother of a friend of mine to tell her that her son, François, was dead. This was in France. In Normandy. When I told her, I was prepared for her grief. It didn't come. She simply beckoned me in, led me to the back room, pulled out a trunk from under an old brass bed, and showed me everything in it. She spoke in very broken English. This little tractor François had stolen from the nursery. He loved it so much she didn't have the heart to make him take it back. These fur boots were worn by both him and his brother, Bertrand, who'd also been killed in the war. They were like twins, only eleven months apart. She moved randomly, now showing me things that had belonged to Bertrand, the balsa-wood glider that his father – also Bertrand, also dead – had made for him. His father had painted it like an American Tomahawk, with a shark's mouth. Then this, her husband's palette and painting set. He'd been a beautiful painter, such a purist. See this, he painted this, that mill.

That's where we used to live, near Narbonne. This is the charm we hung over our door. It's a Spanish charm to protect from acts of God, an *indalu* from Mojacar. She was half Spanish. She showed me the *Fallas* dress she'd worn as a child . . . She spoke frantically, as if I might at any moment leave. But I stayed, all night I stayed as everything was dredged out and accounted for, attached to life. I stayed until finally, exhausted, she fell asleep right on the floor. And I carried her, just as I'd carried Andrew – perhaps that's what made me remember – to her bed, to her sleep, and to her waking.

'We forget, Daniel. It's all about trying not to forget. Wasn't the war itself just forgetfulness? Just as we forget what it is to kiss someone, to make love to someone, we forget what it is to kill. These are things we feel we cannot forget. God knows why. So one kisses to remember kissing, one kills to remember killing.

'Anyway . . . anyway, suddenly there's a knock at the door, and Hamid sticks his head in.

'"Still here! Come and play some cards with us," he said.

'I said, "No."

'"Why don't you go ashore?"

'"Tired," I said.

'"Where's the ghost of Easter present?"

'"Ashore, I think," I said.

'Someone shouted for Hamid. He bid me good night.

'Andrew's body washed up far from the cliffs. Suicide. No investigation. No suggestion of foul play. All the sailors were accounted for. I, at the attestation of Hamid, was in my cabin all night. Andrew had been acting strangely, maundering like a senile man about the deck. He was depressed and antisocial. A few of the sailors had seen him having a terrible argument with his sister in the street just the day before.

'A telegraph was sent to the train station in Valparaiso. Vivian got it as soon as she arrived and was back in Arica two days later.'

36

'I REMEMBER THE TERROR of waiting for her on the platform, of seeing her emerge from the carriage and approach me, her hair bundled up inside a kind of tam-o'-shanter. Her naked face was Andrew's.

'I could feel the stiff trembling of her whole body as I embraced her. She didn't speak, as if a single word would undo her.

'We went first to see the body, which was to be shipped back to Scotland. At the last moment, she couldn't look at it and turned her head into my shoulder as the shroud was pulled off his face.

'I took her back to the ship and our cabin. She sat on Andrew's bunk; I sat on my own. It was here that she spoke for the first time.

'"I shouldn't have broken off the engagement when I did," she said.

'"It wasn't your fault," I said. Then it came straight out of me: "I did it."

'But she wasn't listening. "You did everything you could," she said. "I know you did."

'Getting up, she removed Andrew's blue jacket from the cupboard, and held it out in front of her. The room filled with his odour.

'"He wasn't wearing this," she said. "Must have felt he didn't deserve to."

'I tried to protest again, but she became angry with me and almost shouted: "Well, you must have seen something. Didn't you have any idea?"

'"He was sick." I defended myself. "I begged him to go home."

'Sitting down, folding the jacket carefully into her lap, she went on more calmly, "Do you think he just walked right off? Do you think he just walked right up there and walked right off?"

'"No," I said. "No, that didn't happen. I —"

'"I get so angry," she said, still not paying any attention to what I was saying. "That's what I can't stop. I keep getting so angry with him. He left nothing. He didn't even leave a letter. And the worst thing is that he might have done it also because of what was happening between you and me. I betrayed him. He went crazy when I told him about the two of us. He said he hated me. I'm never going to forget that. Terrible, you can feel that all those years, all that time – our lives together – came to nothing. He died angry; he died hating me."

'All my courage had drained away, and we both languished awhile in an airless silence.

'At last, I said, "With your hair up, you look so much like him." It was my confession in another guise, and now she seemed to sense something, her eyes meeting mine directly, intensely, for the first time.

'"What?" she said.

'"With your hair up," I repeated, "you look exactly like him."

'She stared at me for a moment longer. I asked her, surprising myself, if she'd let me take her there.

'"Where?" She looked frightened.

'"Where it happened," I said.

'She didn't answer, but put his jacket down on the bunk and let me take her hand. I led her off the ship.

'Everything was identical to the night I'd gone up there with Andrew. Indeed, she even broke away from me and walked just ahead, as he had, looking about her, trying to understand and so hold in memory things that merely were: the sea, the setting sun, the sound of the birds.

'Then we came to where the slope levelled off. She stopped for a moment and leaned against that rock upon which I'd sat as my crime had become a dream in the darkness. After a few moments, she walked to the edge of the cliff, looked out over the sea. Then I saw it, pale against the dark ground – the sock. Quickly, I positioned myself between it and Vivian, and embraced her. I could feel her body convulsing gently. She told me I was hurting her and turned in my arms to face me. Fearing she'd see the sock, I took hold of her wet face and pressed it into my neck with an almost violent forcefulness. She reached up to my hand. I thought she was going to peel it away, free herself, but she didn't. In fact, she pressed her hand against mine, crushing her face even harder into my chest as she wept.

'Once again I'd done exactly the right thing. My God,

Daniel, what woman was ever won in such a way? There it began, in the place I'd killed her brother, during that mute and aborted confession, where, in her most vulnerable moment, by the force of an iniquitous embrace, I made her yield up what little strength she had left to bear the truth.

'With that same seemingly tender force, I guided her back.

'The moment I'd broken through her angry, rigid isolation, she didn't want to let me go. I returned with her to that shabby hotel at the docks and – it was the strangest thing – we made love.'

'That night?' Daniel put both his hands on the table, straining forward. 'That night?'

'Yes. That night. I can't convey how surreal it was, in that filthy room with lizards flickering across the walls. It had happened – as such things can in even the most banal circumstances – simply because we had to fill the silence with something.

'During our lovemaking, the margins of that room became crowded with shades, escaping my uninhabitable body. All around us they stood in grim witness: the one who loved her utterly; the one who'd killed her brother; the one who saw her brother's face in hers; the one who realised that this was not even nearly the first time she'd been with a man.'

37

'THE NEXT DAY I RESIGNED from the ship and returned to Lochbroom with Vivian. We married just a few weeks after Andrew's funeral; went back to the same church a month later for her mother's – her decline having been hastened, no doubt, by her son's death. We then moved down to London, where I took a job at the docks.

'Vivian got pregnant almost immediately, but the baby, a girl, Laura, was born with a damaged heart and lived only six months.

'If that hadn't happened, with all the grief and alternate focus it created, things might have come to a crisis in our marriage much sooner. I stopped being able to speak to Vivian, to look her in the eyes, or have any physical intimacy. The lie had become a kind of black hole, drawing in and distorting every other memory, making everything a lie. I could tell her neither about my childhood nor about what I'd been doing just ten minutes before. All was a lie. It was as if I were still with her in that cabin on the *Prince of Scots,* my voice frozen at the moment I should have made my confession.

'I remember one day coming home from work to the new flat we'd moved into just a few months after the death of the baby. Vivian had wanted a fresh start, believing that my behaviour was connected to Laura's death. Painting the flat, she was wearing some of my old clothes, had bundled her hair up into one of my old caps. It was such a shock to see her like this, to find myself confronted by the image of Andrew.

'She asked me how my day had been. Fine, I said. She asked me if anything exciting had happened. As always, I shook my head. Unable to bear the way she looked, I stepped closer and took off her cap to let her hair fall down around her face and shoulders. I often let her hair down if she tied it up, and one time she told me, quite seriously, that she believed I loved her only for her hair.

'Having done this, I knew I couldn't just walk away, so I kissed her. Embracing me, she made that kiss passionate, but I couldn't take it any further. As much as I loved her – and I did love her – I couldn't. So I pulled free and told her I had to go and wash up a bit.

'Before I could get out of the kitchen, she called to me and asked, as I turned back, if I were having an affair.

'I swore I wasn't.

'She said, "I've spent all day painting this bloody flat – our home. Can't you just talk to me? You come in, let my hair down . . . I can't even remember the last time we made love. And that's not as bad as that you just don't talk to me anymore."

'She stared at me, waiting. I went to speak, but couldn't.

'"Whatever it is, say it," she shouted. "Do you love

someone else? Do you want to leave? What are you hiding . . . ? Is it because Laura died? Is that it?"

'"No," I said.

'"Is that why you don't want to sleep with me?"

'"No," I said.

'"I want us to try again," she said softly, "to start trying again."

'It took me a second to understand that she meant children. "Do you think you're ready?" I said.

'"Yes," she said, and asked me if I loved her. I said I did.

'"Because if you don't –"' I cut her off by kissing her. I had to stop her from speaking. As I kissed her, I removed those men's clothes from her body, then lifted her, naked, into my arms, and carried her into our bedroom.

'She said, "You're not just doing this to shut me up, are you?"'

'"Of course I am," I said, feeling a kind of relief at the truth of this.

'We made love then – a confession of sorts: intense, urgent. To make love, as opposed to having sex, is to be deeply silent. It's not joyous, it's hopeless. For more than a year, I found myself able to make love to her again, because it was the one way I could be silent without seeming to reject her. In my eyes, she could see all the pressure of what I couldn't say, and feel it in my body. I have a sense that her body came to know my confession, because she seemed fearful sometimes, or angry. Afterwards, we'd fall away from each other, cleft, useless, like the pieces of a split mould in which had been cast some fresh allegory of Daniel's death.

'Strange to think that our child was conceived from such a coupling.

'But that contact finally tapered off too and, to avoid her, I began to stay in the pub after work with my mates, got home later and later, worked every overtime shift, took any excuse not to be at home. Such agony: I couldn't face her; I couldn't imagine my life without her.

'And one night – it was now two years after Laura's death – I came home at almost three in the morning. The flat had developed signs of neglect, dust everywhere, paint peeling, and I remember a vase of dead daffodils on the mantelpiece.

'I saw the light on in our bedroom and felt a sharp pain in my heart. I entered. She was sitting on the floor surrounded by a pile of letters – just as she'd been a few months earlier with Andrew's letters, when she'd used his words in her voice to seduce us both, for one night, into loving me.

'I asked her what she was doing. With a glance up at the clock beside our bed, she said, more resigned than angry, 'I'm not even sure why you bother to come home anymore.'

'I didn't say anything.

'She told me she'd dug out the letters I'd sent her from the *Prince of Scots*. "I was reading them," she said, "to try to remember what your voice sounded like."

'I knelt down in front of her and pressed my hand

against her cheek. She peeled it off and pushed it away – not aggressively, but as if it were perhaps a leaf that had been blown up against her face by the wind.' Amos was holding out his hand, open, as if he were offering Daniel what it held – her face.

'"I have two pieces of news for you," she said. "I thought of not telling you the first, but I couldn't not tell you. We have enough silence in this house. It's like a disease. The first –" But she changed her mind. "No, let me tell you the other thing," she said. "Funny that this is the *other* thing. But I don't think it'll surprise you. I'm going to leave. Pat will put me up until I can find a place of my own, a place where I don't have to have any trace of you."

'She waited for me to say something, but I didn't, so she went on. "And the first thing is that I'm pregnant."

'Still I couldn't speak.

'She looked up at me, angry, tears welling, and she said, "There's nothing more cruel than silence."

'Then she began to pile the letters up in order to tie them together again with a length of blue ribbon. I think it was the sight of that, of my voice about to be re-bound, that gave me the strength, and I said softly, "Sometimes, there's nothing you want more than silence." Then I knew it was over.

'"I have something to tell you," I said, "something I should have told you a long time ago."

'So, I began, not aboard the *Prince of Scots* but earlier, much earlier. I began in a Dublin sanitarium, a tall orderly standing behind me, his hands on my ten-year-old shoulders; and on the bed in front of me, like a drowned woman, lay my mother, the marks left by the electrodes still on her temples. Began here, Daniel, not so that I could make excuses, but because I had a sense that this is where all my stories began: with a man I couldn't see, a woman I could no longer recognise.

'Each word I spoke seemed to sever one filament of her body's tension.'

Mum –

'She sank before me as I related every smell and gesture, ending at the moment I let his body slip from my arms over that cliff.'

Mum, why didn't you tell me?

'When I was done, she didn't say a word, threw my letters into the chest from which they'd come, went to the spare room, made up the bed, and slept.'

Knowing nothing, I felt everything. You should have spared me that.

'For a month, she didn't speak to me or take any action, a month of unimaginable terror for me. To lose her – I couldn't care less about going to jail or being hanged – to lose her and that child.'

'Then one night I was lying in bed awake.'

She'd transformed.

'I'd barely slept in that month. And I heard the bedroom door open. From the hall, a slant of light cut across the bed.'

Damn your gothic slant, Amos, even now, and the leap of your heart. Surely I would have told it better.

'This was then extinguished as she closed the door behind her. I didn't move, but like a frightened child pretended to be asleep. I knew now that she was coming to tell me that she would leave. But gently, and at this my heart leapt, she got into the bed.'

His smell. Andrew's smell.

'I became aware of a sickly and familiar odour: eucalyptus and cinnamon. I turned to face her.'

Open doors, open windows, all the openings. I would have told it –

'She'd shaved off her hair and was naked but for his blue jacket. She moved towards me. I held her back by her shoulders, but she shrugged me off. I tried to turn away, but she took hold of my face and kissed me, with her brother's lips, kissed me tenderly, and I cried.'

You didn't cry, Amos, she did, and some of her tears got on to your face.

'The next day, when I got back from work, my wife and all her possessions were gone. She'd left every door, every drawer, every window in the house open. Every box, every package, every book. The telephone receiver dangled from its cradle; water ran from all the taps. She'd opened everything. I stood for the longest time right at the centre of these openings. There was nothing else, no note, and that was the last thing that ever passed between us.'

Except my life, Amos. Except my life.

Amos was just shadows. Hardly any light remained, the window was a pale membrane fistulaed with rain, the silver frame a vague nimbus around the Matisse, and on the table the lighter and the ball bearing were illuminated just enough to suggest the forms of the other objects. Daniel became aware of the sound of breathing and realised it was his own. Rain; the rest was silence, an empty room. Empty.

Then two pale hands appeared, like afterimages of light in the darkness, fixed the stem of the pipe into its bowl, and filled the bowl with tobacco. Just these hands visible and a rivulet of light along the ridge of that man's still exposed shin . . . shin. Daniel looked down to see that his own trouser turn-up was still rolled above his knee. He tugged it back down.

One of the hands picked up the lighter, reached towards him, and Daniel felt it being slipped into the breast pocket of his own shirt.

'Don't you need it?' Daniel asked.

'I'm worried you might forget it.'

A noise then – the armchair being shifted.

'Is that it?' Daniel said. 'That can't be all of it.'

Amos was at the window now. 'I wish I could give you more, Daniel, but what have I got to offer? This is my estate.' He made a gesture that seemed to include the flat and what could be seen from the window.

'Two stories up,' Amos said, 'lives a woman called Erin O'Malley. She's sixty-four, and if you go up there, within seconds she'll find a way to tell you about how she came to throw her engagement ring at her fiancé. She'll tell you that she supported him through medical school in Cork for seven years, until she was forty and it was nearly too late for her to have her babies. And how, as soon as he was done, she tried to fix the wedding date and find a house for them. But no date was quite right for him, no house quite suitable until, in a fit of rage, she flung the ring at him. And he seized it. She knows he would have followed through on his promise, strict Catholic that he was, especially after all she'd done for him, and with all she stood to lose – this devout, virginal woman, too old now to have anyone else marry her. But she'd given him his chance, and he clung to that ring like a dead man no matter how much she begged. Less than a month later, he married a twenty-two-year-old air stewardess. Erin got an invitation to the wedding. She'll show it to you.'

'Why are you –'

'Listen. In the flat below this one, Daniel, lives Lucy Evans, who's going senile. She remembers only three things from her life. She remembers seeing the young Queen Mum almost trip on a step, and how gracefully she righted herself. "What grace!" she cries out every time she tells you. She remembers her husband making love to her after England won some football match, how happy he was. And she remembers a cottage in Cornwall that she and her mother had gone to for their holidays. She'll tell you how delicious the steak and kidney pudding was, and about the strange woman who owned the cottage, who lifted her up and held her in front of a mirror and whispered things that Lucy refuses to repeat. She just closes up her little body like a child and shakes it and says, "Awful things! Awful things!"'

'I don't –'

'Then *listen*. Over there.' Amos gestured out of the window. 'Over there on the seventh floor of Drake's House, Bill Cotley is sitting on his bed distraught. He's shared that flat with his dad all his life. For the past fifteen years, they haven't said a single word to each other, avoid each other as much as they can, though their flat is only as big as this one. It began because one of them, I forget which, refused to admit that he'd used a metal implement on the other's nonstick pan. A few hours ago, though, thinking his dad was out of the flat, Bill had walked into the bathroom. But his dad had been in there on the toilet reading a newspaper and had looked up at his son with a shocked face – a suddenly innocent face. And this had caused Bill, standing there with toilet roll in one hand, soap in the other, and a towel flung over his shoulder, to say "Sorry." Just a word, after which he left the bathroom. And now he's tearing his hair out; he just can't forgive himself for being the first to speak.'

'What are you saying, Amos?'

'This is all, Daniel, is what I'm saying. All of me. All I am.'

A flame at the window, playing over the bowl of the pipe. The sweet smell of smoke reached Daniel, and for just a moment he felt it – allowed himself to feel it: love for those shadows, for that man.

Daniel stood, picked up his briefcase, and walked down the musty hallway to the door. As he put his hand on the handle, something seemed to take hold of his heart. It froze him. Beyond this door was his life. He held tighter to the handle, and felt, in his being, a reciprocal pressure. Impossible: to both open out and open in: the perfect lock.

Daniel had believed he could cauterise sadness, longing, cut away all need. He wanted simply to live in a sunny place, without this miserable block of flats, without the diesel clouds of London, the old jerry-rigged machine of this city. He wanted to be a particular sunlight he'd seen years ago, one evening in Nottingham, burnishing the bricks of a defunct coal yard beside a canal. Why couldn't he have been that brief and lovely predicament?

As he turned the handle, Amos spoke. 'Will you forget me, Daniel?' he said.

'I can't,' Daniel said, opening the door.

The door fell away, spun down into the darkness. A bracing wind gusted in, fluttering the pages of the dictionary, blowing the yellowed note on to the floor. The night sky was so beautiful, the clouds like sundering ice around the surfacing moon. He looked down, the whole city spread out before him, all those bridges brightly spanning the Thames. It seemed so naïve, filled him with a strange, deep joy. London, his city, so innocent he wanted to cry for it. He felt completely calm.

'Daniel,' Amos said, 'for you it's so little. For me, it's so much. I must work; I must see. Can't you just forget me?'

'I wish I could,' Daniel said, turning to look at him. 'Amos, I really wish I could.' And with his eyes all the time on those shadows, the ember of that pipe, he stepped out.

38

AFTER PAYING THE CABBIE, Daniel hurried towards work. Late again. He'd missed all his interviews yesterday and three already today.

He'd woken up on his couch this morning, fully dressed and wrapped in the tarpaulin on which the paint cans had been sitting for the past year. The cans were all open, which probably accounted for his headache. It looked as if something had been written in paint over a couple of the walls, then roughly painted out. The phone line had been pulled from the jack, and he wasn't able to bring himself to reconnect it. He was desperate for a smoke but discovered that each one of his cigarettes had been cut open, the tobacco removed and gathered in a pile on the kitchen counter just in front of a vase full of daffodils. He just left the house, didn't even shower or change, and got a taxi. Frightened of what he'd woken up to, he didn't want to think about it. He felt now, though, as if he'd set himself skimming over the surface of the world. If he stopped, he would sink.

He entered the main office. It was like running into a thicker medium, and it pulled him up, his heart racing. The same lines of sullen people waiting to sign on, the same beleaguered co-workers holding their fingers in dikes that had long been breached, or hefting files around like sandbags while the muddy swell rose around them.

A long line of disgruntled clients waited outside his own office. He became aware of how wrinkled his suit was, and of a long paint stain down one of his trouser legs. Someone called his name. It was Richard. Though he was interviewing a client in one of the booths, he got up and hurried over to Daniel.

'Hey, Danny-boy.' He rested a hand on Daniel's arm. 'You look like you slept under the bridge last night.'

'What bridge? Oh . . . oh no, it's . . . Look, I'm late.'

'You been on a bender, matey? When you turned up at Sally's you –'

'No. Listen, Rich –'

Richard squeezed his arm to stop him and called over to Jill, who'd just come out of Daniel's office. Quickly, she walked over to them.

'God, you look wrecked,' she said. She glanced meaningfully at Richard, at which he patted Daniel's arm and told him he'd come and have a chat in a bit.

Daniel noticed that Richard didn't return to his client but went straight to Morgan's office.

'I'm so sorry I didn't say you could come over last night,' Jill said, trying to bring Daniel's thick hair under control. 'I called you so many times. What happened to you yesterday?'

'Look, Jill' – he wanted to get to this right now – 'I don't know what to say about that other night.'

She put both her hands flat against his chest to stop

him. 'I'll tell you the truth, Danny: it seems like it didn't even happen – not,' she hastily added, 'that it wasn't the most astonishing sexual experience of my life.' Neither of them was in the mood for humour, so she went quickly on. 'I just mean that it didn't really seem as if it had anything to do with either of us.'

Daniel didn't know what to say. He hadn't expected this to be quite so straightforward.

The knot at Jill's brow tightened. Both her hands were still pressed flat to his chest. 'Sally's so worried about you.'

'Sally?' Unfamiliar to him at first, the name slowly filled with light: sunlight, mottled and trembling, cast over him and Sally lying in a rowing boat on the Thames more than a decade ago. A rowing boat they'd let drift to the bank, lodge beneath trees. He'd removed her blouse, was kissing the scar upon her back. He could feel it even now, like old braille, like a song in skin.

Richard, reemerging from Morgan's office, returned to his client. Morgan and Perry appeared a moment later. They both assiduously avoided looking at Daniel, and this, as they crossed the office to the information desk, gave them something of the pained dignity of two prim women being wolf-whistled. There they joined Betsy, who was staring openly.

Jill was saying something, but Daniel now cut her off. 'Jill, I know there are clients waiting, but I'm desperate for a fag. Have you got one?'

'I'll have one with you,' she said. 'Stay here.' Quickly,

she went back into his office, emerging a moment later with her coat on and her satchel over her shoulder.

'Don't worry about your clients.' She took his arm. 'We're dealing with them.'

Daniel noticed her glancing back at the information desk, then towards Richard.

Outside on the pavement, she gave him a cigarette and took one herself. He reached into his breast pocket. The feel of the ball bearing was like a crevice opening up at the centre of his body. He removed it and held it out in the palm of his hand. Jill, who'd leaned forward for a light, now pulled back.

'What's that?' she said, taking her cigarette out of her mouth.

But Daniel was already walking away. 'I'll see you tomorrow, Jill,' he said. 'I have to –'

Catching up, Jill caught hold of his arm.

'Danny, stop.' She pulled him around. She was breathing hard, shaking. It made him think of Sally in the garden yesterday. 'I want to take you to see someone. Please, Danny, just come back into the office for a minute.'

'No, I have to go.' He pulled his arm free and forged on.

'Danny, you're not well,' she shouted.

This echoed in his head, confusing him. After a second, he turned to tell her that he was perfectly fine, that there was just one thing he needed to do, but she was already halfway back to the office, running.

Spotting a cab, he hailed it and got in. As it pulled away, he looked through the rear window to see Richard, Jill, Morgan, and Perry spilling out on to the pavement.

Almost an hour later he got to Palm Court. He asked the driver – a gaunt little man – to wait, which the driver agreed to do only after Daniel had paid the fifty pounds he already owed.

Sally was pruning roses. Her hair was tied back in a loose ponytail. At his approach, she stood, alarmed, dropping her shears. 'God, Danny, what happened to you?'

She reached up, perhaps to wipe something from his face, but he intercepted her hand, trapping it gently in both of his.

'Where did you go yesterday?' she said. 'I called you dozens of times from the house and –'

He cut her off. 'I need you to meet someone. You're my . . . It's very important.'

'Oh, Danny, you –' Her voice cracked as she struggled not to cry.

When she'd regained her composure, she said, 'Danny, you seem a little poorly.'

'I'm fine,' he said. Things were so simple, so clear. The thought of bringing her to Amos – of Sally and Amos together in his home – had come to him like a revelation. His faith in this, the unimaginable, was absolute. 'I need you to come with me. Please.'

She didn't speak for a moment.

'I'll come with you,' she said at last, 'if you agree to

come back here with me afterwards and talk to Dr Kenton.'

He couldn't understand why she wanted him to do this, but agreed and began to lead her away.

'I have to change.' Pulling her hand free, she untied her gardening smock and took it off.

'There's a taxi waiting.'

'A taxi?'

Snatching up her hand again, he pulled her, not roughly but a little impatiently, towards the sanitarium. She resisted a little but finally dropped the smock on the lawn and allowed herself to be led through the house and into the taxi.

The taxi dropped them at the entrance to the Windsor Estate. Sally had been trying to talk to him most of the way, but he hadn't been able to concentrate enough to understand what she was saying or to respond and she'd finally gone quiet.

He kept tight hold of her hand as he led her towards Hicks House. The closer they got, the less like herself and the more like sunlight Sally seemed. Not the sunlight that had filled her name, but that which had saturated her when she'd been standing at the threshold to her dark cottage two days ago watching him walk away. God, it felt as if fifty years had passed since then.

Fifty years *had* passed since then. And now, now he was returning home, holding his wife's hand, the hand of a pure, nostalgic sunlight, the light in all the photographs where those in them are dead, and all those who'd ever known them, touched them, felt for them, are also dead. Light without conscience or memory, without pity or malice.

And yet he knew it was his wife, had to keep holding on. Holding on.

As soon as the lift opened on the sixteenth floor, his vertigo hit him – a blinding wash in his head that almost caused him to lose his balance. He staggered to the door. He was holding Sally's hand and could hear her voice, but was afraid to look at her because she still seemed like light to him. He knocked on the door a few times, but there was no answer. Panicked, he began to hammer against it as hard as he could, calling Amos's name. The door to the adjacent flat opened, and a powerful-looking man emerged.

'What the fuck are you up to?' the man shouted.

He looked as if he'd been woken up.

'You were in jail,' Daniel said. 'Were you in jail?'

'What the fuck's that to you?'

'Where's Amos?'

'Are you going to stop making that bloody racket?'

Daniel called for Amos through the door again.

'I have my wife,' he explained irritably to the man. Releasing Sally's hand, he now threw his whole body against the door. The lock gave, and the door slammed in against the wall.

He ran into the sitting room and felt the breeze immediately. All the windows were open, the curtains sucked out into the air. The room began to spin and he fell. He clutched at the floor, which pitched and yawed. Half-opening his eyes, he saw it then, his lighter, lying on the carpet near the open window. He tried ridiculously to reach for it but had to close his eyes again. He would fall into the sky. He would fall. Then he felt a soft pressure anchoring him, a body upon his back. Arms slid around his chest, a damp cheek was pressed to his own.

'Danny.'

'I'm going to fall,' he said.

'You've fallen,' she said. 'You're all right.'

Very softly then she began to sing to him, an old ballad, her brogue emerging, and Daniel was flooded, as animals are when the struggle is over, when the jaws have closed about their throats, with a shock of wonder and bliss.

39

SALLY, JILL, RICHARD, MORGAN, Perry, and Betsy had just finished singing 'Happy Birthday' to Daniel when the woman shouted, 'Vincent.'

Standing just a little distance away on the lawn, she was staring at Daniel. She'd appeared from nowhere – perhaps she'd been in the conservatory. He'd never seen her before. She was a very tall and handsome, if rather careworn, middle-aged woman wearing a navy blue dress suit that resembled an air stewardess's uniform.

Daniel blew out the candles, and the others applauded. Sally, who was sitting on the blanket, leaning against the side of Daniel's deck chair, took the cake out of his lap, and began to slice it.

'Vincent,' the woman called again, shielding her eyes from the bright sun.

'I think she's talking to you, matey,' Richard said.

Jill, who was sitting with her back against Richard's chest, flicked a peanut in the air, and Richard caught it in his mouth.

Morgan, lying on the blanket facing the supine Betsy, rolled over like a bull seal to look at the woman. 'Well, Dan-i-el, seems you have a knack for being mistaken for someone else.'

He rolled back. A little way from him and Betsy sat

Perry, cross-legged on the grass just outside the margins of the blanket. He looked like a bitter little Buddha.

'Vincent!' The woman was getting impatient.

'I'm not Vincent,' Daniel replied.

The woman clearly wanted to come over, but it was as if her feet had been nailed to the ground. She swayed forward, then made a couple of odd, stereotyped gestures with her hands, at which Daniel realised that she was a new patient, not a lost visitor.

'He's not Vincent,' Sally called. 'You've made a mistake.'

The woman didn't seem so much to accept this as to give up hope of crossing the clearly treacherous ten yards between herself and Daniel. She turned around and began to make her way towards the sanitarium. Her progress was agonisingly slow, since she stopped to complete a series of ritualistic motions after each step.

'Man, she's got some funky moves,' Richard said.

'Shut up, you.' Jill threw her hand back to slap the top of his head.

Betsy pointed up at Daniel in his deck chair. 'How do we *know* he's not Vincent?'

'Oh, come on,' Daniel protested, 'do I look like a Vincent?'

'If he were a Vincent,' Richard said, 'he'd be bald, potbellied, and he'd have a *tiny* penis. One out of three's not enough.'

'I knew a Vincent who had a *very* thick head of hair.'

Perry was clearly affronted on behalf of those so named. 'Serbian, he was. Serbians tend to have thick hair.'

'That's what I always think of when I think of Serbians,' Richard said, 'thick hair . . . Oh, and there is another thing. What is that? Oh, yes – genocide. Thick hair and genocide.'

'I never understand what you're going on about,' Perry said.

'Anyway,' Betsy renewed, 'getting back to my point. You just never know.' Morgan was staring at her with drunken adoration. 'I once went out with this bloke, Tristan,' she said, 'whose dad was some bigwig barrister. And when Tris had been a kid, he and his mum and sister had lived in a mansion in Sussex somewhere and his dad worked in London and only came home at the weekends. And one day when Tris was about fifteen, he snuck into town with some mates of his during the week to go to a concert, and he was on the top deck of a bus and the bus stops in traffic and he finds himself looking straight into a flat. And sitting in this flat is his dad in his dressing gown with a little kid in his lap and some woman in the armchair beside him. He had a whole other family in town.'

'Oh, my God, what did he do?' Sally said.

'Wasn't very savoury.' Betsy stifled a belch. 'Essentially blackmailed his dad into giving him buckets of dosh, which he used to travel the world and become a drug addict. That's when I was seeing him. It was fun while it lasted.'

'I'm always being mistaken for people,' Sally took up. 'It's the hair. Because it's a bit unusual –'

'Because it's so bloody beautiful,' Jill interrupted. She was also a little drunk. She reached over and stroked Sally's hair. 'It's our great-grandmother's hair, you know.'

'Really?' Richard said. 'How do you keep it so fresh looking?'

'Har har har,' Betsy brayed.

'That wasn't funny,' Perry said.

'In fact, it happened the other day,' Sally said. 'I was in Kensington High Street and I hear this car screech to a halt. Everyone turns to look. And this bloke gets out and starts running up the street. I didn't think much of it and kept walking, and suddenly I feel these hands on my shoulders and he pulls me round. And when he sees my face – clearly not the face he was expecting – he lets out a horrified yelp and actually backs away with his hands out in front of him as if I were *hideous*. Then he turns round and sprints off.'

All but Perry were laughing. This was such a Sally story. Daniel could feel her hair against the side of his bare foot.

A nurse came across from the sanitarium with Daniel's pill.

'You're not drinking any alcohol, now, are you, Mr Mulvaugh?' she said as she handed it to him.

Daniel shook his head. 'I'm good as gold.'

'Well, happy birthday.' She took back the plastic cup. 'You should be dressed a little warmer, now. There's a bite to that breeze.'

'He should be dressed full stop,' Betsy said.

'One of the advantages of going mad,' Daniel said, 'is that you never have to change out of your pyjamas.'

The nurse returned to the sanitarium. Daniel watched her pass that tall woman who was still engaged in her painstaking ritual of walking away.

Sally looked up at Daniel, squinting at the bright sun. 'You know, it is a bit chilly out here.' She put her hand on his foot. 'God, your feet are freezing.'

'That's okay,' Daniel said. 'I can't feel them.'

'A woman once told me I was the image of Harrison Ford,' Richard said.

Betsy looked over at him. 'What did you do then: put down the knife and let her go?'

Richard wrapped his arms around Jill. 'You think I look like Harrison Ford, don't you, sweetie?'

'Oh, I do, darling,' Jill said, turning back to kiss him. 'And I also believe that the hairs in our nostrils are tiny antennae designed to pick up intergalactic wisdom.'

He tried to bite her neck and she screamed.

Morgan rolled on to his back in order to address them all. 'I have a good friend who owns a boutique on the King's Road, and she once got me into a party at Coco Chanel's house in Chelsea. I didn't know it was a costume party, and I was mistaken a half-dozen times for a notorious transvestite called Miranja Miranjina. One woman laughed so hard at my tuxedo, which she thought was this Miranja's spectacular joke of bad taste, that she ended up choking on a canapé.'

With a slightly troubled expression, Morgan glanced around at all of them and said, 'Do I look like I could be a transvestite?'

'No comment,' Betsy said.

'Only like a very handsome, astonishingly masculine transvestite,' Jill said.

'Thank you, Jill.' Morgan raised his glass to her.

There was a moment of silence, and then Perry took his opportunity. He'd clearly been waiting to say this and couldn't suppress a superior smile. 'I have *never* been mistaken for a person in my life.'

That was it for Betsy: her whole body began to shake with suppressed laughter, which soon broke out of her. Morgan followed, then Richard, Jill, and Sally, all of them drunk and giddy, the laughter flaring each time any one of them looked at Perry, who sat out there, astonished and miserable, like an abandoned baby. Daniel was smiling but hadn't drunk anything. He wanted to feel for Perry, who had to be aware, as Morgan and Betsy's collision became imminent, that he was shifting into a colder, more distant, orbit around Morgan. But all Daniel's feeling was centred on his wife's hand resting upon his foot, on that touch and her relaxed presence so close to him.

She'd wanted him here, and had spent time with him when he'd first been admitted. But after he'd got a little better, she'd begun, as much as she could, to keep her distance. He'd respected that, hadn't gone to the cottage or disturbed her at her work. Instead, he'd written to her, often while he could actually see her in the garden from the window of his room. Plain letters that didn't talk of the past or of his feelings for her. They tried to make a start here, with the nurses and the patients and the books he'd begun to read, and the scent and tenor of each day, and the whole feel of this hollowed Victorian mansion.

Today was his birthday, and on his foot rested her hand, her touch a slender fulcrum upon which the full and precarious weight of his hope was balanced. Almost as if to steady himself, Daniel put his hand on the top of her head. He ran his fingers through her hair, touched her like this for the first time in years. She squinted up at him. She'd been laughing so much that tears were streaming from her eyes; it looked as if she'd been grieving. She then rubbed her face affectionately against the side of his leg – partially, he knew, just to wipe off the tears – and got up to hand out the cake.

Daniel checked on the tall woman's progress. She'd stopped halfway to the sanitarium. She was holding her arms out, as if they were wings or fins, and was moving them hardly at all. In the long middle stretch, she had, at last, found the current that would take her – almost – home.

THE TWO BOYS sat in the branches of the tree, a treasure of horse chestnuts piled in their laps. After hulling them with their penknives, they put the cheese cutters and other good ones into a shopping bag. As they worked, they talked about the rumours that certain boys soaked their conkers in vinegar and baked them hard in the oven. They argued the rule that the victorious conker should take on all the wins of the defeated one. The day was beautiful: sunny and just slightly windy, giving the tree a sighing, caressing life. They'd played truant. It was almost four now and time to go home. A few lonely mothers sat on the grass beneath them and smoked, watching their young children splash about in the paddling pool.

'Galv,' Daniel called. He pointed at a little girl carrying a violin, who was walking past the park with her father.

Careful not to drop his remaining conkers, Galvin pulled himself up from his branch and leaned on Daniel to see who he was pointing at.

'Ah,' said Galvin knowingly, glancing at Daniel. Daniel couldn't quite meet his eyes: in them, recently, there had grown a need he found it difficult to face. 'That man is a Dromadon. He kidnapped that girl when she was a baby.'

'What's her name?'

Galvin thought for a moment. 'Sally,' he said. 'And he kidnapped her, right, because a Dromadon's heart feeds on whatever it's in. It's like a maggot. And he needs something to keep his heart in. She's too young for him to have done it yet, but he's getting her ready, and in a few years –'

'No.'

'We can try to save her, Danny, but it's probably already too late, and with that heart in her, she'll become –'

'No, no, no.'

Galvin sat up, frustrated; he was getting into this one. 'Well, what do you bloody want?' he said.

Daniel watched the little girl, who was looking with shy longing over at the park.

'We've had enough sad ones, today,' Daniel said. 'Save her, Galv. Make her happy. Make this one happy.'

Acknowledgments

My deepest gratitude for invaluable advice, encouragement, and support goes out to the following:

Averill Curdy, Christian Wiman, Amy Scheibe, Louise Quayle, Tom Barbash, Thomas Allen, Rolland Comstock, Sharon Barnes, Erick Kelemen, Ellen Levine, Bill Hamilton, Ravi Mirchandani, and, of course, my family.

Special thanks to Peter Stitt and *The Gettysburg Review*. Daniel and Amos first appeared in *The Writer*, a novella published in *The Gettysburg Review*, Autumn 1995.

Thanks also to the author of that old nautical book I picked up in a library in London many years ago. Details from it added flesh to the crew of the *Prince of Scots*.